# SWITCH HITTERS

## BISEXUAL EROTICA

## VICTORIA RUSH

# COPYRIGHT

*For the uninhibited...*

# VOLUME ONE

---

## ELEVATOR SHAFT

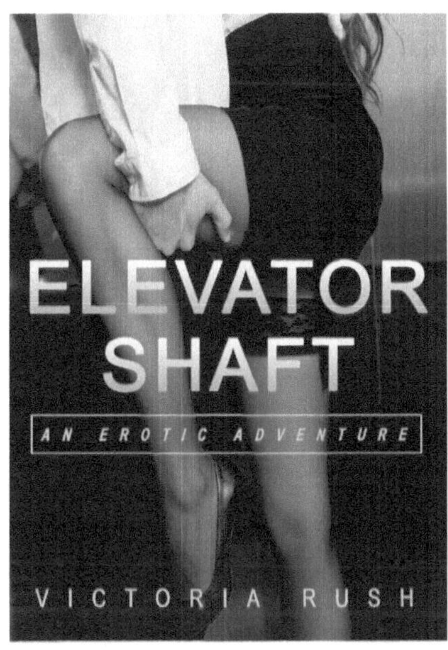

**1**

I breathed a sigh of relief as I stepped into the elevator just after 5 p.m. on the day before Thanksgiving. My meeting with the creative director of Ogilvy & Mather Advertising had gone better than expected, and I felt elated at the prospect of working with the prestigious agency. We'd taken longer than anticipated to discuss the particulars of their Disney Studios campaign, but at the end of the day he'd awarded me exclusive rights to design all their new movie posters.

The view from their penthouse suite atop the Willis Tower was breathtaking. Chicago had been enjoying an unusually mild November, and I could see all the way across Lake Michigan on the clear autumn day. They'd feted me with a late luncheon in the Skydeck Restaurant on the 103rd floor and although I felt fully sated, I was looking forward to the annual feast with my family over the long weekend.

Ogilvy's offices had cleared out early in advance of the

weekend crush, and I nodded toward the two lone elevator occupants as the door slid closed behind us. They were both dressed in expensive suits and looked to be about my age. The man standing to my right had thick ruffled hair, dark eyes, and broad shoulders that curved nicely in his tight wool suit.

But it was the woman standing on the other side of the elevator that caught my attention. Standing almost six feet tall in her Louboutin pumps, her perfectly manicured brows arched over aquamarine-colored eyes and red pouty lips. Like the handsome hunk on the opposite side of the elevator, her busty figure left little to the imagination in her form-fitting skirt and blazer. My pussy twitched as I glanced downward, eyeing her long and shapely legs. Given how far they were standing apart and how hard they were working to avoid eye contact, I quickly surmised that they didn't know each other.

*Funny how perfect strangers always find the quickest way to separate themselves in close quarters*, I thought.

I glanced at the elevator console to confirm the ground floor button was selected, then I stepped to the back of the lift to get a closer look at the two passengers. They looked even sexier from behind, as I shamelessly ran my eyes over their figures. The man had a nice round bump lifting the back of his blazer, and I could make out the muscular curve of his thighs filling in his tight-fitting pants.

*I bet that guy doesn't have much trouble getting his share of the action*, I thought, suddenly feeling warm under my form-fitting suit.

But the woman's suit was even tighter, displaying every

curve and valley of her sexy figure. As I stared at the globes of her firm ass clearly delineated in her snug skirt, my panties began to moisten thinking about how much I'd like to lick my way up her long legs all the way from her pretty feet to her steamy pussy.

Normally I tried to respect everyone's desire for privacy while traveling on elevators, but whether it was the after-effects of my three-martini lunch or my giddiness from landing the prestigious account, for some reason I felt the need to break the awkward silence in the lift.

I hope you guys have as good a reason as I did to work this late on Thanksgiving weekend," I said.

"Par for the course," the man said, turning his head halfway around and smiling half-heartedly in my direction. "Goes with the territory, unfortunately."

"Mmm," the lady grunted, staring impassively toward the front of the elevator. "No rest for the wicked in the urban jungle."

I peered back and forth between the two strangers, sensing some tension between them. Were they ex-lovers or disgruntled co-workers? Maybe they'd just been working late on a problem account and were exhausted after another long day at the office.

"Do you both work at Ogil–" I said, hoping to make some new introductions at the firm.

But as the pressure increased in my ears from the rapid descent of the elevator, suddenly the lights went out and the lift screeched to an abrupt halt.

"What the–" the woman said, breathing heavily.

"Oh my God!" I said, clutching my briefcase next to me as I quivered in the darkness. "What's going on?"

"It's probably just a power failure," the man said. "Everybody's been gearing up for the holidays and the little heat wave has been drawing a lot of power from the grid lately. I'm sure ComEd will have us back on track in no time."

"Are we safe, stuck so far off the ground?" I said nervously. "This is my worst nightmare – being stuck in an elevator suspended hundreds of feet in the air."

"Not to worry," the man reassured. "Modern elevators are equipped with multiple fail-safe mechanisms. An emergency brake automatically engages in the event of a power failure, so there's no way it can drop any further."

"What about the *cables*?" I asked, still petrified at the thought of losing control over the elevator. "Is there a chance they might fatigue or snap if this goes on for a while?"

"No way," he said. "There's more than one cable holding us up and each one is rated for much higher loads than our current weight. As strange as it may sound, this might be one of the safest places to be in the middle of a blackout. I hate to think how crazy it might be on the *streets* right now with all the traffic lights out."

"That's a small consolation," I said, beginning to breathe a little more normally. "I'd rather take my chances out there in broad daylight instead of being cooped up in this claustrophobic death trap."

In the pitch blackness, I could hear the sound of the woman's hands sliding frantically over the blacked-out console.

"What do we do now?" she said. "Can we communicate

with somebody while we're locked up in here? I can't find the emergency call button in the dark–"

Suddenly, the screen of the man's cell phone illuminated and I saw his fingers tapping the surface. A flashlight lit up on the back side, and he pointed it toward the elevator control panel.

"This should help a bit," he said.

We could see a red button near the bottom of the console, and the woman slammed her palm against it repeatedly.

"Can anyone hear me?" she screamed. "We're stuck in an elevator near the top floor of the Willis Tower. Somebody help us, please!"

"The coms are probably down too," the man said calmly. "None of the electronic systems will be working as long as the power is down. I think we just need to wait it out until power is restored or the building's maintenance crew comes to retrieve us."

"Our phones," the woman said, turning her head in the direction of the man's glowing screen. "There are other ways we can call for help."

The two of us pulled our phones out of our purses and tapped 911. A message filled the screen indicating that the mobile network was temporarily unavailable.

"What the fuck?" the woman said. "The *phones* aren't working either?"

As the man lifted his phone to examine his screen, the backlight illuminated his handsome face.

"There's no bars. The power failure has probably disabled the cell towers too."

"Doesn't the phone company have back-up generators or

something?" the woman said.

"Yes, but it will likely take some time for their systems to come online. But even if they do, every person in Chicago will likely be calling their family or emergency services to make sure everything is okay. I don't expect we'll be able to make any calls for at least a couple of hours."

"A couple of *hours*?!" the woman exclaimed. "How are we going to survive in this cramped elevator that long? What about air? Won't we run out of oxygen before then?"

"We're going to be fine, Elle," the man said. "There's plenty of ventilation ducts in the compartment, and with fifty floors above and below us, there's enough oxygen in the elevator shaft to support us for quite a long time."

*So they do know each other*, I smiled.

"You seem to know a lot about elevators for a guy wearing such an expensive suit," I said.

"Working on the hundred and fifth floor of the tallest building in the Midwest will do that to a guy. I'm a little claustrophobic too, so I did a little bit of research before I took this job. We'd *starve* to death long before any malfunction of the elevator would kill us."

"So we just stand here twiddling our thumbs while we wait for someone to come save us?" I said.

"It looks that way. But I'm guessing the emergency response people have their hands full dealing with a city full of panicked citizens. Plus, there's lots of other elevators in this building, so it's likely to be at least a few hours before anyone comes to our rescue. You might want to sit down and relax to make the wait a little more comfortable."

The man squatted toward the floor then leaned back

against the wall and straightened his legs out in front of him. Recognizing that we might be in this for a long haul, I followed his cue and sat down kitty-corner to him against the back wall. Peering up at the woman, I saw that she was still tapping the surface of her phone, trying to make an outside connection.

"Why don't you make yourself more comfortable, Elle?" I said, trying to ease her distress. "My name's Jade. I didn't catch your name–"

"West," the man said. "The least we can do is try to get to know one another better while we're stuck in here. Make the best of an uncomfortable situation."

"It's either that or play Candy Crush on our phones until the power comes back on," I joked.

Elle exhaled a sigh of resignation as I watched her phone slide down the wall to my right while she plopped down on the floor.

"Why not?" she said. "I can't think of a better inmate to spend my time with while I'm locked up in here.".

"You two know one another then," I said. "Do you work together, or do you have some kind of *other* relationship?"

"Hardly," Elle huffed. "Not in a million years."

"We work together at Ogilvy," West said. "We handle two of the firm's largest accounts. I guess there's been a bit of a competition of sorts to see who would make partner first–"

"Not likely, with that lame-ass automotive account you've been handed. Can't you see that's a dying business with more and more people switching to foreign cars these days?"

"Maybe, but at least it's *reliable.* Not like that new tech account of yours–"

Suddenly, our conversation was interrupted with the sound of banging coming from inside the elevator shaft.

"What's that noise?" Elle said.

We paused to listen as the clanging sound grew louder and more frenetic.

"Could it be the maintenance technicians trying to open the doors above us?" I said.

"Unlikely," West said. "I can't imagine they'd be able to respond this fast. Most of them are probably stuck in traffic on their way home already."

"What is it then?" Elle asked. "Are the cables about to snap?"

The clanging noises suddenly changed to a rhythmic pattern of short and long taps.

"It sounds like an SOS signal. Probably from another group of people trapped in an elevator above or below us."

"That's not a bad idea," Elle said, pounding her fist against the wall beside her. "At least we know we've got some company."

"Not that it's likely to do us much good," West said. "There's not much either of us can do from our current locations."

Elle tilted her phone up, scanning the ceiling with her flashlight.

"If you're so clever Mr. Smartypants, maybe you can figure out how to get the lid off this thing and find a nearby exit?"

West chuckled softly in the darkness.

"There's a reason these things aren't designed to be evacuated from the inside," he said. "It takes a special key to open the lid from the outside. It wouldn't be safe for us to exit that way even if we could. Who knows when the elevator might start up again and pin us against the walls?"

"With all the time you spend in the gym," Elle huffed, "I would have thought you could jimmy up the cables to the nearest door."

"Yeah," West said. "I'm sure it's that simple. I'll get right on it."

It was obvious there was a lot more going on between these two than a competitive rivalry. Their little digs sounded more like a high school crush than a workplace disagreement.

"Is it getting hot in here, or is it just me?" I said, trying to break the tension.

I'd begun to perspire under my suit, and I was pretty sure it wasn't because I was afraid of plummeting to my death anymore.

"I feel it too," West said. "The air conditioning systems would have gone offline along with the power. And the radiant heat from outside the building is slowly creeping into the elevator shaft."

"Oh great," Elle said. "So now we're going to *boil* to death while we wait for help?"

"It shouldn't get much hotter than the temperature outside. I expect it will begin to cool as the sun goes down. You can always loosen your clothes to get more comfortable."

"That's the best pick-up line I've heard in a while," I chuckled.

"You have *no* idea," Elle sneered. "He's full of them."

"I guess it wouldn't hurt to take off my jacket and loosen

my shirt," I said. "It's not like we can *see* anything in the pitch dark anyway, right?"

"I wouldn't put it past him to flash his phone you least expect it," Elle said. "We still have a few fleeting sources of power while we're waiting."

"Not for long," West said, peering at the glowing surface of his phone. "I'm already in the yellow zone for power. How about you guys?"

"I'm showing ten percent," I said.

"I'm down to *two* percent," Elle cursed. "I knew I should have replaced my battery during the last upgrade cycle. I can barely get through a full day at the best of times."

"We're consuming a lot of extra juice with our screens and flashlights on full strength," West said. "It's probably best to turn them off or at least switch to sleep mode to save them for when we really need them."

"Awesome," Elle said. "What do we do in the meantime?"

"Why don't we do what people used to do before the advent of modern technology and *talk* to one another," I said. "It sounds like you guys could use some more open lines of communication anyhow."

"What did you want to talk about?" she said sarcastically. "Our favorite hobbies and the unusual weather we've had lately?"

"Well it's probably best to steer clear of work," I suggested. "Tell us something personal about yourself, something nobody else would know. I mean, I'll probably never see you guys again once we get out of this predicament. Who else is gonna know?"

The compartment suddenly fell quiet as each of us

pondered what to say.

"You know, it's strange," West said, breaking the silence. "I've always wondered what it would be like be in a situation like this. It's kind of *exciting* in a way, being left to our own devices without any outside stimulation."

"Kind of like being trapped on a deserted island," Elle chuckled.

"In a way, I guess. Makes you wonder what you'd do to pass the time, so far removed from modern conveniences."

"What do you think *you'd* do to amuse yourself on this deserted island, West?" I said, eager to steer the conversation in a different direction.

"Depends on who I was stranded with."

"What if it were just *you*?"

"I guess I'd have to scrape by on my memories. Or spend my time fantasizing about how to get off the island."

"And if you couldn't?" Elle said. "What would you fantasize about then?

"The usual macho stuff, I suppose. "That I was stranded in paradise with a supermodel–"

"Or two?" I joked.

"The more the merrier," West said.

"You men are always fantasizing about doing it with multiple women at the same time," Elle said.

"What about you then, Elle?" I asked, deflecting the attention away from West temporarily. "What would be *your* ultimate fantasy if you were stranded on a deserted island?"

"I'd probably go stir crazy all by myself after a while. I suppose I wouldn't be much different from West, dreaming about being stuck there with David Beckham or Brad Pitt..."

"Only *men*?" I said, fishing for more details.

"I dunno. I've never tried it with women before. But I suppose if we were stuck on a deserted island long enough, one thing might lead to another..."

"What about you, Jade?" West said, sensing a theme developing.

"I lean more toward women, myself. Although if I didn't have any other choice, I might be tempted to dabble a bit–"

"It *is* getting hot in here," West said as the sound of rustling clothes filled the compartment.

"Hotter than your deserted island fantasy?" I asked.

"It's getting there. All this talk about mixing it up with different partners is making me hot under the collar."

"Don't let us stop you from acting out your fantasy, West," Elle said. "It's just us girls in here. We won't tell if you don't."

"What exactly did you have in mind?" West asked.

"Something tells me you're getting uncomfortable in those heavy clothes for more than one reason," she said. "If you need to free the beast, don't let us stop you from getting your freak on."

"Um..." West paused, unsure if we were thinking the same thing.

"I think maybe West needs a little extra encouragement, Elle," I said. "Why don't you scooch up a little closer to me so he can exercise his fantasy more vividly?"

"This little adventure is getting more interesting by the moment," Elle purred, shimmying her hips across the floor to sit next to me. "I suppose there's more than *one* way to relieve the boredom when you're stuck in an elevator."

## 2

"So, West..." I said, hoping to capitalize on the rapidly developing heat in the room. "Tell us more about your little fantasy. Maybe it'll help keep our minds off this unpleasant situation we find ourselves in."

"Um, well," he said, happy to have a distraction to mask his real desires. "I guess I'd have to get to know these super-models a bit better before we got down to business. I'd have to loosen them up a little before they thought about having sex with me, let alone with each other."

"Oh?" I said, playing along. "What would you want to know about us – I mean *them* – in order to get them in the mood?"

"I dunno, something about their families, I suppose. Maybe their relationship status. I'd need to make sure they were unattached before I proposed any kind of physical engagement. They might be kind of shy about wanting to try anything if they were already in a committed relationship."

"Let's pretend *we're* your fantasy supermodels for a moment," I said, nudging Elle's thigh playfully. "Let's see just how good your pick-up lines really are."

West shifted uncomfortably on the elevator floor and cleared his throat, imagining himself in a bar wedged between two women.

"Okay..." he said. "Well, first, of course, I'd ask them their names."

"I'm Jade," I purred.

"Elle," my partner-in-crime giggled.

"I'm West. Bit of a pickle we've gotten ourselves into. I suppose the first thing we need to do is make sure we have enough food and water to get us through this unfortunate turn of events. We don't know how long this situation might last."

"I've got a candy bar in my purse," I said, pretending to ruffle through my belongings.

"And I've got some bottled water," Elle said.

"That won't get us very far," West said. "But we might be able to catch some fish and create a pit to store fresh water when it rains. I guess our next order of business is to figure out how to send a signal to a passing ship so someone knows we're here. Do either of you carry a lighter?"

"I'm afraid I don't smoke," I said.

"Neither do I," Elle said.

"That's funny," West chuckled. "I always said that would be a deal-breaker whenever I met a pretty girl, but in this case we're going to have to find a workaround..."

"Are you saying you think we're *pretty*?" I teased.

"Well I don't want to swell your heads, but if I have to be

stuck on this island for an extended period of time, I can't imagine two people I'd rather be with."

*He's not bad*, I whispered in Elle's ear.

*He's got his moments*, she nudged.

"So how are we going to let anyone know we're here then?" I said.

West rustled through his suit jacket and I heard a soft tinkling sound.

"I should be able to use my reading glasses as a magnifying lens to start a fire. Then we just need to find some fresh foliage or wet logs to create enough smoke..."

"You seem to know a lot about survival techniques for a guy who works in an office all day long," Elle huffed.

"Maybe I watch a little too much of that show Man vs. Wild."

"Well if you think you can get us out of this situation, we'd be willing to do just about anything you asked," she purred.

"Including eating bugs and drinking your own urine?"

"I'm pretty sure we can find something a little more palatable to eat between the three of us," I said, squeezing Elle's thigh.

"It's too bad we've gotten ourselves into this predicament so close to the holiday," West said. "You both must have been looking forward to enjoying a proper Thanksgiving meal with your families."

"I was just going to have an informal get-together with a few of my siblings at my mother's place," I said.

"What about you, Elle?" West said, fishing for more

details about his colleague. "What did you have planned for the holidays?"

"I was on my way to the airport to visit my folks in LA when we got stuck in here. I hope they don't worry too much when they don't hear from me."

"Is there anyone *else* who'll be concerned about your whereabouts?"

*Smooth*, I nudged Elle. *He's looking to see if you're unattached.*

It was becoming increasingly obvious that West had more than just a working interest in her.

"Other than my *boss*, you mean?" Elle kidded. "Unfortunately, my job doesn't afford much free time for extra-curricular activities. What about you?" she said, turning back to West. "Who were *you* planning to spend some quality time with over the holidays?"

I smiled in the darkness, happy to hear the walls breaking down between the two co-workers.

"Other than my roommate and a few buddies on our house-league hockey team? We were just going to order a pizza and sit down to watch some football over the long weekend."

"You sound like a dyed-in-the-wool bachelor," Elle mused. "I didn't picture you sharing a flat with a buddy."

"Chicago's an expensive city for a single guy. Besides, sometimes it helps to have a wingman to navigate the social jungle. Speaking of living arrangements, it might be a good idea to start looking for a comfortable spot to spend the night–"

"We've already got plenty of shelter in our little corner

under the palm trees," I kidded. I shifted my weight, feigning discomfort. "Although it *is* a little hard. I could use a pillow about now..."

West folded up his jacket and passed it toward me in the dark, and I placed it under Elle's knees, nodding appreciatively.

*He's a gentleman too*, I whispered, trying to encourage their reluctant courtship.

"So you're a *player*, then," she said, still unconvinced. "Where do you and your buddy bring your conquests when you want to have a little fun? Isn't it a bit cramped in your two-bedroom apartment? Or do you two create your own fun with each other?"

"Uh, *no*," West said. "I don't swing that way. What about you two? What are two pretty girls like you doing still single? I might say the same thing about you."

"Oh I like *men* alright," Elle said. "I just haven't found one yet worthy of my attention."

"What kind of man are you looking for?" West probed.

"The strong silent type, I suppose. Someone who knows how to treat a woman like a lady and is good with his hands..."

"Like someone who could get you out of a jam like this?"

"Possibly. But someone who's also a good lover and provider. He'd have to have a stable job and a good build..."

"Fair enough," West said, looking to bring me back into the fold. "How about you Jade? What are you looking for in a potential partner?"

"Someone with long slender legs who can wrap herself around my hips while I fuck her madly–"

"Jesus," West said, adjusting his equipment in the dark. "I've always wondered how you women do that exactly. How you make love without a–"

"*Penis*? Don't tell me you haven't watched your fair share of girl-on-girl porn? We can do pretty much everything a man can do, just without all the mess."

"What about–*penetration*? Don't you ever miss that?"

"We have lots of ways to get that when we're in the mood. Between strap-on cocks, double-sided dildos and all the special sex toys on the market, we can find plenty of ways to stimulate ourselves on both the inside and the outside. In fact, I'm carrying one in my purse right now. You never know when you might feel the need..."

"Really?" West said, his voice taking on a new sense of urgency. "Where do you use it? Isn't it kind of noisy?"

"Not this one. A friend of mine introduced me to it recently. It's called the Osé, designed by a woman. It doesn't vibrate so much as *throb*. It's incredibly lifelike, with a long undulating wand and an opening at the base that provides stimulation remarkably similar to a tongue–"

"*Holy shit!*" Elle interrupted. "Can I see this thing? I've never heard of a woman's vibrator like that."

"Of course," I said, happy to see that see her rapidly warming up.

I opened my purse and handed her the soft silicone instrument. She ran her hands over the long finger-shaped extension, then pressed her hand into the little hole.

"How does it work exactly?" she said. "It's not shaped like any vibrator I've ever seen."

"Feel for a little notch near the bottom of the base.

There's two modes, each of which is activated with a press of the button."

Elle ran her fingers over the base of the object in the dark, then I heard her gasp.

"My God," she said. "It's *moving*. Like a real finger!"

"Exactly," I nodded. "It's designed to simulate the movement and feel of a real person. The curvature of the wand is perfect for stimulating your G-spot. Press the button again and see what *else* it can do."

I heard another click and Elle's body suddenly lurched next to mine.

"What the *fuck*?!" she exclaimed. "That feels just like a–"

"Tongue?" I said. "You won't believe how lifelike it is until you try it for real. Why don't you see for yourself?"

"Right here?!"

"Why not?" I said. "We're all getting pretty worked up with all this talk of sex with different partners. Besides, it's not like any of us can see anything in the pitch dark. If ever there was a safe place to try something like this, this is the time."

"I don't know," Elle hesitated. "It is intriguing, but I hardly know you guys..."

"Come on," I said. "I know you want it. I can feel your hips squirming next to me. Why don't you just slip it under your skirt for a moment? I think you'll get the idea pretty quickly what it's capable of."

Elle paused for a moment, then slowly began to spread her thighs apart. I could feel her hand rustling between her legs, then she gasped.

"Right?" I said. "Not like anything you've ever tried before, is it?"

"No," she panted, spreading her thighs further apart. "It feels more like a–"

"Real person?"

"Mmm," she purred.

"It might not be quite as good as the real thing, but you'll never know until you feel it against your naked flesh. Why don't you take your clothes off? We can place West's jacket under your hips if you're worried about the dirty floor. You don't mind do you, West?"

"Definitely not," he said, unbuckling his belt.

"Maybe for just a few seconds," Elle said. "But no peeking."

"Our phones are turned off, remember? No one will have any idea what you're doing unless you tell us."

"Okay, but no comments from the peanut gallery while I try this thing out. I'm self-conscious enough without you guys taunting me in the dark..."

"Maybe if we *all* took off our clothes together, it would make everybody feel more comfortable. That way, we could each explore our own bodies to the extent we feel comfortable. What do you think, West?"

"Way ahead of you," he said, pulling his pants down across the floor.

"Just go slow as you explore the device's capabilities," I said to Elle. "We'll be enjoying ourselves along with you."

"That does sound pretty hot actually," she said. "I'm getting hornier by the moment."

I lifted my hips off the floor, then pulled my skirt down over my legs and placed it underneath me. Then I grabbed

Elle's hand and pulled it over my bare thigh, inches from my steaming pussy.

"That makes two of us," I said.

"Damn, Jade," she said. "Your skin is so warm."

"That's not the *only* part of me that's warm right now," I said. "Go ahead, let yourself loose."

Elle paused for a second, then unzipped the back of her skirt and shimmied it down over her ankles. Then she lifted her hips and pulled her panties off her legs.

"There," I said. "Doesn't that feel better? Now give our little friend a try against your bare skin."

Elle paused with the vibrator poised inches from her twitching pussy.

"Do you prefer to use the finger or the tongue?" she hesitated.

"Both, depending on my mood. Why don't you start by letting the finger caress you around your opening?"

Elle turned her hand and positioned the Osé so the finger bent toward her in rhythmic motions.

"It feels–*strange*," she said. "Like I'm being touched by a robot."

"But a very *sexy* robot, yes? Just pretend it's Brad Pitt's or David Beckham's or someone *else's* finger caressing you..."

"Mmm," she sighed, tilting her head back against the wall of the elevator. "That does feel better."

"You might want to tease yourself for a while until you get fully warmed up. When you're ready, feel free to insert it inside to experience the full capability of the toy."

"Oh, I'm getting *warmed up* alright," she panted. "How about you guys?"

I spread my legs further apart and rested my thigh overtop Elle's as I began to circle my hand over my clit. With the two of us sitting so close together, she must have felt the movement of my arm against her side as I began to stimulate myself manually.

"I'm burning up inside," I panted as the sound of my fingers rubbing against my wet labia filled the compartment. "How are you doing over there, West?"

"I'm thoroughly enjoying this fantasy," he panted. "I haven't been this hard in ages."

"I'm guessing there's something *else* hard in this room," I said, flapping my thigh against Elle's. "Why don't you put that wand inside you so you can fantasize along with us?"

I could feel Elle's arms tense up for a moment as she held the tip of the undulating finger against her opening, then she groaned, sliding down the wall. As I listened to the sound of the long appendage slipping inside her dripping pussy, I slid the fingers of my right hand inside me at the same time.

"Uhnn," she groaned, pressing the device firmer against her vulva.

"Do you *still* need Brad Pitt on your deserted island?" I said.

"Not with this thing by my side," she purred. "This is better than any man. At least it knows the right places to caress."

"Feels heavenly, doesn't it?" I said, curling my fingers inside my own hole to rub the front side of my G-spot. "Have you turned the tongue on yet?"

"Not yet," Elle panted. "I'm just enjoying the feeling of being stroked inside right now."

"Mmm," I said, feeling my juices beginning to run down the crack of my ass. I was thrilled that Elle had loosened up enough to feel comfortable sharing what she was experiencing. "Take your time, baby. We've got all the time in the world."

"That's what worries me," she grunted. "That we might be stuck in this elevator all weekend."

"I'm sure we can find plenty of other ways to keep ourselves amused if it comes to that," I said. "But don't worry about any of that right now. Just pretend you're stranded in paradise with your ultimate lover. What would you like him to do next?"

"I'd like her to lick me," she slipped. "I mean *him*. I mean whoever."

I reached between Elle's slippery legs and tapped the button on the underside of her vibrator one more time. She pressed the device harder against her body and squealed with a guttural moan.

"Oh my God," she groaned. "That feels incredible. I feel it's tongue. It's so lifelike..."

"Yes, Elle," I purred. "Imagine it's your fantasy lover worshipping your body. You're so hot right now."

"Is this how you do it?" she said. "I mean when you're with other women? This doesn't feel like any *man* I've ever been with..."

"Like I said, the toy is designed by a woman to provide feminine stimulation in the most erotic manner. But you'll never know what it really feels like to make love to another woman until you try–"

"*Fuck*, Jade," Elle growled. "I want to feel you against my body. This feels so good."

"Yes, baby," I whispered, lifting my hand to her chin and turning her face to meet my lips. As we began to kiss passionately, I pulled my hand out of my pussy and slipped it under her blouse, cupping her breasts and pinching her erect nipples. "Imagine it's *me* licking your clit right now."

"*Oh fuck, oh fuck*," she gasped. "I can feel it coming..."

"Yes," I purred, rolling my tongue around the inside of her mouth. "Come inside my mouth, Elle. I want to feel you twitching as I suck your button."

"Oh God!" she wailed. "I cumming, Jade! I cumming so hard. Suck my pussy!"

As we face-fucked each other imagining we were joined at the hips instead of the mouth, I heard West groan on the other side of the elevator as Elle began shaking uncontrollably against my body. Even though I hadn't touched her anywhere near her pussy, with our tongues intertwined and my hand squeezing her shaking tits, I felt incredibly connected to her. As she groaned into my mouth in the throes of a powerful climax, I suddenly gushed out of my opening, spraying my juices all over her bare legs while we quivered together in the darkness.

Something told me this was going to be just the start of our little fantasy adventure...

**3**

———

For the longest time after we came, nobody said anything, as awkward silence filled the compartment. All we could hear was the sound of quiet breathing while we all recovered from our powerful climaxes. There wasn't even any rustling of clothes while we lay there in the dark, completely naked. There was something incredibly erotic about knowing each of us sat inches away from each other, with our exposed genitals still throbbing in excitement.

After a few minutes, I heard Elle reach between her legs and pull the Osé out of her wet pussy with a distinct plop.

"Thanks for letting me share your little toy," she said, handing it to me in the darkness. "I'm sorry that I've made such a mess of it..."

"Mmm," I said, placing the tip of the wand in my mouth and sucking it loudly. "Don't give it a second thought. I like it that way. You taste exquisite. I only wish I could have felt you twitching in my mouth for real."

"With that vibrator's tongue doing its action between my legs and you kissing me at the same time, it was like you were actually there," she said. "I haven't been this turned on in a long time."

"What about you, West?" I said, trying to bring our silent partner into the loop. "Did you enjoy our little fantasy role play? Do you think your supermodels are getting sufficiently warmed up?"

"Damn near," he panted. "That was the most erotic thing I've ever heard. My only regret is that nobody was actually *touching* each other."

"Oh, there was plenty of touching going on, believe me," I said. "And from the sounds of things on the other side of the elevator, you seemed to be enjoying yourself plenty enough."

"Well, yes," he said. "But it's not quite the same as–"

"Having someone *else* touch you? What do you think, Elle? Are you ready to take it to the next level?"

"Maybe," she said, hesitating. "What did you have in mind?"

"Between the three of us, with so many different, um–*tools*–to work with, there's an almost infinite number of ways we can engage. We could pair up to start, then maybe swap partners before the three of us get together. What's your pleasure?"

Elle paused for a minute as she pondered the possibilities. I sensed the walls were beginning to break down between her and West, but there was also no denying her attraction to me.

"I've always wondered what it would be like to make love to another woman," she said. "With you being so much more experienced in that area, maybe you could teach me how to do it properly..."

I grinned at Elle's feeble attempt to mask her real desires. She had no idea what she was in for.

"I can work with that," I said. "How about you, West? Do you think you can hold on a little longer while Elle and I have a bit more fun?"

"Oh, I'll be *holding on*, alright. I'm hard as a rock again knowing I'm about to realize one of my ultimate fantasies."

"Well you go right ahead and enjoy yourself over there while Elle and I get to know each other a little better."

I turned to Elle and squeezed her hand gently.

"Do you want to be the top or the bottom?"

"What do you mean?" she said. "I thought that only applied to men–"

"When two women get together, usually one takes the submissive role while the other takes a more dominant role. It's the same with lesbians as with gay men."

"Okay..." she said. "I guess since I'm the neophyte here, I should assume the more submissive role–"

"Not necessarily," I said. "If you were to take a more active role, you could proceed at your own pace and explore things as they strike your fancy."

"I kind of like the sound of that. How should we position ourselves to start?"

I paused for a moment to think about the best way to give her optimal freedom of movement while still allowing me to touch her freely.

"Why don't you kneel overtop of me while I sit against the wall? That way we can kiss each other while we press our bodies together–"

"Yes," she said. "That sounds perfect. And it will be easier for you to tell me what to do next."

"Possibly. But something tells me you'll pretty soon figure out what to do entirely on your own. But first, take off the rest of your clothes so I can feel *all* of you up next to me."

"Mmm, yes," she purred. "I want to feel every square inch of your body next to me."

While the two of us peeled off our tops and shoes, I could hear West pulling his pants off his ankles and spreading his legs in a wide 'V' on the floor of the elevator. This time, he didn't want anything getting in the way of his enjoying himself while he imagined the two of us making love in the dark.

"Okay," I said, when I heard the last piece of clothing drop to the floor. "Come over here and sit on my lap. I want to feel your wet pussy rubbing up against me."

"Fuck, yes," she growled, swinging her legs over my hips and lowering herself on top of my thighs.

She leaned forward, pressing her tits against mine, and we locked lips as our tongues danced in each other's mouths.

"Mmm," she moaned, twisting her hips on my lap.

I could feel her mound rubbing against abdomen as a trickle of liquid ran down the front of my stomach. I lifted my hands and squeezed her tits, plunging my tongue deeper into her mouth. Elle wriggled her hips over the space between my thighs, trying vainly to get direct stimulation to her burning clit. I reached under her ass and slipped three fingers inside her pussy, and she began to hop up and down on me like a kangaroo.

"Yes, Jade," she panted. "Fuck me with your hand. I want to feel *every* part of you..."

As I listened to the sound of her sopping pussy ramming against my hand, I angled my wrist and pinched her clit between my other two fingers. She pressed her hips harder against my mound and I began to roll her hard button between my fingers.

"*Oh fuck*, Jade," she hissed. "That feels so good. Rub my clit while I fuck your fingers. You're going to make me come very soon..."

Although I wanted to stimulate myself while she rubbed her body against me, with my legs held closed by her vice-grip of my thighs, I decided to give all of my dedicated attention to her.

"Yes, Elle," I purred, slipping down the wall a few inches so I could suck on her tits while she writhed against my dripping hand. "Come for me, baby. I want to feel your pussy squeezing my fingers when you let it loose."

As I sucked on her hard teats, burying my face between her plump tits, Elle suddenly arched her body and wailed at the top of her lungs.

"I'm cumming, Jade!" she screamed. "Suck my tits while I cum all over your sweet pussy!'

The walls of her pussy tightened, contracting over my fingers, and much to my delight and surprise, she began squirting out of her hole all over my mound. With her juices suddenly spraying over my clit, I lurched my body forward as a powerful orgasm suddenly washed over me. While we mashed our tits together and sucked on each other's tongues, I heard West groaning on the other side of the elevator as he flapped his hand wildly against his raging hard-on.

Moments later, the sound of clanging metal began emanating from far beneath us in the elevator shaft. But this time, the banging didn't have any rhythm to it, sounding more like the noise revelers make when they celebrate a new year by thumping pots together. Apparently, our fellow captives had heard the sounds of ecstasy echoing through the shaft and were signaling their approval of our little distraction.

**4**

———

Elle remained seated on my lap for many more minutes while we continued kissing and I caressed her wet labia with the tips of my fingers. It felt wonderful to have given her such a satisfying first lesbian experience, and I reveled in the feeling of her dripping pussy pressed against mine as our sweaty bodies rested against one another.

After a while, she pulled back a few inches and peered at me in the darkness.

"Thank you for making love to me so tenderly," she said. "I never imagined it could be this good. But what about you? This whole time you were focused on me. I want to touch you in the same places and make you feel as good as you did to me."

I smiled, running my fingers through her hair softly.

"I enjoyed that as much as you did Elle, don't you worry. When two women make love, it's more about the journey than the destination. We don't always have to get off to enjoy the experience of loving one another."

"I can see that," Elle said, lowering her head down the front of my chest. "But I've never felt a woman that way and I want this as much as you. Don't you want to feel my lips touching *you* now?"

I grabbed Elle's hair, holding her gently against my stomach.

"I do," I said, imagining her joined with me in a different way. "But not *that* way just yet. I want to feel your lips touching me in a different place."

"A different place?"

"I want to *fuck* you this time instead of making love to you. I want to feel your pussy rubbing against mine when we come together."

"Oh my God," Elle panted. "Yes, Jade. That sounds unbelievably sexy. What's the best way–"

I smiled as a devious thought crossed my mind. Up to this point, I'd felt a little guilty leaving West to his own devices, and I knew he and Elle were just waiting for an excuse to come closer together.

"I want you to get on all fours, facing away from me," I said. "I'll turn the other way around while we rub our asses together."

"But how–"

"Just trust me on this," I said. "I think you're going to like this. We won't just be rubbing our *asses* together."

"Oh," she said, quickly lifting herself off me and positioning herself a few feet away from me in West's direction.

I just hoped he hadn't spent himself entirely listening us making love the last time.

"How are you doing over there, West?" I said. "Do you think you can keep yourself amused a little longer while Elle and I try something a little different?"

"Knock yourselves out," he grinned. "I could do this all day and all night if necessary. I haven't been this hard for this long in ages."

"Don't lose that thought," I said. "We might be able to find some use for a *real* cock soon enough. Save a bit for us when the time comes."

"I'm not going anywhere," he said. "And neither is my dick."

I smiled as I positioned our clothes beneath the two of us, placing my hands and the balls of my feet on the floor, facing away from Elle. Then I shifted my weight backward until our cheeks touched.

"Mmm," Elle purred as she swiveled her buttocks playfully against mine. "I like the feel of your ass touching mine."

"That's not the *only* thing you're going to feel," I said, tilting my hips downward as my wet pussy caressed the inside of her thighs.

"Fuck, yes," Elle panted as she lifted her ass to press her vulva against mine. "This is so hot. I can feel your lips touching mine. Fuck me with your pussy. I want to feel you gushing against me again."

"Mmm," I said, mashing our cunts together. With our vulvas coated in slippery juices, as we slid our pussies against one another, a different kind of slopping sound filled the compartment.

"Fuck *me*..." West groaned, inches away from Elle's face with her body positioned near the base of his legs.

I could only imagine what was going through his mind as he listened to Elle and me fucking each other, and I smiled at how prescient his words were about to be.

*Soon enough, West*, I grinned.

As Elle and I gnashed our pussies together feeling our wet labia sliding over each other, I pressed myself harder against her clit, sliding her further in West's direction. Even though I was lost in the moment fucking her so hard, I had a second agenda for pushing her across the floor. I estimated that she was now only a few inches away from West's throbbing hard-on.

"Look between your legs, Elle," I said. "Even though we can't see each other in the dark, imagine you're watching our pussies rub together and seeing my tits shaking while I make love to you."

"Yes–" she said, then suddenly stopped, with our labia locked in a slippery kiss.

I sensed she'd felt something *else* in the darkness, and I knew her mind was racing about what to do next. But it didn't take long to begin hearing the sound of slurping noises coming from West's side of the elevator, as he began to groan excitedly.

"Oh God, Elle," he hissed. "That feels incredible. I've wanted you for so long..."

As he began thrusting his hips rhythmically into Elle's eager mouth, she hummed in pleasure while I resumed grinding against her pussy.

Knowing that the three of us were joined together in an

erotic daisy chain ratcheted my passion to a higher level. As we all began to moan and whine in tandem, my body suddenly tensed up and I squirted hard between Elle's legs, spraying my juices all over her tits and her face impaled on West's pole. She groaned loudly with West's dick in her mouth, then I felt her buttocks spasming against mine as her body quivered in the throes of another powerful climax. At the same time, West began grunting in rhythmic sequence, jetting his cum deep inside Elle's mouth. The sound of the three of us moaning in mutual pleasure must have been music to the ears of the listening gallery a few floors beneath us, and I wondered if they might soon get the same idea that we had.

Suddenly I no longer cared if anyone came to our rescue for the next few hours. We were having way too much fun finding ways to pass the time on our own little fantasy island.

## 5

For a few moments, we all remained still while we listened to the sound of the three of us panting in the darkness. This time there was no fanfare from others locked in the elevator shaft, now lost in their own distractions. Elle lifted herself off West's dripping cock and shuffled her body back over the floor, resting her back on the wall next to me. I reached out my hand and we interlocked our fingers, squeezing our hands together in acknowledgement of what had just happened.

Nobody wanted to say anything, embarrassed in the way lovers sometimes are the morning after an impassioned night of drunken partying. After all, we didn't really know each other very well, we were simply victims of the strange circumstance we'd found ourselves in.

*It's funny the way a crisis brings people together*, I thought.

I was about to break the silence when the sound of a

distant voice suddenly perked our ears. As we lay still in the darkened elevator, the unmistakable sound of a woman moaning wafted into our chamber. But this time, the noise had a distinct cadence to it, like two bodies slamming up against a metal wall.

"Yes, yes!" the woman said. "Fuck me hard, Chase!"

I smiled, realizing we'd aroused the interest of more than our little group.

"It seems that we've started a chain reaction," West chuckled from the other side of the elevator.

"What else are people going do when they're locked up in close quarters for such a long period of time?" I said.

"It *is* kind of exciting," Elle mused. "Being stuck in the darkness, feeling our way around with a bunch of strangers..."

"I'd hardly say we qualify as *strangers* anymore," West said.

The woman's voice suddenly grew louder and more forceful.

"Oh God, Chase!" she hollered. "Pound my ass!"

"That's certainly *one* way to get to know each other better," I laughed.

"I can't believe I'm admitting this," Elle said. "But I'm actually getting turned on listening to all this sex in the darkness."

The woman's voice reached a crescendo as the banging noises echoed through the shaft.

"I'm coming baby!" she wailed. "Uhn! Uhn! Uhn!"

"Me too," I said. "What about you West? Do you think you have any ammunition left in your cartridge?"

I could hear the shuffling of clothes, as West reached for something to clean himself up with.

"I don't know what it is about this situation," he said, "but I haven't been this turned on since I was a teenager. It's like I'm thirteen years old again. My cock hasn't been this resilient in twenty years!"

"We shouldn't let all that energy go to waste," I said. "What do you think, Elle? Are you ready for some more fun and games?"

"I'm so horny, I could fuck a billy-goat right about now," she said.

I smiled, sensing the opportunity to bring the two colleagues closer together.

"I suspect you've got something a little better endowed on the other side of the elevator. I can feel the sexual energy between you two. If you don't fuck each other soon, there's liable to be a short-circuit in here before long."

"You're probably right," Elle said. "But what about you? What will you do to keep yourself distracted?"

"I'll let my fantasies wander for a little while," I said. I picked up the Osé vibrator resting on top of my skirt and slid it across the inside of Elle's thighs. "I've got my little friend here to keep me amused. You two go get yourselves better acquainted. I'll be just fine for a little while."

"Okay," she said. "But don't get too attached to that thing. I'm looking forward to tasting you with my *own* tongue when I'm finished with West."

"I'll be waiting patiently," I smiled. "Dreaming of all the ways we can pleasure one another."

"Mmm," she said. "Save that thought. I'll be back soon."

"Don't rush things too much," I said. "I'll be enjoying myself just as much as the two of you."

Elle kissed me sweetly on the lips, then skittered over to West's side of the elevator. Moments later, I heard the sound of wet lips kissing and two voices moaning. From the rustling sounds, I guessed that West had remained seated while Elle had assumed the superior position, sitting on his lap.

*This time, she won't have to fish around for something to stimulate her pussy*, I smirked in the darkness. As I imagined her sinking down over West's pole, I plunged the Osé vibrator into my pussy and began rocking my hips back and forth.

"Ohh," Elle moaned as the sound of rhythmic thumping emanated from the other side of the elevator.

"Elle," West panted. "I've wanted this for so long. You feel so good."

"I've been watching you for quite some time," she sighed. "I had no idea you were so well equipped."

"Uhnn," West groaned, slapping his balls against Elle's ass.

"Fuck me with your big dick, West," Elle grunted. "Let's give Jade something to think about."

"Oh, I'm *thinking* about it, alright," I said, tapping the button on the bottom of the Osé, activating it's tongue action. "I'm already fantasizing about what I want to do with the two of you when you're done over there."

"Do you want a piece of West's cock too?" Elle said.

"Maybe," I teased. "It depends on whether I'll have a pretty girl to play with at the same time."

"Mmm, yes," Elle said. "Do you think you might *like* that, West? Having your way with both of us at the same time?"

"*Fuck*, Elle," he panted. "I'm trying to keep it together. Don't make me pop off too soon. That's the last thing I need floating around the office when we get back to work. That I couldn't even last long enough to satisfy you–"

"Don't worry, West," Elle purred. "Your secret will be safe with me. Just imagine sliding your cock between our pussies while we rub our bodies together..."

"Oh God..." West groaned as his mind began to wander.

"Yes, baby," Elle said. "Come inside me as you imagine the two of us tribbing your big cock between our wet lips..."

I smiled at Elle's torment of poor West. But I sensed she was trying to excite someone *else* in the room, and it was working. As I squirmed against the pulsing wand and the slippery tongue caressing my pussy, I couldn't resist getting in on the action.

"Fuck, yes," I hissed. "I want to feel some *real* meat between my legs next time, Elle. I want to feel his pole trembling as he comes all over the two of us–"

"*Damn*," West groaned, as Elle pressed her ass down over his balls. "I can't stop it–"

"Yes, baby," Elle purred. "I feel you cumming inside me. Let it go while you dream about your fantasy supermodels. It's about to happen for real."

"Ohh!" I groaned, pressing the Osé toy harder against me as I began cumming in unison with West. "I feel it too. My cock is twitching inside me too. I'm cumming imagining it's *your* cock fucking me right now, West. Come with me, baby."

"*Uhnn, uhnn, uhnn*," West grunted, as Elle's pussy squeezed his pulsating dick.

By the time he finished moaning, I'd soaked the wet floor and clothes in front of me.

"Holy shit!" I sighed, sliding down the wall in contentment. "That was fucking hot! You two sure know how to drive a girl crazy."

"We're just getting started," Elle said, squeezing West's throbbing cock with the walls of her pussy. "I can feel that West is up for some more fun. It's time the three of us finally came together. Why don't you come over here and join us, Jade?"

"I thought you'd never ask," I said, sliding my body over to their side of the elevator.

I reached my hands out to find them in the dark and felt Elle's back as she sat straddled West's hips with his back against the elevator wall. I spread my knees over his legs and shimmied my body against them, pressing my breasts against Elle's sweaty back.

"Mmm," she purred. "You're so warm."

"And wet," West said, feeling my juices running over the top of his thighs.

"All the better to *fuck* you with," I said, reaching behind my ass to squeeze his balls. "Are you still hard? Because we're not done with you yet."

Elle turned her head to kiss me as she flexed her buttocks, gripping West's pole.

"Oh he's hard alright. But I want to get my hands on you before he gets any ideas. I've been dying to taste you since the moment I laid eyes on you."

"Really?" I said. "I thought you were just into men?"

"So did I until I saw you. There was something about the way you looked at us with that gleam in your eye. I knew I couldn't let you get away the moment the elevator doors closed."

"I guess the power failure happened at a fortuitous time then," I chuckled.

"It's the best thing that could have happened to us," West nodded.

I reached around Elle's back and squeezed her tits gently.

"So how do you want to do this? We better act fast before West loses that loving feeling."

"If you *really* want a piece of him," she said. "I suppose I can let you have first dibs–"

I smiled at Elle's offer, but I had other ideas for West's tool.

"I think we can find a way for him to get in on the action while we still have our way with each other."

"Really?" Elle said. "I'm not picturing it. How can we–"

"Never fear," I said. "I've had a bit more practice with these situations. Get back on the floor on all fours."

"But West has already–"

"Don't you worry about him. He's about to have the experience of his life. I'll lie underneath you in a sixty-nine position so we can lick each other at the same time."

"But I thought you said–" West protested.

"There's plenty in it for you *too*, West" I said. "Get behind Elle's ass and play with her from behind. That way, we can both have access to your boy parts."

Elle lifted herself off West's staff and positioned herself

over top of our jumble of clothes. I slithered underneath her, grabbing the sides of her thighs, pulling my head between her splayed knees. West patted the floor with his hands trying to locate us and when he felt Elle's ass turned up in the air, he positioned himself behind her.

I reached up feeling for his dick and when I grasped his manhood, I gasped. It was bigger than I imagined, at least eight inches in length and six inches around. As I stroked my fingers toward its apex, I smiled when I felt his slippery head. He was still coated in Elle's juices and I plopped it into my mouth, savoring her delicious scent.

"Hmm," I hummed, swirling my tongue around his corona.

Elle could feel my breath blowing out of my nostrils toward her exposed pussy and she lowered herself toward my face, desperate to feel my touch. I pulled West's cock out of my mouth and rubbed the tip against her clit, licking his shaft from the base of his balls all the way to the tip, slathering my tongue over both of their glans.

"Oh God," West panted in delirious pleasure, feeling two women's bodies caressing his sensitive organ for the first time.

"Lick my clit, Jade," Elle growled, elated to feel my mouth against her sex finally. "Make West cum all over my pussy."

"I'd rather feel you come on my tongue," I cooed. "I've got other ideas for West."

I grabbed his shaft and angled the tip toward Elle's hole, and he eagerly sank his manhood into her tunnel. While they both groaned feeling my breath on their genitals, Elle spread her thighs further apart, lowering her vulva closer to my face. I pressed my hands outward against the inside of her knees until her flaming clit touched my lips. As I sucked her nub into my mouth and swirled my tongue over her shaft, she buckled under the weight.

"Oh my God, Jade," she hissed. "That feels incredible. Suck my clit while West fucks my pussy. I've never felt anything this good..."

As West rammed his cock in and out of Elle's hole, I felt his balls swinging against my forehead and I raised my hands to cup his sac, stroking the space in front of his anus.

"Fuckkk!" he squealed, hardly believing he was the lucky recipient of both our attention.

He leaned forward and grabbed Elle's tits from behind, pressing her face closer toward my steaming pussy. Smelling my box inches from her lips, she placed her head between my legs and began licking me like a puppy. As West began pounding her faster, I swung my arms around her hips and pulled her harder into my crotch. The thrusting motion accentuated the stimulation of my clit, as her tongue slapped back and forth against my inflamed nub.

"Mmm," I moaned, feeling Elle's clit growing harder in my mouth. "Suck my cunt, Elle. I want to feel you cum in my mouth as I squirt all over your face."

Elle nodded enthusiastically, trying to mimic the stimulation I was giving her on the other end. She was a quick study, and before long I felt my orgasm approaching as West's balls suddenly tightened and Elle began bucking wildly on top of my face. Within seconds, all three of us were wailing at the top of our lungs, signaling we'd reached the height of pleasure.

As Elle's clit began twitching in my mouth, I grabbed West's balls and squeezed them tightly while he tensed his buttocks and came inside Elle for the second time that day. I could feel his pelvic floor muscle contracting as he emptied his seed inside Elle's pussy, and the combination of sensations was too much for me to hold back. As Elle and West groaned in mutual climax, I tilted my hips and sprayed my juices all over Elle's face planted between my legs. We shook and grunted in unison for what seemed like a full minute before collapsing together on the floor in exhaustion.

But just as I was looking forward to a relaxing respite in the arms of my new friends, the elevator suddenly lurched and the lights came on as it began to descend.

"Holy shit!" Elle said, realizing we only had seconds before the doors opened and we'd be exposed to anyone waiting on the ground floor. "We better get ourselves put together before we're found out!"

We scrambled to put on our wet and wrinkly clothes, and as the elevator jerked to a stop, we looked at each other and smiled.

"That was one hell of a ride," Elle grinned.

As the elevator doors opened, we grabbed each other's hands and nonchalantly strode past the alarmed maintenance crew and rescue workers. The large wet spots and undeniable scent of sex on our clothes left little doubt what we'd been up to in the elevator. When we swung open the main exit doors and walked out onto the building courtyard, a large crowd was waiting to greet us. Without skipping a beat, they spontaneously erupted into a loud ovation.

*I guess we weren't the only ones being entertained while we were locked up this whole time,* I grinned.

Elle and West peered at one another, then leaned over and kissed each other passionately. I was happy to see that I'd been able to create more than one new connection among my friends at the Ogilvy & Mather Advertising Agency.

---

**R**eady for more erotic chills and thrills? Enjoy the next volume in Jade's Erotic Adventures:

*Some girls have a little more to work with than others...*

**Sneak peek:**

*But when I reached the base of her mound, instead of finding a little clit, I felt a huge, throbbing phallus pointing upward toward her stomach. Hardly believing what I was feeling, I placed my fingers around the shaft and squeezed it tightly to see if it was real. Unlike any strap-on dildo or faux penis I'd ever felt before, this one felt warm and spongy in my hand. And unlike the usual plastic or silicone fake dick, hers pulsed in my hand as I felt the rush of blood coursing through its shaft...*

## READ MORE...

# VOLUME TWO

---

## PARLOR GAMES

1
———

**THE INVITATION**

This had to be the strangest party invitation I'd ever received.

And the most titillating.

It was from my friend Madison, and the subject heading simply read *Parlor Game*:

*You are cordially invited to a special party at Madison's house, Saturday, June 15, at 9:00 p.m. sharp. Dress code is optional. It's a sit-down affair, but I assure you it will be anything but boring. Be prepared to be entertained like you've never been before. Come alone, but come often!*

*Mad*

*P.S.: There will be special arrival procedures. Text me five minutes before you get to the door. Please be punctual because the game cannot be interrupted once started. RSVP by Friday, 6:00 p.m.*

*WTF?* I thought upon first reading the invitation. *What kind of parlor game is 'dress code optional'? Did that mean we were free to wear whatever we wanted, or did it mean we were meant to wear no clothing at all? And why couldn't I bring a date?*

But I liked the *come often* idea.

*What was Madison up to this time?* I knew she had a kinky side, but I had no idea what she had planned for this event. Who could turn down such an invitation? Her parties always had the most interesting people, the best music, and plenty of unexpected hook-ups.

I picked up the phone and called her as soon as I got the message, dying to get all the dirt on this shindig.

"Whassup, gurl?" Maddie said when she answered my call, recognizing my caller ID.

"You've definitely got my attention now," I said.

"You got my message?"

"Uh–*yeah*. That is one crazy, cryptic invite. What are you getting us into this time?"

"Sorry, I can't provide any more details," she said. "Need to know only. Everything will be explained when you arrive. Are you coming?"

"How could I *not*, with that kind of invitation? But I'm confused about your dress code comment. I have no idea what to wear."

"It doesn't matter what you wear. I assure you no one will be paying attention to any of that."

"Oh, *come on!*" I said. "Now you've really got me squirming in my chair. You have to give me at least a *hint* at what's going to happen. Is it at least *legal?*"

"Of course," she said. "We're all consenting adults. But

there will be an opt-out clause for anyone who doesn't feel comfortable participating. I'd never put my friends in a compromising position."

"Okay, you've twisted my arm," I said. "But what's this calling five minutes ahead business? I've never heard of such a thing beyond the usual RSVP."

"It's just to ensure the privacy and confidentiality of our guests. It's the anonymity of the affair that makes this party so special."

*Anonymity?* I thought. *So I'm not going to know anyone who'll be attending? How does she propose to maintain everyone's privacy?* This thing was getting weirder and more exciting by the moment.

"Fine," I said, shaking my head in frustration. "Your house, your rules. But this better be everything it's cracked up to be. Because now you've seriously raised my expectations."

"I hope that's not the *only* thing I've raised," she purred over the phone. "See you Saturday at nine. Don't be late!"

When I hung up the phone, I could feel my heart pounding in my chest. The call had done nothing to lessen my confusion about the event, only to further arouse my curiosity and excitement. And yes, she'd definitely succeeded in raising more than just my expectations. Feeling my clit hardening in my panties, I opened my blouse and squeezed my erect nipples.

I wasn't sure what I was getting myself into, but my rapidly moistening panties told me this wasn't going to be a party soon forgotten.

**2**

---

## IN THE DARK

On the night of the event, I circled Madison's block at least three times trying to get a better idea about this mysterious game she'd cooked up. But all I could see was a slow procession of strangers approaching her door, one at a time. In each case, she opened the door to greet them, then closed it just as quickly. I had no way of determining how many guests had arrived or what was going on inside. I thought I recognized a few cars parked on the adjoining streets, but there was no way of knowing for sure if they belonged to people I knew.

*Note to self. Next time take a pic of my friend's plate and attach it to their contact listing on my phone. You never know when that might come in handy.*

On my fourth go-round, I called Maddie from the next street over five minutes before nine. I didn't want to be the first one to break protocol and miss any of the fun.

"I'm here," I said when I heard her pick up.

"Cool," she said. "Find a parking spot close to the house, then come up to the door in five minutes. I'll greet you and get you all set up."

*Set up?* I thought, hanging up the phone. *What does that mean? And what's with all this careful spacing of guests? Isn't a party supposed to be all about getting to know one another and meeting new faces?*

No matter, I thought, circling around the block and finding a spot on the side of her street four houses down. Judging by the number of cars queued up, it looked like it was going to be an intimate affair. I walked up to her door and tapped the bell. Madison opened the door and after glancing outside to make sure I was alone, she ushered me into her foyer.

"Glad you could make it," she said, smiling at me. "I was afraid I might have scared you off."

"Are you kidding me?" I said. "Wild horses couldn't keep me from coming to this party. If only to see what you've got cooked up."

"I'm glad," she said. "It wouldn't be the same without you."

She pulled a thin black cloth out of a bag resting on the floor and handed it to me. "First up, I need you to put this on."

"A *blindfold*?" I said, widening my eyes. "What for?"

"You'll see," she said. "Maybe not in the *literal* sense, but everything will become apparent soon enough."

She carefully positioned the bandana over my eyes then tied it firmly behind my head.

"No peeking," she said. "That'll ruin all the fun. Not to mention everyone's privacy."

"I couldn't even if I wanted to," I said, feeling the soft fabric wrap snugly over my nose and cheekbones, blocking out my entire field of vision. "Are you going to escort me inside so I don't break a leg?"

"Of course. But you'll have to strip first."

"Say *what*?" I said, cocking my head.

"Oh *please*," she said. "You've never been shy about showing off your amazing body before."

"Well yes, but that was usually with a modicum of cover or around people I know. In this case, I have no idea who'll I be exposing myself to."

"Nor will they. That's why everybody *else* will be blind-folded too."

"Okay," I said, beginning to understand why she'd been so careful not to let anyone see her arriving guests. "But is it safe? I mean, how do I know I'm not going to be accosted by some stranger once I get to the meeting room?"

"You've got nothing to worry about. Everyone will be seated two feet apart on separate chairs. And remember, you can always pull out anytime you feel uncomfortable. I've got your back, girl."

"Jesus, Mad," I sighed. "You are one twisted bitch. I'm just going to have to trust that you know what you're doing."

I started removing my clothes and handed them to Madison and when I was completely naked, she escorted me down a hall into another room where I heard her place my belongings on a table. Then she took my hand and led to me to terrycloth towel-covered chair and eased me down onto it.

"I'll be back after the next guest arrives," she said. "You're welcome to chat with the other guests already here while I'm away. Just don't reveal any names and keep your blindfold in place to maintain the secrecy. The party will get started shortly."

I heard Madison head back to the foyer then for the next few awkward moments, silence filled the room.

"Welcome, new guest," a baritone man's voice said.

I couldn't place him, but he sounded about my age, mid-thirties.

Okay, so at least I know it's a *co-ed* affair.

"Hello," I said timidly, placing my right leg overtop of my knee to protect my modesty.

"It's okay," a woman's voice said. "We were just as freaked out when we got here too."

"Good to know," I nodded, happy to hear another woman's voice in the crowd. The idea of sitting stark naked in a room full of naked strangers was disconcerting to say the least, but strangely arousing. I shifted uncomfortably in my chair, hearing the sound of plastic squeaking underneath me.

"That's a voice I recognize," a familiar-sounding woman said.

It sounded like my friend Lily from last year's camping trip. We'd shared a brief but passionate fling on our one-week excursion into the woods of northern Canada, and suddenly I felt the space between my overlapping thighs become slippery with lubrication.

"Is that–?"

"Sh!" she quickly interrupted me. "No names, remember? You don't want to get kicked out before all the fun starts."

"Mmm," I nodded, squeezing my thighs even tighter

together, feeling my clit twitching in excitement between my legs.

I could hear the sound of another guest arriving and quiet murmuring from the other end of the house, then Madison escorted the person into the room and sat him down with the rest of the group. From the minimal smalltalk we'd engaged in during her absence, it sounded like everyone was arranged in a circle roughly twenty feet in diameter. I smiled at Madison's ingenuity concocting such a bold idea, and as I listened to the group of strangers talking around me, my mind began to wander with what she intended to do with us.

When the last guest was seated, I heard her take a seat a few feet to my left as she opened the proceedings.

"First off," she said. "I want to thank everyone for coming. I know it was a pretty vague invitation, and I can't blame any of you if you're wondering what you've gotten yourself into. But I know each of you well enough to know that you're open to new adventures and that you're reasonably uninhibited, if that's the right word."

"If we weren't before, we sure as hell are *now*," the husky-voiced man said.

Everybody chuckled nervously, then Madison continued her briefing.

"Okay, I won't keep you in suspense any longer. What I had in mind was a kind of free association body exploration between willing partners. I thought it might be kind of fun to receive, and then later on, provide some physical stimulation to a chosen partner one at a time, without anyone actually knowing who was doing the giving and who was receiving the stimulation..."

"And by *stimulation* you mean–" I heard Lily enquire.

"Whatever your partner feels comfortable providing. And what you feel comfortable receiving. Because of the blindfolds and the no-name rule, each of the connections will be anonymous. I'll make the initial introductions, and then it's up to each couple to decide how far they wish to proceed. In some cases, you'll be able to guess the gender of your partner, and in some cases you may not. But in all cases, you won't know who it is you're engaging with.

"Unless, that is," Madison said. "You have a prior history with that person and you're specially attuned to your partner's technique and endowments."

"What about–?" someone said, voicing what all of us were thinking.

"For heterosexual combinations, I've put aside a set of condoms on each of your tables to your right. Along with your choice of beer, wine, or cocktails in unspillable containers. Sorry for the sippy cups, but I thought some of you might need a little extra lubrication to get started, and we don't want to make too much of a mess."

"Speaking of–" another woman said.

"You'll also find a tube of lube on each of your tables, should you feel the need. As for cleanliness and diseases, each of you is on your honor to step away or refuse to participate if you have any known issues."

Awkward silence suddenly filled the room.

"Is there some kind of *goal* or *prize* with this parlor game?"

I asked. "Or are we just supposed to go with the flow and take everything it as it comes?"

"There will be special prizes later on in the evening for each partner who correctly guesses who received and who provided stimulation. But I suspect the main reward will be enjoyed while you're *living* the experience."

I could hear nervous laughter around the circle as everyone knew exactly what Madison meant.

"Okay," she said. "Now that you understand the rules of engagement, anyone is free to withdraw if you're feeling at all uncomfortable, or abstain from participating once given the choice. I've assembled a small enough group that everyone should have a chance both to receive and give before the evening is over. Does anybody want out?"

Awkward silence filled the room again as I listened to the sound of guests shifting uncomfortably in their chairs. Whether it was because they were nervous or because they were already becoming aroused, I couldn't be sure, but I certainly knew which it was in *my* case.

"Okay then," Madison said. "Let the fun begin. Raise your hand if you want to be the first to give it a try."

I heard the sound of shifting a few chairs away, but I decided to hold back to see how things played out at first.

"Good," Madison said. "I see some of you guys came to play. We've got our first two candidates."

I heard Madison rise from her chair and walk to the other side of the circle, then a pair of footfalls approached a chair a few feet to my right.

"You may proceed at your leisure," Madison said. "If at any time you feel uncomfortable or wish to stop the engagement, simply cross your arms and/or legs and your partner will stop immediately. However, if you're enjoying what you're experiencing, I encourage each of you to let down your guard as much as you feel comfortable and open yourself up to all the possibilities."

"Can we *talk* to our partner while we're engaged in the process?" a man's voice said in front of the chair.

"By all means," Madison said. "Feel free to provide whatever guidance, requests or feedback you feel heightens the experience. The only rule is no revealing of names, and no peeking at any time."

As I listened to the sound of the man kneeling on the carpet in front of the chair, I placed my hands in my lap and pressed my fingers down over the front of my mound. Even before I'd been touched by anyone, I was already feeling more excited and aroused than I'd been in a long time.

3

# MF

For the first couple of minutes, I could only hear the sound of the man's hands caressing someone's skin and the subtle squeaking of a chair to my right. I didn't even know if it was a man or a woman who he'd been paired with, and my mind raced with the idea of stretching each of our sexual boundaries. Although I considered myself pansexual, I suspected many of the other guests considered themselves straight who wouldn't under normal circumstances engage in intimate relations with another person of the same sex.

But this was far from typical circumstances. Madison had created a unique, non-judgmental environment for open-minded strangers to explore each other's bodies while focusing only on the sensations they were giving and receiving. It was a brilliant idea, and I could feel the terrycloth towel under my butt already moistening from the stream of juices beginning to run down my vulva. Now I knew why she'd covered each of the chairs with a plastic screen and a towel. I was pretty sure I wasn't the *only* one getting this turned on listening to the two strangers exploring each other's bodies in the dark.

Suddenly, I heard a woman moaning where the man had been placed, and the sound of plastic squeaking under her seat.

*Okay,* I thought. *So this first pairing is a man giving pleasure to a woman. Madison's playing it safe to start, hoping to ease everybody's nervousness about engaging with an unidentified stranger.* Although I preferred lesbian sex myself, I was not above enjoying other people's intimate relations, especially at a safe distance.

"Mmm," I heard the woman purr, squeaking her chair more loudly.

It was obvious to all of us that whatever the man was doing, she was enjoying his attention while she squirmed her hips on the chair.

"That feels good," she said, encouraging him to continue. "I want to feel your hands on my breasts. Squeeze my tits and pinch my nipples."

"Hmm," the man hummed in acknowledgment, shifting his position closer to her body on the plush carpet below my feet.

"Yes," she hissed, feeling the man's hands caressing her tits. "Whoever you are, I like your touch. Now suck my nipples while I run my fingers through your hair..."

I heard the sound of wet lips smacking on skin as the woman groaned, and I spread my knees apart, circling my clit listening to her getting more and more turned on by the man's ministrations. There was something incredibly sexy about not knowing who was engaged in the veiled sex act or what they looked like.

While the smacking and moaning sounds continued a few chairs away, I began to hear the squeaking of chairs and subtle sighs of *other* people around the circle. It was obvious that many of the other attending guests had become just as aroused as I was from what was going on beside them, and they felt brave enough to touch themselves knowing nobody else was watching.

*Nobody except Madison,* I smiled. *You scheming bitch. You designed this scenario not only for the enjoyment of your guests, but so you could shamelessly watch everybody while they pleasured one another and themselves.* I could only imagine what she was doing while this was all going down. It must have been a feast for her eyes watching the naked couple exploring each other's bodies, not to mention all the guests touching themselves while they listened in.

"Can you feel how hard my nipples are getting?" the woman said as the man continued sucking her teats.

"Oh yes," the man murmured with his face buried in her cleavage.

"Start licking your way down the front of my stomach. There's something *else* getting hard that needs your attention."

"Mmm," the man purred, kneeling back on the carpet as he lowered his face down her body.

"Yes," she moaned. "Just like that. Rub your rough face over my bare mound. I want to feel your stubble scratching my skin before you fuck me."

*Jesus*, I thought, spreading my legs further apart while I jilled my clit furiously. I could feel the towel underneath me getting wetter by the moment as I listened to these two strangers ramping up the action. There was a whole extra level of excitement from not being able to see what was going on and only being able to listen to the two lovers as they touched one another. It was true what they said about our other senses being heightened when another one is compromised. My whole body was buzzing like it had an electric current running through it.

I could hear the scratching sound of the man's whiskers rubbing against the woman's skin, and knowing how close his face was to her most sensitive part was driving me crazy with anticipation. And from the sound of the rustling plastic all around me, apparently I wasn't the only one who felt this way.

"Now put your face between my legs and lick my lips up and down," the woman instructed. "I want you to taste my juices while I feel your bristles between my legs."

*Holy shit*, I thought, placing my palm over my snatch, rubbing my entire vulva with my hand. *I love the way she's bossing him around like he's her slave. It must be driving him crazy not being able to be touched himself. Kind of like the rest of us, except we've got a little more freedom of expression not having other distractions getting in the way.*

"Fuck, yes," the woman groaned. "Your tongue feels so warm on my lips. Now stick it inside me and fuck me while I pull your face into my crotch."

I could hear the sound of wet skin slapping against each other as other voices around the room began to moan and sigh in concert with the woman next to me. Imagining it was me on the receiving end of the man's attention, I stuck my middle finger in my pussy and began fucking myself while I circled my nub with my other hand.

"Deeper," the woman moaned. "I want to feel you probing into my deepest recesses. You're sucking my cunny like a good boy."

"Um-hmm," the man hummed, obviously enjoying the feedback he was getting from his partner while he ate her pussy.

As I listened to the muffled sound of his voice, I imagined her grabbing the back of his hair while she held his face against her cunt. I placed both of my hands between my legs and closed my thighs around them, envisioning it was the man's head pressed against my sex instead of my hands. I could feel my pleasure beginning to rise, but I wanted to hold off coming so I could enjoy the woman's orgasm fully.

"That's it, baby," she growled. "Fuck my pussy with your tongue. I'm getting close now. Lift your head and take my button into your mouth. Suck my clit like you've never sucked on anything before. Make me cum all over your face."

"If you insist," the man murmured with gentle laughter filling the room.

This whole experience was turning out to be even more exciting than I had envisioned. Multi-gender partner swapping with the mystery of not being able to see the couples in action, and even a little humor.

*I have got to try this blindfold thing with more of my own partners*, I thought. *What a great way to get more attuned to their touch and learn to give better feedback.*

Suddenly, the woman gasped as the plastic on her chair squeaked from the shifting of her ass on the seat. There wasn't much mystery as to what they were doing to each other now. As the licking sounds escalated in volume along with the movement of her hips in her chair, everybody knew he was now sucking on her clit while she pressed his face between her legs.

"Yes," she panted. "Suck my bean and swirl your tongue over it like you're licking a lollypop. I'm going to come in your mouth soon."

"Mmm," the man hummed in assent, not wanting to interrupt the rhythm of his tongue action.

I could only imagine how hard he must have been kneeling between her legs as he sucked her pussy, listening to the sound of her escalating tension. I could almost *see* the cum dripping from the tip of his penis onto the carpet below her chair while he focused on maximizing her pleasure. I nodded at how clever Madison had been in separating the acts of giving and receiving so that each person could enjoy the experience to the fullest without any other distraction.

"That's it, baby," the woman grunted. "Suck me harder. I'm going to come any second."

As I listened to the sound of the woman's chair squeaking and her breath rising in pitch, I spread my legs further apart and pinched my clit between my fingers while I rubbed it up and down. I was ready to come along with the woman, and there was no longer anything holding me back from expressing myself fully. I didn't care if my seatmates heard what I was doing or how much pleasure I was giving myself. This blind exploration experience had turned out to be more arousing than any explicit porno I'd watched on my computer on lonely nights.

"Yes!" the woman grunted. "Don't stop. Oh God, I'm going to cum! I'm gonna cum so hard in your mouth. *Fuckkk*!"

As I listened to the woman wailing at the top of her lungs, I felt my own orgasm wash over me while I clamped my legs together and gushed all over my hands. After my climax began to ebb, I became more aware of the sounds of the other people in the room as they experienced their own climaxes listening to the sexy couple. With everybody grunting and gasping in collective ecstasy, I turned my head to face Madison, knowing she was watching the whole scene only a few chairs away.

*You little fucker*, I smiled. *You knew exactly what you were getting us into.* I was so turned on I wanted to jump out of my chair and grind my pussy against her face just like the woman had done with the man.

But I knew that would have to wait. There were still too many *other* possibilities to explore in the meantime.

---

After a few moments, I heard the sound of the woman's breathing return to normal and the man pull away, wondering what to do next. Although she'd just had a powerful orgasm, there were still many other ways they could connect, and he must have been bursting in anticipation. Sensing his discomfort, the woman sat up in her chair and cleared her throat.

"God damn," she said. "You sure know how to satisfy a

woman with your mouth. Can I see what *else* you've got to work with?"

I heard the man rise up from his kneeling position and take a step forward. I could imagine his hard pole dripping in anticipation as he pressed it closer to her face, when Madison, who'd been silent up to now, suddenly interrupted their proceedings.

"Remember the rules," she said. "Each interaction is limited to giving or receiving only. The gentleman will have his opportunity to receive equivalent attention in due course. You can't touch him sexually yet–only *he* can touch *you*."

"That hardly seems fair," the woman huffed. "I'm dying to feel the rest of his package. Can't he touch me with his *cock* also?"

"If that's what you'd like," Madison said. "You just can't touch him in return. At least not *that* way."

"So *other* parts of my body are allowed to touch him, as long as he's taking the lead?"

"Um-hmm," Madison nodded.

"You heard the lady," the woman snarled, shifting her weight in her chair. "Assume the position. I'm ready to feel something *else* in my pussy now."

"If you insist," the man said as the rest of the room chuckled softly.

"But go slow," the woman instructed. "Since I can't touch you with my hands, I want to savor every inch of your cock as you slide inside me. Lift my legs over my shoulders and point your python into my hole."

I heard the sound of the plastic squeaking loudly, then

the chair creaked as the woman's weight shifted further back toward her backrest.

"Yes, baby," she purred. "I'm so wet for you. Let me feel the head of your cock pressing into my cunt. Let's savor this moment together."

With the sound of her dirty talk getting me all worked up again, I lifted my feet on top of my chair seat, spreading my knees far apart like I imagined hers were. Suddenly I wished I'd had the foresight to bring one of my favorite dildos to fuck myself at this moment, but I wasn't sure that would be allowed under Madison's rules. Then I remembered that she said each of us had a tube of lube next to us on our side tables. Desperate for anything to put inside me, I reached over and tapped the table gently until I felt a cylinder-shaped object.

*Thank God*, I thought, running my fingers over the round cap and the tapered end of the tube. *This stuff is going to come in handy in more ways than one.* I picked up the tube and placed the round end against my hole, half expecting her to stop me. Fortunately, her attention seemed to be directed elsewhere, and I groaned as I pressed the tube into my slit.

"Do you need me to–?" the man said, remembering the instructions Madison had given us earlier regarding protection.

"It's already taken care of," the woman purred. "I want to feel your bare skin inside me. I've got my *own* protection."

The man exhaled heavily. I wasn't sure if it was from relief at not having to worry about fumbling with a condom or because he'd reached the limit of his self-control. He lifted the woman's thighs up toward her chest and took a step closer to her. Suddenly both of them groaned as they joined in congress.

"Fuck yes," the woman moaned. "Your dick is so warm. And *thick*. Tease me with your head while I imagine how much more you've got to give me."

The chair began to squeak softly as the man shifted his weight back and forth, lubricating the head of his cock with her juices.

"Mmm," the woman said. "That feels good. "Is it good for you too?"

"Uh-huh," the man grunted.

For a brief moment, I considered lifting my blindfold just enough to see his pole probing her slit, but I dared not be the first to break Madison's rules. I didn't want to interrupt their rhythm with another reprimand from my friend. And besides, she'd put so much forethought and planning into this event, it would be unfair to spoil the fun.

"Okay," the woman continued. "Now slowly push your dick further inside me so I can feel every inch of your burning meat. I want to feel you impale me all the way to the hilt."

"Uhnn," the man groaned as he pressed himself further into her hole.

"God damn," the woman purred. "That's one hell of a joystick. I can feel you spreading me apart the further you go inside me."

"Yes," the man grunted. "You're so tight and wet. Squeeze me while I give you all eight inches."

I heard a few gasps around the room, and smiled imagining how turned on many of the women and some of the men were imagining themselves on the receiving end of his snake.

"Oh God," the woman groaned, feeling him press more and more of his length inside her. "Fill me up, baby. Let me feel all of you inside me now. I want you to pound your meat inside my pussy."

The man grunted as he thrust his full weight against her splayed legs, and she shuddered when he reached the end of her tunnel.

"Holy shit!" she gasped. "You weren't kidding about the size of your cock. I can feel you pressing up against my uterus. Be careful you don't slam me too hard. You might *kill* me with that thing."

"No worries," he said. "I'll be careful. Just let me know if I'm hurting you."

"Ahh," a few women muttered around the room, apparently equally taken by his sexiness as by his concern for his partner.

I pressed the tube of lube as far into my hole as I dared, gripping the tapered end tightly with the fingers of my right hand. The last thing I needed was to lose it inside my pussy and have to go to the hospital to have it removed. Besides, I had *other* purposes I was saving my pussy for. I needed to keep it unoccupied in case Madison decided to hook me up with a man later.

It didn't take long for me to hear the unmistakable sound of the man's penis thrusting in and out of her pussy as their wet bellies slapped together and the woman's chair squeaked loudly next to me.

"Fuck yes," the woman grunted. "Fuck me with that spear.

You feel so good. I want to feel you shooting your load inside my pussy."

"Uhnn, uhnn, uhnn," the man groaned as he slammed his cock in and out of her hole. I could hear the sound of his balls flapping against the underside of her vulva as the sloshing sound of her dripping pussy filled the room.

But that wasn't the *only* thing I heard in the room. From almost every direction around the circle, I could hear the grunting and moaning sounds of both men and women pleasuring themselves as they listened to the couple copulating only a few feet away.

I pulled the tube out of my pussy for a moment, then flipped open the cap and squeezed a dollop of lube inside my hole. Then I closed the lid and thrust it back inside me while I trilled my fingers over my burning clit.

"Yes, baby," the woman panted. "I want to feel you come inside me. I'm getting close–"

"Ahem," Madison suddenly interrupted again. "I hate to disturb your fun at this delicate moment. But I want to remind both of you of the rules. Remember, this engagement is designed for the *woman's* pleasure only. Unfortunately, I must ask the gentleman to resist the temptation to consummate the act. Your focus must be on *giving* pleasure for the moment, not receiving."

"Argh," I heard the man groan in frustration.

"Are you *kidding* me?" the woman complained. "If the goal is to give me pleasure, nothing would make me happier than to have my partner experience the penultimate pleasure along with me."

"That may be true," Madison said. "But he'll have to wait

his turn. That's the main attraction, focusing on *one* person's pleasure at a time. If you break the rules, I'm going to have to ask each of you to sit out the rest of the proceedings in a passive role."

"Alright Tiger," the woman said, readjusting her position in her chair. "I'm close. Do you think you can hold off long enough until I climax?"

"I'll try," he said. "Maybe if you take over more of the rocking action. The harder I thrust inside you, the harder it will be not to come."

"Okay," she said. "Just hold steady while I do all the work. Pretend you're a rock while I fuck your magnificent penis. Someone *else* is going to have a wonderful awakening later this evening when they take matters into their own hands."

I heard the woman grip the arms of her chair and begin to rock her hips forward and back as the plastic squeezed under her ass while she fucked the man's pole with her slippery pussy.

"I'm fucking you baby," she panted. "I'm fucking your red-hot poker with my dripping cunt. I'm going to come all over your balls. Are you ready?"

"Uhhh," the man groaned, straining with all his might to resist popping off inside her.

"Here it comes baby," she said. "I'm going to cum all over your big firehose. Oh! Oh! *Uhhhn*!"

As I listened to the sound of the woman grunting in the throes of another orgasm, I pulled my knees together and clamped down over the tube of lube planted inside my pussy while I hissed in ecstasy from the feeling of my own orgasm taking hold of me. This time, there was less reluctance on the part of the rest of the crowd to hold back as they grunted and groaned in orgasmic unison with the woman a few seats over.

While I rocked forward and back in my seat with my entire body quivering in excitement, I couldn't help thinking about the man who'd been forced to contain his pleasure while she rolled her flapping pussy over his giant organ. With any luck, I thought, I'll be the one to finish him off later this evening. I was already beginning to think about how I could make it up to him.

## 4

### FF

For a few moments after the woman came, the only thing I could hear in the room was the sound of other people shuffling in their seats and towels rubbing up against bare skin. It was obvious that I wasn't the only one who'd made a mess cumming so hard listening to the sexy man and woman next to me. I envied Madison being able to spy on everybody pleasuring themselves while each couple engaged in their own sexual exploration. It was a brilliant idea on so many levels, and I resolved to hold my *own* blindfold party at the first opportunity.

"So what happens now?" the woman next to me said after she recovered from her orgasm. "My partner is still hard, and I can think of many other ways he can still satisfy me."

"I'm sure he could," Madison said. "But I think it's time to let some of our other guests share in the fun."

*As if they haven't already*, I grinned under my blindfold as

I wiped the dripping tube of lube off with the towel under my seat and placed it back on the table next to me. It felt strangely liberating being able to touch myself with my body on full display, knowing that nobody could actually see me.

"If the gentleman could, um, *extricate* himself now and take his seat," Madison said, seeing the man's cock still impaled in the woman's pussy. "I'd like to ask for a new set of volunteers to continue the entertainment."

I heard the sudden squeaking of plastic all around the circle as everyone threw up their hand.

"Whoa!" Madison exclaimed. "We can't take everybody at once. What do you say we mix it up a little bit this time? If you guys are game to try something a little different, I've got a couple of candidates in mind."

I could almost picture everyone's head nodding as they begged to be chosen next. But knowing Maddie, I knew she'd want to stretch the next couple's boundaries.

"Okay," she said, walking to the other side of the circle. "I think I've identified another interesting pairing. Let me take your hand and escort you to your next partner."

I heard a pair of footfalls crunch across the plush carpet to the opposite side of my circle, three or four chairs away.

"I'll leave you now in the capable hands of your partner," Madison said. "But remember the rules. Only one person at a time can enjoy each coupling. Like the gentleman before, one of you will have to save yourself to receive similar attention later in the evening. Are you guys ready to resume the festivities?"

I heard the shifting of a body in the chair to my left, then the sound of someone kneeling on the carpet in front of the chair. I smiled at how tentative each of the partners were in beginning each engagement, first wanting to identify the other person's sex before deciding to become more actively involved. I still had no idea who'd been paired together, and my pussy throbbed in anticipation as I held my breath dying to find out what Madison had concocted this time. Moments later, I heard the sound of soft hands caressing someone's thighs and a woman purring.

*Good*, I thought, pressing my hand back down over my dripping mound. At least there's another girl involved. I couldn't place her voice yet, but I was excited to see if it was someone I knew.

"Your hands are so soft," the woman said. I cocked my head recognizing the timbre of her voice. "I like the way you're caressing my thighs."

I recognized the voice instantly. It was my sex therapist friend Hannah, who I'd had more than one sexy rendezvous with myself.

"Mmm," another woman's voice purred between her legs.

*Fuck yes*, I smiled, feeling my nipples hardening. *This is what I've been waiting for—hearing two women get it on.* I spread my thighs further apart, pressing my fingers against my twitching clit.

"Don't be shy," Hannah said to her hesitant partner. "Feel free to touch me in *other* places."

It seemed obvious that this was the first time her partner had touched another woman this way, and I felt a stream of juices run down the crack of my ass as my pussy twitched in excitement. With nobody else watching, I hoped that the new girl could be encouraged to explore Hannah's body more directly.

I heard the sound of the girl's hands moving further up Hannah's thighs, and she moaned softly.

"Yes," Hannah said. "Press your hands up against the side of my vulva. Can you feel the heat between my legs?"

"Mmm–mmm," the girl hummed.

"Is this your first time touching a woman this way?" Hannah said.

"Mmm–mmm," the girl nodded.

"Feel free to explore at your own pace," Hannah said. "There's no expectations or pressure here. It's just you and me, and nobody else is watching."

"Okay..." the younger woman's voice said.

"Hold your hand over my pussy to see how wet you've made me," Hannah instructed.

I heard the girl shift her body a little closer to Hannah's chair then the sound of wet skin being touched.

"Yes," Hannah moaned. "Your hand feels warm against my cunny. Caress my lips and probe deeper. That feels good."

"Mmm," the girl purred as I heard the smacking sounds grow louder.

"You're making me get all warm and puffy," Hannah sighed. "Can you feel how plump my lips are getting?"

"Yes..." the girl said.

"Press your finger inside me. I want you to see how tight and wet I am."

As I listened to the two women interacting, I suddenly

became aware of how quiet the rest of the room had become while everybody strained to listen. Not wanting to interrupt the girls' rhythm, I circled my clit quietly with two fingers while I sat mesmerized on my chair.

Suddenly Hannah groaned as she pressed her body lower in her chair, taking the girl's finger deep inside her pussy.

"Oh God," she panted. "You have no idea what you're doing to me. I love feeling you inside me. Place another finger into my slit and curl your fingers toward the front of my pussy. I want to feel you caress my G-spot."

A few chairs around the room suddenly squeaked as some of the guests adjusted their position uncomfortably. It was obvious I wasn't the only one getting turned on listening to two girls touching each other–especially knowing that for one of them, it was her first lesbian experience.

"Fuck yes," Hannah panted. "Just like that. Can you feel my pussy squeezing your fingers while you caress me inside?"

"Mmm–hmm," the girl hummed shyly.

"That feels incredible the way you're stroking me. Can you see my clit pushing out of its hood?"

"Yes," the girl groaned, becoming aroused watching Hannah's splayed pussy mere inches in front of her face.

"Let me feel your breath on my pearl while you caress me."

"Okay..." the girl said, shifting closer to Hannah's dripping pussy.

"Mmm," Hannah purred. "I feel you so close to me now. Blow on my clit while I imagine you watching me."

I heard a soft blowing sound then Hannah groaned more loudly.

"Oh God," she said. "You're driving me insane. Can I feel your lips on me? Even if for just a brief kiss?"

I smiled at how Hannah was gently coaxing the girl to take progressively bolder steps exploring her body. She was an experienced therapist who'd had many years of experience bringing similarly uptight women out of their shells.

I heard the girl press her body slowly forward, followed by a wet smacking sound.

"Yes, baby," Hannah purred. "Take my jewel between your lips. Feel how hot and hard I am for you. Let me feel you suck my bean while I squeeze your fingers. Can you see what you're doing to me?"

"Mmm," the girl moaned into Hannah's pussy.

"Swirl your tongue over my button now," Hannah said, continuing to guide the girl. "Show me how a woman is properly made love to."

"*Fuckk*," Hannah groaned, gripping her chair's armrests tightly with her hands. "Your tongue feels so hot on my clit. Suck me harder into your mouth while you swirl your tongue in circles over my nub."

Suddenly, the familiar sound of squeaking chairs from around the circle filled the room as the rest of the group began to get more and more aroused listening to the two women. I thrust three fingers into my pussy and began pressing them in and out of my hole, trying to imagine what Hannah was feeling.

"Yes baby," she panted more deeply. "Now curl your fingers against the inside of my pussy while you suck and tease my clit. You're doing an amazing job. I haven't felt someone excite me like this in a long time."

I suspected Hannah was stretching the truth a little bit there, knowing how often the two of us had shared a passionate encounter, but I liked how she was continuing to give her partner positive encouragement.

"Are you enjoying this as much as I am?" she said to the girl.

"Mmm-hmm," the girl hummed in agreement.

"Do you want to make me come with your sweet mouth?"

"Mmm–hmm," she hummed even louder.

"Press your fingers deep inside me while you keep caressing the front of my pussy. Maintain the steady action of your tongue over my clit. Flick it from side to side, then roll your tongue over it in figure-eight motions. I want to feel you sucking my whole gland."

I heard the girl shift her weight to get more comfortable between Hannah's legs then Hannah uttered a deep guttural moan.

"Fuck *yes*, baby," she said. "Just like that. God damn, you sure know how to eat a girl's pussy. Suck my clit. I'm going to cum soon. I'm going to cum all over your sweet face."

For the next thirty seconds, all I could hear was the escalating sound of Hannah's breathing and the accelerated squeaking of her chair a few feet to my left. Every so often, I heard the soft moaning and grunting of other guests pleasuring themselves as they listened to the two girls, and I began to jerk my hand harder up against my snatch, feeling my own pleasure beginning to build.

"That's it, baby," Hannah hissed. "Don't stop. That's

perfect. I'm going to come soon. Oh God...I'm cumming! *Nnngh!!*"

This time I managed to hold off coming long enough to listen to the sounds of pleasure emanating from all around me in the room. My pussy twitched while I listened to Hannah climaxing in her partner's mouth then the rest of the group coming one after another.

"I'm still cumming baby!" she panted. "Don't take your mouth off me. Can you feel me pulsing on your fingers?"

"Mmm," the girl moaned, thoroughly enjoying how well she'd managed to please her partner.

"*Uhnn, uhnn, uhnn,*" Hannah grunted with each powerful contraction of her pussy.

It seemed to take almost a full minute for her to stop thrashing in her chair before silence filled the room once again.

"Whoever you are," she sighed after finally coming down from her climax. "You're a quick learner. That was amazing. Come up here and kiss me. I want to thank you properly for your amazing performance."

The girl lifted herself up off the carpet and pressed her body closer to Hannah then I heard the sound of the two women kissing.

"Come sit on my lap, baby," Hannah said after a few moments. "I want to feel your tits pressing up against me."

I heard Hannah's chair squeak as the girl placed her legs through the open armrests and sat down spread-eagled on her lap.

"Your body feels so hot against my skin," Hannah said, kissing her face softly. "Your tits are nice and full. And your nipples are hard. Do you like it when I squeeze them like this?"

"Yes," the girl panted.

I heard the sound of Hannah's hands roaming over the girl's body, then the familiar sound of someone's fingers pressing into a moist pussy.

"How about *this*?" Hannah said. "Do you like it when I touch you *here*?"

"Fuck, yes," the girl panted.

"Ahem," Madison said, clearing her throat. "Don't forget the rules. This is supposed to be a *one-way* engagement only."

"But she's obviously enjoying this," Hannah protested. "And since it's her first time with another woman, can't we make an exception?"

"She'll have her chance soon enough," Madison said. "If you two can't control yourselves, perhaps it's time to separate..."

"Wait," Hannah said as the girl began to lift herself from the chair. "I'd like to try one more thing. Can you change your position so you're facing the other way, with one of your legs threaded through one side of the armrests? That way we'll be able to touch our pussies together and I can enjoy this connection in a *different* way. That's allowed, right Madison?"

"As long as your partner will be able to contain herself," she said. "But I have my doubts. I'd hate to see her miss out on her own one-on-one opportunity later tonight."

"Just try it for a few seconds," Hannah said to the girl. "I want you to get a taste for what it feels like when two women join together in the most intimate way. Don't worry about making me come again if you find it too hard to continue. Let's just have a little fun together."

"I like the sound of that," the girl said. "But you might have to show me how to position my body correctly. I've never done it like this before."

"Stand up and turn your body around so your ass is facing my hips," Hannah instructed. "Then put your right leg through the armrest on the right side of my chair and sit down on my lap. I'll take care of the rest."

"Okay," the girl said.

I heard her shift her feet on the carpet then the squeaking sound of the chair as the girl sat down over Hannah's hips.

"That's it," Hannah said. "Now lean forward while I tilt my hips up. Can you feel the heat between my legs?"

"Yes," the girl panted.

"Just a couple more inches and–"

"*Uhnn!*" the girl suddenly groaned.

"Can you feel that baby? I'm touching my pussy against yours. Can you feel our wet skin joining together?"

"Oh God," the girl moaned. "That feels incredible. I never even imagined–"

"It only gets better," Hannah purred, grabbing the girl's hips, pulling her harder toward her snatch. "God, you're burning up against me."

"Yes," the girl groaned. "Fuck me with your pussy. Rub your cunt against mine. I want to feel *every* part of you rubbing up against me."

"Mmm," Hannah moaned, as her chair began to squeak rhythmically.

"Does that feel good, baby?" she said.

"Fuck, yes," the girl moaned.

"Lean forward a bit more while I tilt my hips higher..."

"Nnngh," the girl groaned more loudly.

"Do you like that? Can you feel my clit rubbing up against yours?"

"Yes," the girl said. "Don't stop. That feels so good."

As I listened to the two women's breathing rate escalate toward the inevitable tipping point, I knew even before she said anything what was going to happen next.

"You have no idea how much I hate to do this," Madison interrupted again. "But I'm going to have to ask you two to slow down or separate. I don't think your partner is going to be able to hold out much longer."

"You are *so* cruel, Madison!" Hannah huffed. "How can you deny this beautiful creature her chance to enjoy her first lesbian experience to the fullest?"

"I promise I'll give her a chance to consummate the experience later. Why don't you finish up now so we can move on to the next couple? But I suggest you try a different position to avoid putting your partner over the edge."

"Jesus," Hannah said. "I was just about to come. What do you think, baby? Do you mind finishing me off another way then I'll try to make sure you're properly taken care of later?"

"I'll try," the girl said, still breathing heavily. "What do you want me to do?"

Hannah paused for a moment, contemplating the

simplest way to get off, then she shifted her position in her chair.

"Can you lift yourself up a few inches and reach between my legs? I'd love to feel you finish me with your hands while I caress your body."

The girl straightened her legs and lifted her body off Hannah a few inches, then I heard her hand moving over Hannah's wet vulva as she began moaning in pleasure again.

"Yes, baby," Hannah said. "That's perfect. Rub your fingers in circles over my hard clit while I squeeze your tits. It won't take long to make me cum this time."

"Mmm," the girl purred as the chair began squeaking from the weight of her hand propping her body up on the side armrest.

"Your nipples are so hard," Hannah moaned. "Next time I want you to fuck me with your tits. I hope this won't be the last time we have a chance to be together."

"Absolutely," the girl said. "This is way better than fucking a man. They're only interested in one thing, and they're always in such a hurry to get it over with. I'm not sure I'll *ever* go back after this."

"That's my girl," Hannah purred. "I'm ready now. Press your fingers harder against my clit and move them around in circles over my shaft. I love the way you're touching me."

"Yes," the girl purred. "I want to feel you come in my hands. Spray your juices all over me."

"Oh *fuckk*!" Hannah suddenly howled, losing control hearing the girl talk dirty to her. "I'm cumming, baby. I'm cumming so hard. *Uhnnn*!"

Suddenly, I heard the whole room erupting in a

cacophony of grunts and groans as the other men and women around the circle could no longer contain their pleasure listening to Hannah having another powerful climax. I'd been holding back for the big finish too, and as I listened to Hannah gushing all over the girl's ass perched inches above her flapping pussy, I grunted loudly as I sprayed my own juices all over my seat.

5

—————

**MM**

"Okay then," Madison said after giving Hannah a few moments to recover. "That certainly was exciting. Who'd like to give it a try next?"

I heard some chairs squeak as a few more guests put up their hands.

"I'm glad to see you're all enjoying this enough to want to participate directly. But I'd like to stretch everyone's horizons a bit this time and test some new combinations."

There was some shuffling sounds a few feet to my left, then a group of footfalls moved across the carpet to the other side of the circle.

"Allow me to escort the lady back to her chair to make sure nobody trips over each other. Now, let's see," Madison paused. "Yes–I think *this* might make for an interesting pairing."

I heard some heavier footsteps being escorted to the

opposite side of the circle, then Madison sat back down in her chair.

"Remember," she instructed, "there's no pressure to do anything you don't want to do. That applies to both of you. But you never know how much you might enjoy something until you try it. So I encourage both of you to explore each other at your own pace and open your minds to some new possibilities."

*Hmm*, I thought, rubbing my slippery thighs together. *This sounds even more interesting than the last two pairings. What has Madison cooked up this time?*

The room was quiet for a few moments, then I heard the sound of someone kneeling on the carpet in front of the designated chair. There was a brief scuffing noise that sounded like hands rubbing against hairy skin, then it stopped almost as abruptly.

The room filled with awkward silence for a few moments, then Madison interjected to break the tension.

"I can see both of you are feeling a little squeamish. Remember, this is all about sharing new experiences and enjoying the attention of different partners without any judgment or preconceptions. I encourage both of you to open yourselves up to try something new. *All* of us have fantasized about exploring new sexual boundaries at one time or another. This is one place where it's completely safe and judgment-free. Am I right, ladies and gentlemen?"

A soft cheer rose from around the circle as the guests clapped quietly.

"See?" Madison said. "Nobody here cares who's connecting with whom, and they'll never know anyway unless you choose to reveal it later. Live in the moment and enjoy yourselves for a while!"

There was another awkward silence then I heard the squeak of a chair and the crinkling of plastic as someone spread their legs further apart. The other person hesitated for another long moment, then I heard the sound of hands moving over rough skin.

*Okay*, I nodded. *That definitely sounds like a man's thighs this time, unless someone hasn't shaved her legs in quite a while. The only question now is, is his partner a man or a woman?*

The scratching sound seemed to get rougher and rougher until I heard the familiar sound of skin rubbing over stubble.

*There we go*, I smiled. *At least someone's done some grooming down there.* I could almost see the man's cock slowly inflating as his partner caressed his bristly pubis and private parts.

"Uhnn," a husky-sounding man groaned, shifting his position again in his chair. "That feels good, whoever you are. You're making me hard."

I heard his partner exhale deeply and wondered if it was because they were getting turned on watching the man get aroused or because they were nervous about proceeding.

"If you just want to touch me with your hands, that's cool," the man said, sensing his partner's hesitation. "I've never done it with a man before, but so far it feels just as good as with any woman I've been with."

*So it's an all-male coupling this time*, I nodded excitedly. I'd always been fascinated watching gay men have sex online, and the thought of two *straight* guys hooking up excited me even more. I spread my legs apart and began stroking the sides of my vulva, trying to imagine what he was feeling.

"Yeah, play with my balls, man," the receiving man groaned. "That feels good. I can never get my girlfriend to give me enough attention down there. They always think it's all about the cock."

"Mmm," his partner hummed in agreement.

*Fuck, this is hot*, I thought, feeling my juices begin to run down over my slit. Listening to two guys who knew what they liked was utterly fascinating. I wondered how many straight women around the room were making mental notes of how to better please their partners, just like the *guys* were when Hannah and her partner were getting it on.

"Fuck man," the husky-voied man purred. "I'm hard as a rock. My dick is flapping up against my stomach. Grab my shaft and feel how hard I am."

"Uhnn," the other man grunted, his breathing beginning to grow more ragged.

Straight or not, it was apparent he was getting just as excited as his partner feeling another man's hard cock in his hands. I suddenly wished I could lift my blindfold again to see his lengthening cock swinging between his legs while he leaned over to touch his partner. The scene was becoming more exciting by the moment.

"Yeah, man," the first man groaned. "Grab me with two hands. Squeeze my shaft while you stroke me up and down."

As I strained to listen, all I could hear was the sound of both men breathing heavily.

"Fuck, yes, that feels so good. Can you feel my head popping in and out of your hands while you stroke me?"

"Uh–huh," the other man nodded.

"I'm getting sticky on top with precum. Do you mind

putting some lube on my dick to make it more slippery? I want to enjoy this handjob properly."

I heard a tapping sound as the other man reached over to the side table, then a pop as he flipped open the lid and squirted some lube over the top of the other man's cock. Seconds later, I heard the familiar slapping sound of skin rubbing against wet skin as the first man began to moan louder.

"Yeah, man," he groaned. "That's so much better. Squeeze me hard while I pump my cock in your hands. Are you getting hard too?"

"Uhnn," the other man grunted, which I took to be a yes. Now I *really* wanted to take my blindfold off to see the two of them getting aroused touching each other.

"God damn, that feels good," the first man moaned. "I like your tight grip on my dick. Can you feel my cum dripping out of the tip and down over your hands?"

"Yeah," the other man spoke for the first time.

I couldn't place either person's voice, but that didn't stop me from enjoying the experience to the fullest. While I listened to both of them grunting and breathing heavily, I circled my clit and moaned softly along with them.

"Play with my balls again," the first man said. "Squeeze them with one hand while you work the head of my dick with the other. Yeah–that's it, squeeze them tighter. Is that the way you like it too?"

"Uh-huh," the other man groaned.

"Listen," the first man said. "I could come any second now, but I'd love to feel your dick before I pop off. Can you stand up and let me touch it for a second? I've never felt another man's hard cock before either."

*This is fucking awesome*, I smiled, feeling my pussy twitch listening to the two straight men exploring each other's bodies. It's even better than I imagined. Madison must have known when she selected the guests what she had in mind, and I nodded in appreciation at her courage in pairing these two up. Nobody's ever a hundred percent straight. Sometimes they just need a safe place and the right opportunity to explore the other side of their sexuality.

I heard the other man rise up from his kneeling position then take a step forward. Suddenly he groaned, as his partner grasped his cock in front of his face.

"Damn, man," the husky-voiced man said. "That's a pretty impressive piece of equipment you've got there. It feels like you're circumcised like me. And you're dripping, too. Can you do me a favor and touch your cock against mine? Maybe we can *both* have a little fun if that's okay with Madison."

"No problem on my end," Madison chimed in. "As long as your partner doesn't get too carried away."

The other man knelt back down on the carpet as the first man shifted his weight forward on his chair. Then I heard the lube container flip open again while the second man squirted some on top of his own hard-on.

"Yeah, man," the first man said. "I've always wondered what this would feel like. Place the underside of your dick up against mine, then let me hold them together while we jerk our cocks together."

I heard some more shuffling sounds, followed by a rhythmic smacking noise while both men moaned together.

"That feels incredible having your dick rubbing against mine," the deep-voiced man groaned. "Your cock feels so hot. Is this feeling as good for you as it is for me?"

"Yeah," the other man grunted. Whether he was just being shy about revealing his identity or he didn't want to show how much he was enjoying his first man-on-man encounter was unclear.

But *I* was sure as hell enjoying it. And from the sounds of other men and women around the circle, so was everybody else.

*God damn*, Madison, I thought. *This idea was absolutely fucking brilliant. Not only are you giving everybody a chance to stretch their individual boundaries, you're also giving the rest of us a chance to live out our wildest fantasies listening in on the action.*

"Can you picture our cockheads rubbing together while I grip our shafts with two hands?" the first man said.

"Fuck yeah," the other man grunted.

"I wish I could see it too," the husky-sounding man said. "Maybe Madison will give me a chance to switch positions with you later."

"Maybe..." Madison grinned a few seats away.

"Damn, man. I can feel your *balls* rubbing up against mine too. This is even hotter than I thought it would be. I'm getting close, how about you?"

"Yeah," the other man panted.

"Okay guys," Madison suddenly interrupted. "As much as I'd love to watch the fireworks, I'm going to have to ask you to disengage. Let's focus primarily on stimulating the gentleman in the chair. As you said, your partner will have his chance for reciprocal action soon enough."

"I'm sorry, man," the first man said. "But I promise to make it up to you later. I love the feel of your cock in my hands. I can't wait to watch you spew all over my dick. Do you mind finishing me with your hands?"

"No worries, man," the second man said.

I smiled listening to the dynamic between the two men. If this was how straight guys spoke when they had sex with each other, I found it kind of amusing. There was none of the usual love-talk between regular gay men. For some reason, it was turning me on even *more* listening to them pretending to sound all macho.

I heard the second man shift his position a few inches further away from the chair, then the rhythmic, wet smacking sounds resumed.

"Fuck yeah, man," the first man said. "I can feel your sticky cum coating my dick. Your hands feel so warm around my cock. It won't take long now. Squeeze my balls while you stroke my dick. I'm going to cum hard in your hands."

"Do it, man," the second man spoke up, momentarily forgetting where he was. "This is so hot watching your dick flare in my hands. You seem to be getting even bigger the closer you get to popping off."

"Yeah man," the first man huffed. "I can feel it. I'm gonna cum any second now. Let me cum all over your chest."

Suddenly, I heard the second man shift his position again, and the husky-voiced man let out an unearthly groan.

"Oh my God," he grunted. "Yes, suck my dick into your mouth. Your lips feel so hot on my dick. I'm gonna cum, man. Oh fuck, I'm gonna cum so hard in your mouth."

"Um-hmm," the other man hummed, obviously ready to accept his load.

"Yeah, baby," the first man growled. "Here it comes. Squeeze my balls. Oh *fuckkkkk*!!"

As I listened to the man howl in ecstasy, I could picture him pouring his load into the other man's mouth. It must have felt incredibly exciting for the other man to feel him pulsing in his hands while his partner exploded in his mouth. Whether he was swallowing his cum or letting it drip out of the side of his mouth, I had no way of knowing. But from the sounds of all the other grunting men all around me, it was apparent he wasn't the *only* one spilling his load.

**6**

---

**FF**

After the two men had their turn, I eagerly awaited Madison's next choice of partners. She once again asked for a show of hands, and when she took my hand and escorted me to the other side of the circle, my pussy throbbed in anticipation to see who she'd paired me with. When I knelt down in front of my partner's chair and placed my hands on her thighs, my heart pounded when I felt the smooth, soft skin of a woman.

It had been weeks since I'd felt another woman's body next to mine, and I smiled at the opportunity to give the mysterious guest some girl-on-girl attention. I still had no idea if she was straight, bi, or lesbian, but it hardly mattered. I was about to give her a sexual experience like nothing she'd ever experienced before.

At least nothing she'd experienced *blindfolded*.

Her breathing began to deepen when she felt my hands on her legs, and I slid them slowly up the outsides of her thighs until I reached her ass. I took a moment to caress the sides of her buttocks, squeezing her muscles as she reflexively contracted them into two tight globes. I still had no idea who I was touching, but one thing was for sure. She hardly had a stitch of fat on her body, and her ass must have been a magnificent thing to see from behind.

The woman still hadn't uttered a single word, not even a moan or a sigh, but I could hear her breathing rate beginning to escalate the further I pressed my hands upward. With my face so close to her pussy, it was tempting to move closer toward her genitals, but with her seeming to hold back, I decided to press further up her body to see if I could get her to open up. I pressed her knees gently apart and pushed my breasts into her gap as I slowly lifted my hands up the side of her stomach toward her chest. When I felt the curvature of her breasts, I cupped them with both hands and pressed my tits against her wet snatch. I smiled feeling the river of juices cascading over my skin, belying her attempt to pretend indifference.

*Damn*, I thought. *This is one uptight girl. This calls for some more aggressive action.*

I raised myself up from my kneeling position, then threaded each of my legs through the armrests on both sides of her chair and lowered my ass onto her steaming lap. Then I slowly leaned forward until I felt her hard nipples touching my own. Twisting my torso from side-to-side, I flicked her teats with my tips then pressed my tits hard against her as I tilted my sopping pussy toward her quivering stomach.

As I leaned in closer toward her, I turned my face toward the side of her head.

"Do you like what I'm doing so far?" I whispered into her ear.

"Uh-huh," she squeaked softly.

I smiled as I nibbled and sucked on her ear, feeling her hot breath pulsing against my neck. Then I pulled back a few inches and squeezed her firm breasts, kneading her tips between my fingers. When she uttered a deep guttural growl, I leaned forward to kiss her. She pursed her lips, resisting my intrusion at first, and I bit her lower lip gently, sliding my wet tongue under the rim. When she parted her lips unconsciously, I thrust my tongue into her cavity, pressing my face hard against hers.

With my tongue probing her insides and my hands pinching her nipples, she slowly began to surrender herself as she tilted her hips upward, pressing her mound against mine. When she began moaning in my mouth, I grabbed both sides of her head, pulling her harder toward me. She responded by swirling her tongue around mine while rocking her hips, trying to increase the stimulation between her legs.

After a few seconds, I pulled back and smiled at the woman, sensing she was ready for the next stage in my exploration.

"Would you like me to move a little *lower* now?" I asked.

"Yes," she panted.

She still hadn't said enough for me to place her voice, but not knowing who it was turned me on even more. There was something about the idea of intimately touching a stranger–especially a straight woman–that I found insanely exciting.

I pulled my legs out from between the armrests and

kneeled back down onto the carpet between her legs, determined to draw her further out of her shell. This time, as I pressed my hands up the insides of her thighs, I found them coated with a slippery film while she parted her legs, inviting me to move closer. When I pressed my hands against the side of her dripping vulva, she groaned softly and placed her hands on top of my head, running her fingers through my hair.

"That feels good," she said softly.

I thought there was something in her voice that sounded familiar, and I moved my face closer to her pussy, encouraging her to provide more verbal feedback. Normally, I would have been inclined to tease her some more with my hands, but I could feel the heat emanating from her pussy and her juices running down over my fingers, and I leaned in to encircle her flaming nub between my lips. When I sucked her clit into my mouth and began rolling my tongue over her exposed bulb, she groaned deeply, pulling my head in harder toward her slit.

"Oh God," she groaned. "That feels so good. Lick my pussy with your tongue."

I paused for a second trying to place the voice, then it suddenly struck me. It was my married neighbor, Valerie, who'd invited me to a pool party a few weeks ago at her house on the opposite side of my yard. We'd ogled each other's bikini-clad bodies for much of the event, but neither of us felt comfortable making a move with her husband and friends milling so close nearby. I was amazed how tight and shapely her figure was for a mother of two teenagers, and I couldn't take my eyes off her shapely ass the whole time I was there. For a long time after, I spied on her whenever she went outside to swim in the pool, masturbating to orgasm many times, wishing I had the courage to approach her directly.

Knowing I finally had my sexy neighbor exactly where I wanted her drove me crazy with desire, and I grabbed her ass with both hands, pulling her pussy hard against my face as I flicked her hard pearl with my lips and tongue.

"Fuck yes," she panted, losing herself in the heat of the moment. "Suck me into your mouth. Your lips feel so hot against my pussy."

"Mmm," I nodded, happily lapping up her juices as she rolled her hips over my face.

Her breathing beginning to quicken and become more ragged, and I knew it wouldn't be long before she came. Whether it was because I was doing such a good job eating her pussy or because she was excited feeling another woman's lips on her clit for the first time, I wasn't sure. All I knew was that I wanted to enjoy her orgasm to the fullest when the moment came.

I held the tips of two fingers against her widening hole, then I pressed them slowly inside her. She gasped when she felt me penetrate her, and as I began to curl my fingers forward caressing the front of her G-spot, she bunched her fingers into a fist, clutching my hair with two hands. While I swirled my wet tongue over her clit, she pulled my hair harder and harder as she unconsciously clenched her hands approaching the peak of her pleasure. When she finally hit the tipping point, she screamed out loud, jerking her hips hard against my face in spastic twitches.

While the walls of her pussy clamped down against my fingers in rhythmic pulses, I held my face against her vulva as I felt my own juices running down the insides of my thighs in sympathetic union. When her contractions finally began to subside, she loosened her grip on my hair, and I pulled away smelling the sweet musk between her legs.

"I'm sorry if I hurt you," she said. "It's just that I haven't felt a woman touch me like that and I guess I got a little carried away."

I wanted to tell her it was no bother, but she still hadn't guessed who I was, and I didn't want to spoil the mystery, so I simply nodded and mumbled *um-hmm* to indicate that I was fine. But I was far from being finished with my sexy neighbor. Before the evening was over, I wanted her to experience the full spectrum of girl-on-girl sex, and I had more plans for her. I leaned forward, pressing my breasts between her thighs, then I grabbed one of my tits and swiped it up and down over her slippery vulva.

"Oh my God," she panted. "Is that your–? Yes, fuck my pussy with your tits. You're so soft. Much softer than my–"

"Husband?" I purred.

"Yes," she said. "And slower and more sensuous. I love the way you tease me with *every* part of your body."

"I'm far from finished teasing you with the rest of my body," I purred.

When I felt Valerie's fingers reach down over her mound and begin to circle her clit above my breast, I reached out and stopped her with my hand.

"I think we might be able to find another way to stimulate you there," I smiled.

"Yes," she panted. "Rub my clit again. I want to come again."

I thrust my arms under her thighs and pulled her closer toward the edge of her chair, then I pushed her knees up toward her chest, placing my legs over the top of her armrests. Grasping the sides of her backrest for support, I lowered my pussy down on top of her flayed legs. When she felt my hot cunt press against her vulva, she groaned loudly in my ear.

"Do you like that, baby?" I said, mashing my tits against hers while rocking my hips against her dripping pussy.

"Fuck yes," she panted in my ear. Then she pulled my head closer to her face, breathing against my neck. "I know who are, Jade. I've fantasized about making love to you ever since you moved in next door. You're even sexier than I imagined. Rub your cunt against me. I want to feel you come against my lips."

"I'm not sure Madison's going to allow that," I whispered back. "But at least I'll be able to feel you coming against me. Until *next* time, that is."

"Oh, there's definitely going to be a next time," she panted.

"Hold on babe," I purred. "Cause I'm going to ride you like a bucking bronco."

As we began to rock our hips back and forth, the loud smacking sound of our two vulvas began to echo around the room, and I wondered how many of the guests knew just how tightly the two of us were pinned together. From the sound of all the moans and sighs around the circle, I guessed their imaginations were already wandering to some interesting places.

As Valerie and I pressed our bodies harder together, I reveled in the feeling of her hot, slippery skin rubbing up against my tits and pussy. It must have been a feast for Madison's eyes being able to watch both of our exposed pussies pushing over the edge of Valerie's chair as we gnashed our cunts together. While I tribbed my clit hard against Valerie's hard nub, we moaned in unison, feeling our passion rising in tandem.

"Hold on ladies," Madison interrupted, right on cue. "Are you going to be able to–"

"I *got* this Maddie," I said, holding out a finger from the side of my body. "Just give me one more minute."

"You're threading the needle here," she said. "I'd hate to stop you before your partner is fully satisfied."

I pulled my arms against the side of Valerie's back rest, drawing my face closer to her ear once again.

"Come all over my pussy, Valerie," I said. "I want to feel your cunt twitching when you come."

"Uhnnn," she groaned into my other ear as I felt a dribble leak out of her slit and down the crack of my ass.

"Yes, baby," I purred. "Come for momma. Grind your cunt against me while I feel you gush into my hole."

"Oh God..." Valerie suddenly grunted. "Yes, I'm coming! I'm going to cum so hard against your hot pussy. Here it comes. *Aieeeee!*"

Listening to Valerie scream in my ear as she clamped her pussy against mine in the throes of another powerful climax took all of my willpower to contain myself from coming along with her. But I knew from Madison's viewing angle that I wouldn't be able to hide my usual flood of waterworks. So I simply held Valerie close to me and purred into her ear, encouraging her to enjoy her orgasm to the fullest.

"Yes, baby," I said. "I feel your pussy pulsing against me. Come all over me, baby. I love feeling your sexy body against mine."

"Oh Christ," she panted. "I'm still coming. I'm still coming against your beautiful, hot pussy. *Uhnn, uhnn, uhnn...*"

I smiled, feeling the contractions of her vulva syncing with her loud grunts in my ear. I hadn't fucked another woman like this for a very long time, and I reveled in every twitch and groan of my newly liberated straight friend. Something told me this wouldn't be the last time we stole a few clandestine meetings away from the prying eyes of our nosy neighbors.

## 7

## FM

For the next hour and a half, Madison continued selecting random participants from around the circle until just about everybody had had a turn both ways. But I'd just had a single turn so far, and I was eagerly looking forward to my next pairing, especially since I'd been prevented from fully enjoying the last episode. But when she grabbed my hand and pulled me out of my chair, indicating that I'd be the giver not the receiver again, I paused and turned my face toward her inquisitively.

"But I thought–"

"Something tells me you'll enjoy being the one in charge of this next encounter," she smiled, leading me to the far side of the circle.

When I kneeled down in front of my partner's chair and placed my hands on their thighs, I hesitated when I felt the telltale bristly skin of a man. I usually preferred making love to women, but in this case I was prepared to make an exception. I'd been biding my time patiently touching myself listening to everybody else get off, but the tube of lube just wasn't cutting it for me any longer. I needed a proper, full-sized cock in my pussy to finish things off.

And besides, I thought. It would be kind of fun to explore a man's body while blindfolded, learning what turned him on without the benefit of any visual cues.

Not knowing the identity of the person she'd coupled me with, I decided I'd have a little fun teasing him with a slow build-up. I placed my hands on top of his legs and gradually slid them up toward his crotch, pressing my fingers into the inside of his thighs.

"Mmm," a husky-sounding voice purred. "This feels a little different than the last time."

My heart raced knowing it was the same deep-voiced man I'd heard earlier in the evening when he'd been paired with another guy. I was excited to feel his organ in my hands and give him a different perspective this time. Knowing he was straight, I suspected he preferred having sex with women, and I planned to give him an experience he wouldn't forget.

As I slowly spread his knees apart with my shoulders, I caressed the inside of his thighs with the tips of my breasts. I could feel his hairs standing on end while my hands slid over the goose bumps on his skin.

"Yes?" I purred. "Do you like feeling my tits against your thighs? Are you ready for a *woman's* touch this time?"

"*Fuck* yes," he panted, spreading his legs further apart.

"Mmm," I smiled, pressing my breasts up against his balls, feeling his cock already pointing straight up at full flagstaff.

"Is there anything in particular you'd like me to do with my special endowments?"

"Yes," he moaned. "Rub your tits on my balls. Then tit-fuck me with those nice melons of yours."

I smiled at the crude labels men often used to describe women's lady parts, but it didn't bother me this time because I knew I'd be the one in the driver's seat controlling the action. And before our turn was over, I planned to make him *beg* me to do his bidding.

I grabbed the sides of my tits and lifted myself up a few inches, surrounding his cock in my cleavage. It was hard for me to tell just how big he was without touching him directly with my hands, but there was plenty of dick still poking out from the top of my tits even though I was bustier than most women.

"That feels incredible," he groaned, angling his hips upward, pressing his balls tightly against my chest. "Your tits are so soft and warm..."

"Softer and warmer than a man's hands?" I teased.

"Yes," he grunted. "I far prefer feeling a woman's skin against my body."

"You didn't seem to be complaining too much last time."

"Yeah well, when you're horny, just about anything will do the trick. But chicks turn me on a lot more than men."

"Well you better strap yourself in then," I said. "Because I plan to give you a hell of a ride."

Although I could feel his hard pole burning up between my compressed tits, it was hard to get traction rubbing dry skin on dry skin, so I leaned over toward his side table and grabbed the tube of lube, pouring a generous dollop over the head of his throbbing member.

"Yeah, baby," he said. "Lube me up. I want to fuck your tits and come all over your face."

*Fat chance of that*, I smiled. Apparently, he still needed to be shown who was in charge here.

I grabbed his dick hard with two hands and slowly pulled them down the length of his shaft, coating his hard-on with the lube.

*Jesus*, I thought, feeling his thick phallus in my hands. This guy is the real deal. By the time my hands reached the base of his dick, I estimated he was at least nine inches in length. I wasn't even sure if it would fit inside me.

*I might need to change up my plan of attack after all.*

I wrapped my tits around his shaft, pressing them tightly against his organ, then I began to slide myself up and down his steaming erection.

"Yeah, baby," he moaned. "Fuck me with your tits. Feel my big pole sliding in and out of your pit. Stroke the whole length of my tool."

*He sure is full enough of himself*, I thought as I slid my breasts over his flagpole. *He knows he's got it and he likes to flaunt it.* But to be honest, I was digging it almost as much as he was. I enjoyed feeling a man's cock from time to time, and this one was far bigger than most.

I tilted my head up, hoping to get a glimpse of his head poking in and out of my slippery breasts, but Madison had tied my blindfold carefully enough to prevent even the slightest peek. As I listened to his dick slurping between my lubricated breasts, I felt the head of his pole poking up against the underside of my chin, and for a moment I was tempted to angle my face down and take him into my mouth.

"Oh God, baby," he groaned. "I want your mouth over my dick so bad. Can you suck the tip while you fuck me with your tits?"

I'd given enough blowjobs in my straight days to know how to satisfy a man, but I wasn't really into that anymore having long since shifted my preferences to women. And besides, I never much cared for the taste and texture of a man's cum, and I wasn't about to let him pop off in my mouth without warning.

On the other hand, I *did* want to drive him crazy with desire before I finished with him.

I pulled away from his beanstalk for a moment and leaned in, slowly licking him from the base of his pole to the flaring crown. I could taste his precum spilling out of his slit and dripping down his shaft while I continued licking him like a giant Popsicle. I was enjoying making him squirm, and I wanted to give him just enough of what he craved so that when we reached the end he'd explode with the biggest orgasm of his life.

"Mmm," I moaned, pretending to worship his giant phallus. "You're so big. I can feel every inch of your python with my tongue."

"Yeah, baby," he grunted. "Lick my dick like an ice cream cone. Make sure you swirl your tongue over the head to catch my drips."

Knowing his most sensitive part was the soft tissue under the ridge of his crown, I pointed my tongue and slowly circled my head around the edge of his rim.

"Oh my God, baby," he panted. "Yes, lick my head with your tongue. You know how to drive a man crazy..."

"As well as another *man*?" I smiled, feeling his dick pulse in my hands as two more drops of precum spilled over his helmet.

"Yes," he said. "Suck my cock, baby. I need you to swallow me. Let me feel my cock in your mouth."

I was prepared to give him a little bit of latitude, just enough to let him think he was still in control. But I had a plan, and it didn't involve him cumming in my mouth.

I lifted myself up a bit further, then I paused with my mouth poised over the tip of his cock. He could feel my hot breath on his cum-coated glans, and he pressed his hips upward, desperate to feel my lips around his shaft. I pursed my lips and emitted a long stream of spit that landed on top of his flaring head with a soft splat.

"Oh, fuck yes," he groaned. "Lube me up with your spit. I want to fuck your mouth so bad."

Feeling temporarily sorry for him, I lowered my mouth to his burning head and spread my lips, feeling his girth stretch me open until I had his full circumference inside me. I was shocked at how thick he was, and I gripped his shaft tightly with both hands to make sure he didn't press himself too much further into my mouth. As I began to bob up and down gently on his pole and swirl my tongue under his ridge, he placed his hands on my head and pushed down gently.

I was glad that I'd had the presence of mind to grip his dick hand-over-hand so there was only two inches or so at the top of his hard-on that he could comfortably insert into me. But that was plenty enough. With his coke-can-sized girth, my jaw soon became sore from being stretched so wide, and after a minute or two of sucking his tip, I pulled away to catch my breath.

"What's the matter, baby?" he said. "Am I too big for you?"

"You *are* pretty fucking huge," I panted, wiping his precum from the sides of my mouth. "Maybe you're better suited for a man's equipment after all."

"I'm sure there are *other* parts of you that can accommodate me more easily," he grinned. "If you can deliver a baby, I'm pretty sure you'll be able to fit my dick in your pussy."

"Maybe," I smiled. "But I'd like to have a little more fun playing with that thing first. I want to feel your joystick throbbing in my hands while I pleasure you. Would you like to see how a woman's handjob compares to a man's?"

"Absolutely," he snarled. "Let's see if your little hands can handle my big poker."

Chuckling at his arrogant attitude, I clasped his dick again with both hands and squeezed it as tightly as I could. He felt hard as a rock, and his manhood burned in my hands.

"Yeah, baby," he grunted. "Squeeze the cum out of my dick. Rub my shaft while I fuck your pretty little hands. Can you feel my cock throbbing?"

"Oh yes," I purred.

"Don't forget to play with my balls. It feels so much better when you stimulate every part of me down there."

I moved my right hand up to his crown then cupped his balls with my other hand, squeezing him tightly.

"Yeah, baby," he groaned. "Squeeze my balls. That feels awesome."

As I squeezed the tip of his cock with the fingers of my

right hand, more precum oozed out the top, mingling with the lube, creating a loud smacking sound as the air pocket under his frenulum filled with the sticky mixture. I could hear the sound of other men from around the circle flapping their dicks as they imagined me giving them a similarly dedicated hand job. I was pretty sure every one of them fantasized about a naked woman kneeling in front of them, giving them every bit of her attention while she gazed admiringly at their manhood.

*Men are so predictable,* I thought. *They really are all about the cock after all.*

"Yeah, just like that, honey," the man grunted. "Work my head while you play with my balls. Do you want to feel me cum all over your tits?"

"Mmm," I said, pretending to play along. "Do you *want* to cum on my tits?"

"Yeah, baby," he hissed. "I just need a little longer, then I'm going to spray all over your pretty breasts."

Seeking to heighten his fantasy cum shot fantasy, I lowered my left hand below his balls, caressing the space between his testicles and his ass. I knew this was another sensitive space for most men, and one his previous partner hadn't explored.

"Yes," he hissed. "Tickle the area below my balls. That feels incredible. I'm getting close..."

"Knowing he was close to cumming and wanting to make him climax on my own terms, I slid my hand lower, pressing my little finger toward his pucker. When I rolled my digit over his sphincter, he groaned and pushed his body lower in the chair, pressing harder against me.

"Oh fuck, baby," he grunted. "Whatever you're doing, don't stop. I've never been touched there before. That feels incredible."

When I heard his breathing begin to escalate and felt his precum pour out of his slit over my hand massaging his head, I knew he was close to the point of no return. With a huge grin on my face, I pressed my little finger harder against his sphincter until it slipped inside.

"Fuck," the man moaned, angling his hips harder against my finger until it was buried two knuckles deep in his anus. "I'm going to cum baby. I'm going to cum all over you face. Fuck me with your finger–"

Suddenly I pulled my finger out of his butthole and pulled back, listening to his dick flap excitedly against his stomach.

"What the *fuck*, man?" the man groaned. "I was just about to come! What are you doing?"

"Don't worry, man," I said, imitating his macho-man language. "I have something even better in mind to finish you off with. You didn't think I was going to let you waste all that hard meat coming in my *hands*, did you?

"You mean–?"

"Yes, baby," I smiled. "I'm going to finish you with my pussy. Would you like to cum inside something a little warmer and wetter?"

"*Fuck*, yes," he growled. "Give me anything you've got. I need to cum so bad."

"Do you think you can hold off long enough for me to have a little fun first? With a weapon like that, I assume you've practiced firing it enough to learn how to properly satisfy a woman."

"I'll try," he said. "But maybe you should hold off stimulating me like that until you're ready. I don't know how much longer I'll be able to hold out."

"Never fear," I said, standing up and turning around with my back facing his chair. "I'll take care of it the rest of the way."

Knowing I'd just finished my period, I wasn't worried about protection. Besides, I wanted to feel his hot flesh inside me when he shot off his cannon. I grabbed his tool between my legs then slowly lowered my hips over his lap as I felt his mammoth organ spread me apart.

"Uhnnn," I groaned, feeling his dick sliding inside me.

"Fuck, baby," the man panted. "Your pussy is so tight. Fuck me with your pretty cunt. I'm going to cum so hard inside you."

"Yes, baby," I purred, flexing the muscles in my legs as I bobbed up and down on his pole, feeling his balls slapping up against my wet vulva.

As much as I wanted to squeeze his testicles rubbing up against me, I didn't want to risk of setting him off. I'd planned this scenario pretty much from the moment Madison had planted me in front of him, and there was no way I was going to let him come before I'd enjoyed myself to the fullest.

The man grabbed the sides of my hips and began pistoning his cock harder inside me, and with his breathing becoming more ragged, I knew I didn't have much time left. I moved my right hand over my clit and began circling my nub furiously. The combination of his big dick filling me up together with my already heightened state of arousal from having him almost cum in my hands had already taken me close to the brink. As the two of us moaned louder and louder ramping up our rocking pace toward the inevitable climax, I suddenly heard Madison clear her throat.

I held up my hand in front of me, pointing it toward her like a traffic cop ordering a driver to stop. There was no way she was going to deny me this last chance to enjoy my orgasm while impaled on this beast of a man. Knowing we were the last pairing of the night, there was no need to save ourselves for anyone else. Signaling that I was ready to let him come, I reached between his legs with my other hand and squeezed his balls tightly.

"I'm ready, baby," I panted. "Let it rip. Let me feel you spray your firehose inside me. I'm going to cum with you."

"Fuck yes," he groaned, pulling my hips tighter over his cock. "I'm going to cum in your tight pussy. Here it comes, baby! *Ngahhh!*"

As the man emptied his gigantic load inside me, I clamped down hard over his dick, gushing like a waterfall all over his tight balls. Between the howling sound the two of us were making and the sound of my waterworks splashing over his testicles, it must have sounded like an erotic symphony for rest of the listening guests. While we wailed together in orgiastic union, I heard an orchestra of squeals and groans coming from all sides of the circle around me. I smiled in blissful delight, knowing that we'd provided a fitting finish to Madison's exciting blindfold game.

## 8

## GUESS WHO

After the man and I recovered from our orgasms, Madison escorted me back to my seat. For a few moments, there was an uncomfortable silence in the room as everyone waited to see what would happen next. She'd mentioned at the beginning of the party that we'd have a chance to guess who we were paired with and that there would be prizes, but it was hard to imagine how we could do that blindfolded. With everybody sitting buck naked facing each other in a circle, the only question now was just how much we'd have to reveal.

"Well I don't know about you guys," Madison said. "But *I* certainly enjoyed this experience."

"Woo-hoo!" isolated cheers came from around the circle as everyone applauded loudly.

"Part of the fun in doing this of course," she said, "was in guessing who your partners were. I know for *some* of you, we stretched a few boundaries, and I'm really glad you opened yourselves up to a new type of sexual exploration. I hope we opened your eyes, figuratively speaking, to the myriad possibilities for sexual expression, even if it only allows you to better understand and appreciate the preferences of our LGBTQ brethren."

"Absolutely," one of the women hollered, with the rest of the group applauding even louder.

"So now, as we approach the end of our little parlor game, the question is—how comfortable do you all feel taking off your blindfolds and revealing yourselves in front of your fellow participants? I promised there'd be prizes for those of you who guessed correctly who your partners were, but we can only do this if we reveal our identities."

There was an awkward silence as Madison paused to let her comments sink in.

"I don't want to make anyone feel pressured to expose themselves to a bunch of strangers if you don't feel comfortable. So, if you'd like to exit now with your modesty intact, there will be no judgment, and I can escort you to the front of the house where you can get dressed and leave quietly. If so, please raise your hand now, and we'll allow you to make a graceful exit."

I cocked my head and listened to the telltale squeaking of seat plastic to see if anyone was raising their hand. But the room stayed pin-drop quiet as everyone held their breath waiting for the next step.

"Okay then," Madison said. "You're welcome to remove your blindfolds then and take a look around the room to see if you can find any clues as to who your partners were."

I pulled off my veil and swiveled my head slowly around

the circle, smiling as I recognized a few familiar faces. In addition to Hannah, Valerie, and Lily, whose voices I'd recognized earlier, there were a few other familiar faces in the crowd. There were my friends Bonnie and Emma from last year's camping trip, Cheryl from my favorite sex shop in town, and my friends Dylan and Jake and from my previous job.

But at least half of the group were a mix of people I'd never seen before. As everybody crossed their arms and legs trying to cover up their naked bodies, a few of us chuckled when we recognized some of the obvious suspects. I was surprised to see even *Madison* completely naked, sitting erect in her chair with her firm breasts pointing proudly out from her chest.

"I see some of you know each other already," she said, "while many others are meeting for the first time. And yes, I've *also* been naked this whole time, enjoying the proceedings along with the rest of you. I didn't think it would be fair being the only one covered up, especially since I could see everybody else in the buff."

"Who are you *kidding*, Mad," I huffed. "You just wanted to have as much fun as the rest of us while you watched all of us getting down and dirty."

"You might be right about that," she smiled, being careful to conceal my identity among the other guests who didn't yet know me. "And enjoy it I *did*."

"So," she said. "Who'd like to go first guessing who your partners were?"

"Are we guessing as the *giver* or the *receiver*?" Hannah asked a few seats to my left.

"Both," Madison said. "There will be prizes for each correct guess."

"It might be easier if each of us said something first to help us place the voice," Cheryl suggested. "Or at least uncrossed their arms and legs to give us some more clues about their special endowments."

"Fair enough," Madison nodded. "But for those of you who already know each other, I'm guessing you won't need too many extra clues."

Valerie was the first to raise her hand as she peered at me with a lopsided grin.

"Yes, ma'am," Madison said, giving her permission to proceed.

"Are we allowed to use names, or should we just *point* to our partners?" Valerie asked.

"That's between the two of you. Whatever makes you more comfortable."

Valerie lifted her arm and slowly pointed in my direction, making direct eye contact with me.

"I have to confess that I recognized Jade's voice while she was touching me. And I'd recognize those magnificent breasts anywhere. I've spied on her swimming in her pool from the other side of our yards for quite some time."

"Did you enjoy your first face-to-face, or should I say *body-to-body*, connection this evening?" Madison smiled.

"We'd met previously at a few neighborhood get-togethers, and this wasn't actually the first time we'd touched each other. But somehow it seemed even more exciting not being able to *see* her this time."

"I'm so glad you enjoyed the experience," Madison

nodded. "What about when you had *your* turn to provide the stimulation? Do you recognize who that might have been?"

"Well it was obviously another woman," she blushed. "But I didn't recognize the voice."

"Would the recipient like to reveal herself, now that you've heard your partner's voice?"

Everybody sat quietly in their chairs, then Lily raised her hand, smiling shyly at Valerie.

"Ah yes," Madison smiled. "That was a memorable coupling, as I recall. Did you both enjoy your connection?"

"Oh yes," Lily purred. "Valerie has quite a way with her hands, not to mention her talented tongue."

"Well I'm glad you both enjoyed the encounter," Madison said, reaching beside her into a large canvas tote bag on the floor. "Because you answered one of your connections correctly, Valerie, I have a special prize for you."

She lifted a Pocket Rocket vibrator out of the bag and passed it down the circle toward her.

"I hope this little sex toy will keep you entertained on lonely nights when you think back on this experience."

Everybody cheered as Valerie took possession of the toy, pretending to rub it against her vulva.

"How about if we mix it up a bit now?" Madison said, looking around the circle. "Do any of the *men* want to try guessing their partners?"

Everyone paused for another long moment, then a muscular, hairy-chested man raised his hand slowly.

"Yes, Neil," Madison said, nodding in his direction.

"I *also* recognize Jade's voice now that she's spoken," he said, grinning at me sexily.

"As the giver or receiver?"

"Well actually, I think maybe she was one of the lucky ones who experienced it *both* ways we me."

"I think you might be right about that," Madison said, turning her head to smile in my direction. "She *did* break the rules, but we might have to give her a pass since it was the last coupling of the night. And what about your *other* partner, do you have any idea who that might be?"

He glanced around the room at the other men in the circle, pinching his eyebrows suspiciously. Then one of the men on the opposite side slowly parted his legs, gazing him in the eye. Neil glanced down at his swelling equipment and smiled.

"I can't be a hundred percent certain," he said, pointing at the other man. "But based on the size of the gentleman's cock, I'm guessing it might be him."

"What do you say, Ryan?" Madison said. "Do you recognize the gentleman's voice or anything else about him?"

"Ah, *yeah*," he said, glancing down at Neil's semi-tumescent monster. "That's not the *only* thing I recognize."

Everybody around the circle chuckled as they watched the two men's cocks beginning to swell again in recollection of their memorable connection.

"Well, Neil," Madison said, reaching into her prize bag again, this time pulling out a purple silicone ring toy. "For guessing the *lady* half of your equation, I'm passing around this lovely vibrating cock ring. Though I'm not entirely sure you'll be able to fit into it."

Then she reached behind her into a large duffel bag, pulling out a full-size inflatable doll. The round mouth had a large hole with a bright red ring of painted lipstick around it, and between the doll's legs was a large red slit.

"Maybe you'll be able to fit yourself more easily into this lovely inflatable companion?" Then she pulled another doll from the bag, this one with a puffy cock pointing up between its legs. "Or would you'd prefer to have the *male* doll?"

"I'll take the female one, thanks," he smiled as the rest of the group erupted in laughter.

For the next twenty minutes or so, Madison continued around the room until everybody had had a turn to guess and reveal their partners. Once again, she saved me for last, and I cocked my head smiling at her, guessing what she was cooking up.

"So I guess that just leaves Jade without a parting gift," she said. "Each of your partners have already revealed who you were paired with, so it doesn't seem fair to hand out two prizes. But because you've been such a sport saving yourself to the end this evening, I'll let you decide which prize you'd prefer."

She held up each of the inflatable dolls in her separate hands, looking at me with a devilish smile.

"You seemed to have an *equal* amount of fun with each of your partners," she smiled. "Something tells me you'd be able to entertain yourself for hours with either one of these dolls."

Then she reached into her bag and held up one of my favorite sex toys, the two-pronged Osé vibrator.

"Or perhaps you'd prefer this special toy which simulates the movement of *each* sex against your private parts?"

I peered at Madison through narrowed eyelids while I parted my legs slowly.

"*Actually*, Maddie," I said. "I've been thinking about a different kind of prize all evening. After everyone leaves, I'd like to have *you* all to myself."

"Why wait until everybody leaves?" she grinned. "Why don't we get it on right here and now where everybody can see?" She looked around the group and held out her hands, seeking input. "What do you say, guys–would you like to enjoy one last pairing without the restriction of the blindfolds?"

A loud cheer rose from the circle as everybody clapped loudly, egging us on.

"Which would you prefer this time?" Madison asked me. "To give or receive?"

"Fuck that idea," I said, lifting myself out of my chair and lying seductively on the plush carpet in the middle of the circle. "I want to fuck you every way possible. It's time you got some of your own medicine."

"With pleasure," she purred, crawling across the carpet in my direction.

As she moved toward me, I glanced around the circle and noticed many of the men had separated their legs, revealing their hard poles pointing straight up in their laps. Something told me this party was far from being over, and that before the end of the evening there'd be quite a few more connections made among the hot and still-horny guests...

R eady for more erotic chills and thrills? Enjoy the next volume in Jade's Erotic Adventures:

*Some cultural exchange programs are more rewarding than others...*

## Sneak peek:

*I found myself holding my breath as I strained to listen to the sound of the razor scraping Luna's skin and the water sloshing over her naked body as she shifted her position periodically in the tub. After a while, the scraping sound stopped and for a while I couldn't hear anything in the washroom. Then I slowly began to hear the sound of ripples lapping against the side of the tub, and I wondered what she was doing. Straining to listen, I heard her begin to mew as the sound of rippling water began to escalate in pitch and frequency...*

## READ MORE...

# VOLUME THREE

---

## THE DARKROOM

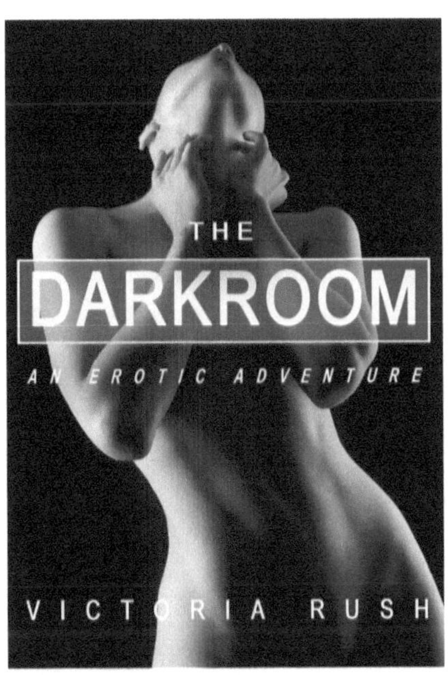

## 1

# IN THE SHADOWS

After my exhilarating experience at The Dinner Party, I was ready for more sexual exploration. The idea of being watched and watching other people releasing our inhibitions in a group setting was incredibly erotic. There was something about being with strangers that took the encounter to an entirely new level.

But it was more than that—it was the *anonymity* that made it especially appealing. With my mask on, I felt empowered to try new things, to do things I would never do in my regular guise. It was like I had superpowers. With my identity hidden, I could try anything, and the results were equally surprising. The sexual feelings were stronger and the climaxes were more powerful than anything I'd experienced before.

I wanted more. But I also wanted something different. I wanted to stretch my boundaries to see how far my new powers of sexual expression could take me. What other exotic destinations might I discover in the erotic underworld?

One day late at night, I sat down in front of my computer and typed in the search words 'anonymous group sex'. Among a litany of listings for gay bathhouses, swingers parties, and wife-swapping groups, I found a cryptic heading on the bottom of the second page, reading *The Dark Room: Explore Your Sensuality*. I clicked on the link and a video opened with a naked dancer undulating under the mesmerizing effect of black and white zebra-like stripes illuminated on her body.

I watched, transfixed, as the light patterns flowed over every sensuous curve of her body. In the background, soft instrumental music added to the trance-like effect. The alternating dark and light patches provided just enough camouflage to mask her identity. But as the light parts moved over different areas of her physique, they briefly revealed her erogenous zones. The curve of her shapely breasts, a fleeting glimpse of her bare nipple, the glorious cleft in her tight round ass. She was completely naked, but I had to look carefully to recognize the naughty parts.

And what a sight it was to behold. As the illuminated stripes curved and stretched around every contour of her body, they accentuated her gorgeous figure. When she moved closer to the screen and briefly revealed her face, it had the same effect. I could see the fullness of her lips and the sensuous curve of her cheekbones. But the light never stayed in one place long enough to betray her identity, even if someone knew who was hidden behind the unusual light effects.

*Now this was something completely different,* I thought. *Erotic, stimulating, and anonymous.*

*But where were her playmates?*

As exciting as I imagined it might be to dance naked under the relative obscurity of these light effects, it would be infinitely *more* fun to participate actively with others in such a room. I scanned the webpage and noticed a heading in the menu at the top of the page titled 'Group Packages'. I clicked the link and three more video thumbnails appeared on the page: one labeled 'Men', one titled 'Women', and another marked 'Mixed'. I tapped on the first one, and another video started playing, showing multiple figures gyrating to the music.

This time, the light-projections were in different colors, shifting and bending around the moving figures like a psychedelic kaleidoscope. The bodies were masculine, with broad shoulders, muscled chests, and washboard stomachs. Occasionally, the men would brush up against one another and move their hips in a feigned anal intercourse motion, but the action was too slow and measured to be real. And the camera never strayed far below the subjects' bellybuttons, so it was impossible to tell if they were actually aroused. Even though they occasionally embraced in lip lock, it all seemed staged and dispassionate, like strippers putting on a show in a dance club.

I wasn't much interested in watching gay sex anyway, even with buff Chippendale characters such as these, so I clicked the next video thumbnail labeled 'Women'. This was definitely more my thing, and I could feel the stirring in my pussy as I reflected back on my last lesbian encounter at The

Dinner Party. The video began with three slim and shapely women dancing sensuously under a new light effect. Instead of black and white alternating zebra stripes, this time the illuminated light resembled streaking raindrops.

The effect was even more captivating than the previous videos. Like an animated expressionist painting, the streaks danced across every curve and valley of the women's bodies as they swayed their hips and torsos in tantalizingly rhythmic ways. I had to concentrate even harder to catch fleeting glances of their breasts, nipples, and midsections, with the light patches even sparser than before.

At least in the women's videos, the camera panned below their waists to highlight the resplendent shape of their hips and buttocks. I strained to recognize the telltale protrusion of their mound or catch a glimpse of the mysterious slit between their legs. But as my pussy began to moisten imagining what was hidden behind the dancing raindrops splashing across their figures, the models never bent in such a way to reveal anything explicit.

Maybe this was the intention of the producers—to tease our interest just enough so we'd want to click for more information, leading to some kind of sale. This was, after all, the tried and true model for virtually every porn site—to show the viewer just enough to get them worked up until they were horny enough to pay for the real thing. Although in this case, I was still confused as to what the 'real thing' was this website was selling.

Was it just beautiful videos, orchestrated to appear as legitimate art? Were they just trying to sell me a fancy video version of a self-portrait that I could share with my husband or partner? That might be intriguing, but I was looking for more. As I continued watching the video, the three women moved closer to one another, eventually rubbing their hips and torsos together like in the all-male video. But this time, I could see their lower bodies as they caressed one another.

I watched them rub their hips and breasts together as the light streaks raced across their erect nipples. They were kissing one another far more sensuously than the men, like they were really losing themselves in the moment. It was definitely a turn-on and I imagined myself in the mix, caressing their beautiful bodies in the darkness with the streaks of light providing fleeting glimpses of their figures. As I thought about what it would feel like to have a stranger stroking my body in the dark, I slipped my fingers under my panties and began to play with my clit. But just as the action started flowing in the video, the clip suddenly ended.

*Fuck!* I screamed. *Just as I was getting turned on! Even a normal porno is better than this. At least they go all the way and offer some release.*

I was tempted to divert to my favorite porn site and watch some good lesbian tribbing action to get off when I noticed the last video thumbnail on the screen, labeled 'Mixed'. At least *this* one, if it was real, would be hard to hide the state of arousal that heterosexual men would experience in the presence of sexy naked women—light or no light.

I clicked on the icon, and the last video started to play. This time the light effects were in the form of multi-hued geometric circles, stretching and undulating over the curves of the naked figures like a rolling spirograph. I had to give it to the video producers—they were certainly creative in using unusual light effects that looked beautiful when projected onto shapely naked bodies.

And there was no denying that the bodies were gorgeous. Both the men and the women were firm and well-toned, with curves in all the right places. Every one of them was seriously fuckable. But much to my chagrin, the interaction between the subjects in the video once again seemed practiced and restrained. Even the men hardly seemed into it, rubbing and caressing their partners like in a cheesy black-and-white B-movie. The camera never strayed below their waistlines, but I didn't need to see their flaccid penises to recognize play acting when I saw it.

*If this is what happens in these dark rooms, you can count me out,* I thought.

It was all too antiseptic and 'soft-porn' for my liking. I wanted some *real* sex—actual *touching* and *penetration*—where I could feel myself and my dark room partners getting aroused and getting off. I didn't just want to be in some kind of frou-frou art production, I wanted to participate in a live orgy! I was about to click out of the website when a chat bubble popped up in the lower right corner. A text message appeared in the bubble.

'Hi!' someone named Sara wrote. 'How can I help you? Did you want to learn more about our products and services?'

*Products and services? Maybe it's worth investigating this a little further after all. Let's see what other 'services' they have to offer...*

## 2

## EYES WIDE SHUT

'How can I participate in these dark rooms?' I typed in the chat window.

'If you come to our studio,' Sara replied, 'you can join any room of your choosing at any time.'

*Studio? This was sounding more and more like some kind of photography service to me.*

'How many people will be in the rooms with me?' I typed.

'That depends what time of the day and week you come. Friday and Saturday nights are busiest, but we also schedule sessions during the day, between 2:00 and 4:00 p.m. You can book a session by clicking on the tab for Appointments at the top of the page. We normally only have two or three people in the afternoon rooms and up to ten maximum on Friday and Saturday nights.'

The word *sessions* was beginning to sound more intriguing to me. I decided to probe for more information.

'What kind of clothing should I wear in these sessions?' I asked.

'You can wear anything that makes you feel comfortable, but most of our patrons choose to wear a minimum of accoutrements.'

'Including nothing at all?'

'Yes—if that's what makes you feel most comfortable.'

I loved how Sara kept dancing around the obvious question.

'How do the people in these dark room sessions typically *interact*?' I typed.

'That depends on what you're looking for and the kind of people that join you in the room.'

I hesitated for a moment before typing my reply.

'Is *touching* permitted?'

'Absolutely. That's what makes the experience particularly enjoyable. You're encouraged to explore each other's bodies in the privacy and safety of the dark room. Subject to the consent of each partner, of course.'

*Now we're talking,* I thought. Exploring each other's bodies was exactly what I was looking for. But I still had lots of questions pertaining to the privacy and safety parts.

'What if I don't want somebody to touch my body? How can I ensure my personal space will be respected?'

'We have a simple rule for everybody entering any of our dark rooms. All you have to do is brush someone's body away if you don't wish to be touched. Everyone is issued a safety bracelet before entering each room. If you feel threatened or forced to do anything against your will, all you have to do is press the alert button and an audio intercom will be activated. Any violators will be immediately removed from the room. You can ask for help at any time, but we rarely receive complaints from any of our patrons.'

I paused to let Sara's comments sink in. I liked the safeguards they had set up, but I didn't like the sound of audio recordings or being leered at by a bunch of security guards.

'What kind of privacy will I have? Will any audio or video recordings be made while I'm in any of the rooms?'

'Never,' Sara said. 'What goes on in the security of the dark rooms is between you and your consenting partners.'

I liked the sound of that.

'What about the video clips on your website?' I asked. 'Those were obviously recorded. Were those actual participants?'

'Those were paid actors, using our own models. I assure you, you will never be recorded while in one of our dark rooms.'

'What about your security personnel or anyone outside the room? Can they see what's happening inside?'

'Each dark room is enclosed in one-way glass all around,' Sara replied. 'You can't see out, but outside observers can see in. This allows patrons to observe the action in the room before committing to go inside. We find this adds to the excitement level for both those watching and those being watched. But the light effects in the room are always moderated in such a way to ensure your identity will be masked. The only thing outside observers can see, including our security staff, are the silhouettes of the people inside.'

*Oh my god,* I thought. *That sounds so hot.*

The idea of being watched, both within the room and

from outside the room, while I got down and dirty with my dark room partners sounded incredibly stimulating. I suddenly became aware of how soaked my panties had become as I continued the dialog with Sara.

'What about...*hygiene*?' I asked tentatively. 'What protections do I have against the spread of diseases?'

Sara and I finally seemed to be talking about the same thing. I decided to dispense with any further niceties and cut right to the chase.

'Every dark room participant must provide a recent blood test from an accredited medical lab,' she replied. 'You must report negative for all known sexual or communicable diseases. You'll also need to submit to a brief exam with our accredited medical doctor on staff to ensure you do not have any open sores or infections that could be spread by physical contact. This is for the safety of all participants.'

*Holy shit, these guys don't fool around. A gynecological exam is never fun, but if it's performed by a real doctor and it's not too intrusive, it's better to be safe than sorry.*

'Will the exam be performed by a gynecologist? Is the doctor male or female? May I ask for his or her credentials before I submit to the examination?'

'It will be with a female gynecologist for female examinations and a male urologist for male examinations. Their credentials will be on display in the examining office, which is also maintained with the utmost hygienic cleanliness. The examination is external only and very brief.'

*Okay,* I thought. *Now that we know exactly what we're talking about here, let's get down to brass tacks.*

'What are your fees? And is this...you know, *legitimate*? I mean, it sounds like I'm paying for sex.'

Sara paused for a moment before replying.

'This is a private club in a private residence. Whatever consenting adults choose to do with each other on private property is entirely legal. There is a modest subscription fee to join the club. You can see our fees under the tab marked Rates.'

It was all starting to come together. Just like The Dinner Party erotic club I attended a few weeks ago, they had similar terms of service. In fact, their professionalism and attention to detail made me wonder if it might be run by the same operators. I just had a few remaining questions.

'Are there separate rooms for men and women?' I asked. I was definitely ready for some more girl-on-girl action, but I wasn't ready to rule out a little hetero fun too if the mood struck me.

'We have separate rooms for men-only, women-only, and mixed gender. You may enter the single-gender room that matches your sex and also the mixed gender room, if you so wish, during your visit.'

I was definitely getting more interested by the moment and based on how fast the wet patch between my legs was spreading in my tight jeans, so was my aching pussy.

I wondered if there'd be any equipment to recline onto if things got hot and heavy enough.

'Are there places to relax in each of the rooms, or are they standing room only?' I typed.

'There is small upholstered furniture in each of the rooms, as well as Liberator sex cushions to adjust your position. Everything has neon piping around the edges to help you find it in the dark, and the coverings are laundered after each session to ensure cleanliness. Your safety and comfort is our universal goal.'

*Wow*, I thought. *These guys have thought of everything.*

This obviously wasn't going to be some kind of seedy swingers' party where just anybody could walk in and fuck anything that moves. This sounded like a first-class operation that was sure to titillate and satisfy all my senses.

I paused as I considered any other questions or concerns that I might have before venturing out to their club.

'How long can I remain in each room?' I said. 'And when I wish to leave, where can I go to freshen up and get dressed?'

'We have separate change rooms and showers for both men and women. Strobe lights are used in these and other public rooms of the residence to protect your identity at all times. From the moment you enter any of our dark rooms to the moment you leave the building, no one will be able to identify you. The only person who'll ask for ID is the doctor who examines you. He or she will verify your blood report belongs to you and the physician is sworn by doctor-patient privilege to maintain your privacy.'

I unconsciously exhaled a long deep breath as I began to relax. All my concerns had been addressed and all my expectations were satisfied. This was the perfect outlet I was looking for.

'Thank you for being patient with all my questions,' I typed. 'I'll check your rates and schedules and book a session in the near future.'

'It's been my pleasure,' Sara said. 'I hope our club satisfies all of your desires. Feel free to chat again if you have any more questions. See you soon!'

*Satisfy my desires, indeed. I had no doubt that it would. But right now, I needed some satisfaction that no one else could give me.*

I tore off my leggings and threw them on the floor as I reached into my nightstand for my favorite rabbit vibrator. Then I turned the rotating beads and rabbit ears on maximum and plunged the dildo into my aching pussy, moaning in delight as I imagined the pleasures that awaited me in the mysterious dark room.

## 3

## FOREPLAY

As I thrust the vibrator deep inside my snatch, I watched the all-girl dark room video on continuous loop. I was absolutely hypnotized by the swirling light effects rolling over their luscious bodies. Whenever the streaks illuminated their bare nipples and mounds, it made the effect all the more electrifying. My pussy made sexy slurping sounds as my juices sopped up the slick dildo sliding in and out of my hole.

I moaned like a dog in heat thinking about what it would be like to watch and touch these women in a *real* dark room. This experience would take my Dinner Party adventure to a whole new level. Instead of just sitting and watching passively while other people did things to me, in these spaces I could participate actively with whomever I pleased. My mind raced with all the things I wanted to do with these women—and maybe even some of the men in the mixed room. I wanted to fuck and be fucked by these mysterious apparitions.

When the women in the video started touching one another and rubbing their nipples together, I lifted my hips off the bed and thrust the vibrator deeper inside me. I angled the shaft so the oscillating tip massaged my G-spot, while I pushed the fluttering rabbit ears hard against my swollen nub. I could feel my orgasm building and I opened my mouth to kiss one of the models in the video as she did the same. When the tide finally swept over me, I clamped down hard over the pulsing vibrator and spasmed a long stream of powerful contractions.

I hadn't cum this hard since Jasmin had jilled me under the dinner table at the Dinner Party retreat. As I lay on the bed rolling my hips in post-orgasmic bliss, I closed my eyes and imagined myself dancing with the geometric light effects projected on my body. For a thirty-six-year-old, I still had a pretty damn fine figure with a tight ass, perky breasts, and a yoga-toned stomach. I wouldn't be the only one in the dark room admiring the physiques of my fellow participants.

I pulled the vibrator out of my pussy and stood up to admire myself in my full-length dressing mirror. I began to sway my hips and caress my breasts like the women in the video. I looked pretty good, but something was missing. I turned off the bedroom light and closed the drapes, then opened the bathroom door just enough to emit a thin sliver of light. I moved back from the mirror until the ray of light projected a narrow beam on my body.

It wasn't nearly as fancy as the light effects shown in the dark room videos, but it was enough to make me imagine I was there. I experimented with different positions as I watched the light illuminate different parts of my body in the darkness of my bedroom. Just as in the videos, it was fascinating to see how I could briefly reveal the naughty parts by moving in and out of the light. It was almost as exciting to watch my own body as it was the models in the video, and I began to caress my curves like a stripper in a dance club.

*I'll have to work on my technique,* I thought, analyzing my moves.

I had to be as irresistible as the models in the video if I hoped to attract the attention of men and women with similarly toned bodies.

*But that can wait for later.*

Right now, the only thing I could think about was booking an appointment for a dark room session as soon as possible. My vibrator, as entertaining as it was, would be no match for the real thing. I sat down again in front of my computer and clicked on the tab marked Rates.

*Let's see if I have to pay an arm and a leg to touch some of these arms and legs.*

It wasn't as bad as I imagined. There was a one-time subscription fee of $300, plus another $200 for each session. *Seems reasonable,* I thought. The gyno exam alone would cost that much or more in a regular doctor's office. Two hundred bucks for two hours or more of safe, titillating sex with multiple partners seemed like a bargain.

"Sign me up!" I thought out loud, clicking the tab for Appointments.

A registration page opened where they asked me to create an account. I paused for a moment as I considered my next move. I could use an alias and a fake email account, but I knew they'd also want a credit card to pay for the subscription.

*So much for nobody knowing my identity other than the doctor who'll examine me.*

I looked further down the page and saw a disclaimer promising that my email and credit information wouldn't be shared with anyone else, and that I wouldn't be sent any marketing information other than the confirmation of my appointment.

*What the fuck,* I said to myself. *Anybody running an internet business these days knows the surest way to lose customers is to share someone's online details without consent. Besides, I reveal a lot more personal financial information when I pay bills and do my banking online—this is pretty minor in comparison.*

I filled in the required fields to complete my registration, then scanned the schedule for available sessions. All the Friday and Saturday nights on the booking calendar were grayed out for the next three weeks.

*This place is popular,* I thought. *I guess that's a good sign.*

I imagined that meant most sessions would be pretty full and that I'd have my pick of partners to choose to engage with. I remembered Sara saying the daytime sessions were not as busy as the night sessions, so I clicked on the first available weekday. A new window opened indicating that I was about to reserve an afternoon session for the indicated date, then it asked me to fill in the credit card information to complete the transaction. I filled in the required details then clicked the Submit button. After about ten seconds of processing time, a window popped up from my email account confirming the payment and appointment.

*Well, that's it,* I thought. *I'm committed now.*

I could feel the blood flowing back into my pussy as my mind already started going where I'd been fantasizing for the last hour. I stood up and positioned myself again in the sliver of light emanating from the washroom.

*Damn girl,* I thought, admiring my figure as my fingers strayed down toward my warm cunny. *This is going to be fun...*

4

—————

## PEOPLE IN GLASS HOUSES

On my appointment day, I could barely contain my excitement. I drove out to the address provided in my email confirmation and was pleasantly surprised when I arrived at the destination. As with my previous experience at the dinner party, the facility was in a large country chateau. Just like the last place, I had to provide my registration username and password to be permitted access through the security gate. I drove up the long tree-lined driveway to an even larger mansion than before.

If this was any indication of the step up in the level of services that awaited me, I was all-in. I parked my car alongside five or six other cars in the guest parking section and walked over a cobblestone path up to the front door. I tapped on the large brass door knocker and was greeted a few seconds later by an attractive young woman in a smart business suit.

*I guess there'll be no naked attendants in masquerade masks this time around,* I frowned. *Maybe this place is run by a different operator, after all.*

Nevertheless, the interior appointments and finishings were on a par with the previous home, and I was eager to explore its special rooms.

"You must be Jade," the woman said, taking my coat and hanging it in the closet. "My name's Ali, and I'll be your host for the evening. Can I get you something to drink? Coffee, tea, a glass of wine?"

I was pretty charged up already and thought a bit of alcohol would help relax some of the inhibitions I was beginning to feel about getting naked with a group of strangers.

"I'd love a glass of white wine if you have it, thank you."

Ali motioned to an adjoining room with large French doors.

"Feel free to relax in our waiting room," she said, handing me a piece of paper and a pen. "If you can take a few moments to review and sign this waiver, this will help ensure our expectations are aligned. I'll be back in a few minutes."

I walked into a beautiful room with tall Palladian windows and sat down on the large leather sofa. I quickly reviewed the document, which was mostly concerned with the rules of engagement in the dark rooms. Only women were permitted in the women's dark room it said, and only men were permitted in the men's dark room, but they could commingle in the mixed room. It reiterated the 'golden rule' about touching others only with consent. A simple brush of the hand or step back from an advancing partner indicated that you did not wish to be touched. Any violators would be immediately removed from the room and banned from using the facility in future. I signed the document with my alias Jade and placed it face-up on the coffee table.

I noticed some picture books lying on the table with familiar photos of naked people illuminated with similar light effects to the videos I'd watched earlier. I opened one of the books and flipped through the pages as I admired the beautiful figures of the models and the different light effects displayed in each image.

*I hope the people in my dark room will be as pretty as these,* I thought, feeling my panties start to dampen again.

A minute later, Ali returned with a large glass of wine, setting it down on the coffee table.

"I see you've been familiarizing yourself with our light productions," she said, noticing the open book laid out in front of me. "Did you have any questions before I take you to the viewing room?"

*Viewing room? The voyeur in me liked the sound of that.*

"So I'll have a chance to watch some of the dark rooms before I choose to enter one?" I asked.

"Of course," Ali said. "That's part of the fun. All of our dark rooms can be observed from the outside through one-way glass. You'll be able to watch the participants but they won't be able to see you. Most of our patrons find this to be a stimulating experience that helps put them in the mood. If you like what you see, you can then proceed to the doctor's office for a brief exam, after which you're welcome to enter your appointed rooms. Did you bring your lab test report with you?"

"Yes—of course," I said, fishing in my purse for the blood test.

Ali held up her hand to save me the trouble.

"Bring it with you and show it to the doctor when she examines you. Are you ready to head downstairs?"

"Absolutely," I said, pleased that just as Sara had promised earlier, no one had yet asked for anything that could reveal my identity.

"Allow me to escort you, then. Would you like to leave your wine glass here or bring it with you?"

"I think it's better that I leave it here. Something tells me that I'm going to need my hands free for other things."

Ali simply smiled and nodded. I followed her out of the sitting room and across a marbled foyer, where we paused at the top of a declining circular stairway.

"Our dark rooms are in the lower level, where we can control the light more effectively. There are three exits, including a direct exit to the guest parking area. You may leave at any time, or return to the main floor if you need further help."

Ali reached into one of her pockets and handed me a black wristband.

"This is your security bracelet. Please wear it at all times until you leave the building. If you feel uncomfortable at any time, all you have to do is press this button on the side of your bracelet and a security agent will come to your assistance immediately. But I think you'll find it will be quite unnecessary. Our patrons are very respectful of the stipulated rules. I believe you'll find the experience very safe and satisfying."

I nodded my head as I fastened the bracelet buckle behind my wrist.

Ali escorted me down the stairs and opened a door at the base of the steps. A white strobe light and soft instrumental music emanated through the open portal.

"It may take you a few moments to get comfortable with the flashing light, but this will protect your identity while you stay on the lower level. The light is sequenced in such a way to allow you to find your way around while also maintaining your anonymity. Each of the exits are clearly marked, as is the entrance to the doctor's office and the change rooms."

She motioned to three large glass cubes in the center of the cavern.

"Each of the dark rooms is marked according to gender. Which room would you like to see first?"

"Um..." I said, hesitating for only a moment. "I think I'd like to see the women-only room first."

Ali gently grasped my hand and escorted me to the first glass-enclosed cube. It was much larger than it appeared from the other side of the room, measuring roughly twenty feet square on each side and ten feet tall. Inside the floor-to-ceiling glass panels, I could see the familiar movement of furtive figures illuminated under the kaleidoscopic light. The rest of the room was pitch black so the only things illuminated by the projected light were the moving bodies.

I unconsciously moved closer to the glass, captivated by the swirling light effects and soft music. This wasn't some cheesy strip club with pounding music and bright lights illuminating a gaudy stage. The soft instrumental music combined with the pretty light effects projected a feeling of real class. My eyes widened as I watched the naked participants move around inside the room.

Just as in the video, they were swaying their bodies and caressing each other. But there was something different this time. Their hands and bodies were no longer touching each other with fleeting, artificial gestures. This time, they *lingered* and *probed* one another. Their action looked *purposeful*, not like the play acting in the video. Near the front of the glass, two women were locked in a tight embrace, passionately kissing and grinding their hips together in familiar motion. I could see their buttock muscles flexing as they rubbed their mounds together under the swirling light.

My eyes raced around the inside of the enclosure as I took it all in. In the far corner of the cube, I noticed some neon piping tracing the outline of a large sofa. I squinted my eyes to decipher a commingled figure twisting together as the geometric lights swept over a mass of tangled arms and legs. At first, it looked like a single person doing some kind of yoga movement, with her leg stretched over her shoulder. But as I looked more closely, I could see that the raised leg belonged to a woman lying on the sofa with her legs splayed apart. Another woman was resting on her knees, squatting between the prone woman's legs, rubbing their vulvas together, fucking her with rapid swings of her hips while she clasped the prone woman's elevated leg tightly against her breasts.

I gasped audibly and slumped over, unconsciously mimicking the movement of the woman on top.

"Shall I leave you now to enjoy the show?' Ali said, somewhere to my side.

I'd completely forgotten she was still there. I turned and saw her familiar outline flashing beside me under the white strobe light.

"Yes, I'll be fine now," I said, catching my breath and trying to sound composed.

"Wonderful," she said. "You're welcome to remain outside the rooms and watch as long as your session is booked, or enter your allotted rooms at your leisure. The entrance to the dark rooms is via the doctor's office, who'll validate your blood report and conduct a brief external exam before you move on. Remember that if you need help at any time, all you have to do is press the button on the side of your bracelet. I hope you enjoy your stay and that we'll see you again soon. Bye for now."

It was strange watching her talk as the white light flashed over her face. I could see her lips open and close in delayed jerky movements that didn't synchronize with her speech. It was a bit disconcerting and nothing like the flowing movement of the light projected inside the dark room, but it was sexy and mysterious in its own way. Just as she and Sara had promised, it was impossible to recognize her face through the intermittent flashes.

"Thank you, Ali," I said. "I'll let you know if I need anything."

I was glad to see her leave, because my pussy was pounding and my crotch was soaked from watching the action in the cube. As soon as she closed the door leading to the stairs behind her, I unclasped the top button of my jeans and thrust my hand under my panties. My fingers immediately found my opening and I inserted three fingers as far as they'd go inside me while I rubbed my palm against my aching clit. It couldn't have taken more than ten seconds for me to cum hard in my jeans as I watched the women scissoring on the couch in the dark room.

It was difficult to see the expressions on their faces under the shifting light, but I noticed the mouth of the woman on top widen as her movements became increasingly frenetic. Then she suddenly stopped and arched her back as she pulled her partner's elevated leg against her torso and spasmed her body in obvious climax. I longed to be there with them, feeling what they were feeling and listening to their moans of ecstasy as their love juices washed over one another.

After I came down from my orgasm, I suddenly became aware that I wasn't the only one standing outside the cube watching what was going on inside. I noticed another figure standing about five feet to my side, and I glanced in her direction. The flashing light showed just enough to reveal a pretty woman with long hair and high cheekbones. Although I'd never recognize her in the plain light of day, her full lips and gently sloping jawline betrayed her beauty. I glanced down at her body and noticed the bulge of her full breasts in her blouse and the curvature of her hips and ass in her tight jeans.

I blushed in the dark thinking that she might have noticed me rubbing myself in the dark like some kind of creepy flasher. But she just peered at me and smiled.

"Pretty hot, huh?" she said, in a soft, sexy voice.

"Yeah," was all I could manage to pant.

"Are you going in?" she asked, matter-of-factly.

"Definitely," I said.

"Perhaps I'll see you in a few minutes then. I'm going to watch for a little longer to get my nerve up."

"Enjoy," I said, imagining her getting just as turned on as I did watching the action in the cube. Sara was right—it was almost as much fun *watching* the action as participating in it. But I was eager to feel the touch of another woman and experience the hypnotic light effects first-hand.

*But those aren't the only body parts I'll be using*, I thought as I headed toward the examining room.

## 5

## INTO THE LIGHT

The gyno exam wasn't as bad as I anticipated, though it was pretty embarrassing walking into the examining room with a big wet patch in the crotch of my jeans. The doctor didn't bat an eyelash and simply asked me to disrobe and lie down on the examining table. The whole thing was over in a couple of minutes.

She examined me for any sign of open sores then reviewed my lab test and checked my driver's license to verify the report. Fortunately, I'd made a recent visit to my aesthetician to clean things up down below. My smooth pussy was bald and spotless, which made the examination all the faster and easier.

When she was done, she handed me a note with a number and a key code then directed me through a door leading into the women's change room. As with the other public sections of the lower level, a soft strobe light permeated the change room. In between the flashes, I could see a few women in various stages of undress going about their business in the locker room, but I paid them no attention. Part of me wanted to search for the pretty woman who I'd chatted with briefly outside the women's dark room, but I decided it was best to respect everyone's privacy. There'd be plenty of opportunity to engage more directly once I got inside the actual dark rooms.

I located a bank of lockers with combination locks and pulled out the slip of paper the doctor had handed me. I matched the number on the slip with the corresponding locker and entered the code on the tumblers to undo the lock. Inside the locker, there was a freshly-laundered terrycloth robe and towel. I removed my clothes and placed my belongings inside the locker, then put the robe on and carried the towel to one of the shower stalls. I could still feel the vestiges of dried-up lubrication coating my inner thighs, and I wanted to be as clean and fresh as I could be going in to the dark rooms.

As I turned on the shower and stepped under its gentle spray, I reflected back to the video with the rain drop effect. I imagined myself dancing in the dark room as the light streaks flowed over my body, turning and bending my figure to reveal every sensuous curve. I opened a fresh bar of soap and rubbed the silky pod across my breasts, under my arms, and between my legs. My body felt electrified, and for a moment I was tempted to rub another one out, but I decided to save myself for the real thing. I didn't want anything tempering the pleasure that awaited me. I finished the shower, then dried myself off and returned my towel to my locker. I hesitated for a moment, deciding whether to hang my robe in my locker too, or wear it out into the open spaces of the lower level.

*Screw it*, I said, placing it on the hook. *This whole experience is about letting myself go and losing myself in the moment. Besides, between the strobe lights outside the dark rooms and the light show inside the rooms, no one will be able to recognize me anyhow.*

I closed the locker and scrambled the tumblers, making a mental note of my locker number and combination code. Then I walked out of change room into the open space of the lower level and looked around. It felt liberating to be stark naked in the cool air of the basement under the pulsating strobe lights.

Each of the three dark rooms were bathed with different colored and patterned light effects. On each side of the cubes, illuminated gender symbols clearly indicated who was inside. The glass cubes looked from a distance like a holographic dance show, with three different 'theaters' to choose from. I walked toward the cube displaying two familiar circle-and-cross symbols, knowing the all-girl show was what had initially attracted me to the program.

When I got closer to the cube, I noticed the light patterns inside had changed from when I viewed it earlier. This time, the patterns were in the form of orange and black spots, making the figures inside the room look like human-shaped leopards. I could make out four distinct figures inside the enclosure. Two of the women were quite slim, with tight ballerina figures. The other two were more voluptuous, with full breasts and wide, curving hips. But they all looked mouth-watering gorgeous, bathed in pretty feline leopard spots.

I was transfixed watching the women circle one another like prowling cats in the dark. It didn't take long for the figures to blend together and begin rubbing against one another. I stood spellbound as they huddled their bodies together like a group of leopards feasting over prey.

*I want to be their prey,* I thought, swaying my body in synchronization with the women.

I looked around the enclosure and didn't see anyone else standing in the flashing light, so I decided it was time to join the action inside the room. A sign on one side of the cube read Open. I ran my hand over the glass near the sign and felt a handle, pulling the glass door toward me. For a moment, the outside strobe light intermixed with the flowing orange spots inside the room, and I was conscious of how chaotic it suddenly appeared. I immediately closed the door and the one-way glass blocked out the outside light, returning the room to its flowing orange and black leopard motif.

By now, the four women in the room had paired off and seemed preoccupied with their partners, so I stood to the side and swayed my hips to the music as I watched the hypnotic movement of their bodies. The women circled around one another as if stalking each other. It was exciting to watch them play-act to the theme of the light show. But the acting soon turned more serious as the couples moved closer together and began rubbing their bodies together. Soon, their lips locked together and I could see them kissing passionately as the light and dark spots flowed over their faces.

I was dying to get in on the action, but I didn't want to interrupt their connection. As I watched their hands slide down each other's bodies, my hands mimicked their movement. When their hips briefly separated and their hands moved between each other's legs, so did mine. I was the odd woman out, but somehow I didn't mind. I could feel the juices flowing down my thighs as my pussy watered in sympathy with the gyrating couples.

I began circling my button and was just about to push my fingers into my slit when suddenly the light in the room was interrupted once again by someone opening the door. The shape of the body in the flashing light looked familiar, and I recognized the shoulder-length hair of the woman who'd stood beside me earlier. She closed the door, then paused for a moment as she looked around the room. Before long, she began walking in my direction then stopped about two feet in front of me. She smiled as the leopard spots flowed over her face and I suddenly felt weak at the knees once again.

Her body was even more beautiful in the buff than in her tight blouse and jeans. Her breasts were a full and firm, with a gentle ski-jump slope on the top. These were no fake balloon-shaped artificial tits—these were the real thing. I glanced further down and watched the leopard spots flowing over her hips as my mouth began to water. There was just enough light flowing over her pubic area to show that she was shaved bald like me. As she danced sensuously in front of me in the dark, her bare mound swayed slowly from side to side.

"My name's Emma," she said in a soft voice.

"Jade," was all I could reply, hypnotized by her beauty.

"Beautiful, isn't it?" she said, turning her face toward one of the couples locked in a passionate embrace.

"Stunning," I said, happy the music was playing softly enough to engage in quiet conversation.

"You look like quite a tasty feline yourself," Emma said.

"You too," I replied lamely.

Emma inched closer toward me, until we were about six inches apart. I could see her looking directly into my eyes as she smiled sexily at me.

"May I?" she asked.

I wasn't sure exactly what she had in mind, but whatever she wanted to do with me, I was game.

"Please," I panted.

She closed the remaining distance and I could feel her breasts push against mine as she locked lips with me. A jolt shot through my body as if I'd been lit on fire. I could feel the heat of her body and the perspiration on our chests as our breasts slid sensuously over one another. She slipped her tongue between my lips and I sucked on hers as we swirled our tongues together. Our hips met and we gently ground our mounds together. When she moaned in my mouth, I practically came from the passion of the moment.

There was something electrifying about being in the dark with a perfect stranger, our bodies pressed together, with these mysterious and beautiful light effects highlighting the curves and shadows of our bodies. I could feel my nipples hardening, and we separated for a moment as we tweaked them together, watching the orange spots highlighting our swollen tips.

I was hypnotized by the sights and sounds and I could feel the juices in my pussy building by the moment as they began to run down the inside of my thighs toward my knees. As if reading my thoughts, Emma's right hand began tracing a line down the side of my waist and curved over my hips toward my love box. I quivered as her hand got closer to my pussy. When she finally slipped her fingers into my cleft and traced them slowly up toward my clit, I gasped out loud.

"Yes," I exhaled onto her bare shoulder as I slumped my body against hers. I wanted her to plunge her fingers deep into me and bring me to a quick orgasm. There would be plenty of time to experiment with other things and for me to return the favor in a moment. Right now, I desperately needed to get off.

She inserted two fingers further inside me and stroked my G-spot, and our mouths joined together once again. Our tongues swirled and sucked one another while she caressed my insides. But her palm remained stubbornly fixed in place over my mound. I wanted her to move her hand over my aching clit, and I swiveled my hips in a vain attempt to create more friction. But Emma seemed to be holding back, savoring the moment, as if intentionally denying my pleasure.

"Let's move to the sofa," she said, taking her hand out of my pussy and weaving her fingers between mine as she led me to the neon-outlined rectangle at the far edge of the cube. I hardly even noticed the other women as we walked straight by them, my head was so swimming in anticipation of what Emma wanted to do with me on the sofa.

When we got to the neon lines marking the perimeter of the couch, she gently pushed me down onto its surface. When my buttocks rested on the cushion, she kneeled down beside me and kissed me hard on the lips while lowering me slowly onto the couch. Emma lay on her side beside me while she ran her left hand over my breasts and stomach, then she leaned in and sucked my erect nipples. It felt incredible and I hoped she'd soon move lower and administer the same kind of action on my aching clit.

But she seemed content with running her hands over me as she explored every curve and crevasse of my body. When her hand passed over my bare mound, I lifted one of my legs to permit freer access to my pulsating cunny. Instead, she swept her arm under my knee and pulled my other leg up until both legs were pointed straight up in the air. Then she stopped kissing me and lowered her face closer to my hips.

*Finally!* I thought. She's going to give me attention where I most needed it—in my aching pussy.

She positioned herself behind my exposed ass, then spread my legs apart until they formed a bent V-shape, with my thighs resting against my chest. My entire vulva was now exposed to her and I could feel my wetness trickling down my perineum toward my anus.

*Now, Emma,* I screamed inside. *Suck my aching twat, I* begged. *Take me into your mouth and lick my clit like you were playing with my tongue earlier. Slip your fingers inside me and fuck my twat like there's no tomorrow. Because right now, time is standing still and I'm not sure there's going to be another tomorrow.*

Emma paused, and I lifted my head to look in her direction. She looked up at me and smiled with a mischievous grin as the leopard spots flowed over her pretty face. Then she lifted herself up and positioned her hips over top of mine as she rested her thighs on top of mine and slowly lowered her vulva until it touched mine. The feeling when our pussies touched was indescribable.

We were both aflame in passion and soaked through and through between our legs. I could feel her labia interlacing with mine in a different kind of lip lock, and I threw my head back against the sofa cushion in utter ecstasy. I began rubbing my cunt furiously against hers, listening to the sound of our juices commingling as they slurped and sloshed in glorious union. It was dirty and raunchy and sexy, and something I'd been longing to try ever since my last lesbian encounter at the Dinner Party.

Just when I thought it couldn't get any more intense, Emma shifted forward a few inches and our clits suddenly touched.

"Fuck, yes!" I cried out loud as our eyes locked in the strange orange and while shifting lightness.

Her face looked exquisite as we began to grind our pussies together and she fucked me harder. I could feel the hardness of her clit as it flicked and over mine, and I moaned in blissful abandon. I felt the ache deep in my core beginning to build, but I wasn't ready to cum yet. I wanted to savor this moment and play with Emma on the precipice of pleasure as long as I could make it last.

Emma leaned forward and began to kiss me passionately as she began fucking my gaping hole more vigorously. We both moaned into each other's mouths as we savored the union of our most private parts in the soft orange light. Suddenly, Emma lifted her face above mine and moaned an otherworldly sound. I felt a gush of liquid spraying against my open pussy, filling me with her juices. Emma was squirting her wetness against me while she came hard between my legs. Any chance of holding back my orgasm any longer quickly evaporated as I fell over the cliff, spasming a long serious of hard contractions against Emma's sex. While our bodies jerked and spasmed at the height of pleasure, we watched each other gasp and moan in the swirling lightscape.

When our climactic contractions finally subsided, Emma collapsed onto my body and kissed me softly on my lips. For the longest time, we simply lay on our sides with our legs intertwined, kissing and giggling like two little girls.

"That was incredible," Emma whispered in my ear.

"We're not done yet," I said, smiling into her eyes. "This cat still has a lot more fight left in her."

## OVER THE RAINBOW

Emma and I played for another hour or so in the women's dark room, experimenting with different positions and techniques, and we both came many more times. I was tempted to engage with some of the other women in the room, but I wanted to save myself for something else. I exchanged email addresses with Emma and we promised to stay in touch, then I exited the cube.

When I stepped back into the flashing light of the lower level, I glanced over at the men's room. There was something intriguing about watching men have sex with one another, and I was drawn to their shapes moving under a different kind of light effect. As I got closer to the enclosure, I noticed the light looked like little white tadpoles, swimming over the men's bodies while they moved about the room. Just as in all the other rooms, it was beautiful and hypnotic to watch.

Three men were facing each other near the front of the glass, grinding their hips together in a triangle formation. As they swayed their bodies, I could see they all had erections and were rubbing their cocks together in a coordinated frotting action. It was fun watching them slap their swords together like they were Three Musketeers in a playful fight.

Suddenly, the man nearest the glass knelt down and began licking the other two men's penises. It was incredibly erotic to watch him caress their hard-ons with his tongue and lips. It was hard to tell exactly how worked up the men on the receiving end of his ministrations were, but the little white tadpoles racing across their stomachs simulated the effect of sperm shooting out of their cocks.

Then the kneeling man moved up to the heads of their cocks and took both penises into his mouth. I'd heard of double penetration before, but this was an entirely different version from what I'd never seen. As the two men humped their hips slowly together, fucking the kneeling man's mouth, they began to kiss passionately. I was surprised how turned on I was getting watching the action, and I was soon ready to experience some dick of my own in the mixed room. As much as I enjoyed making love to Emma, sometimes all I wanted was a hard, throbbing cock pounding my pussy to its limits.

As I turned toward the cube housing the mixed-gender participants, my kitty beginning to tingle even more strongly. This time, the light effects stretched and curved around the figures in beautiful rainbow-colored stripes. I recognized three figures in the cube: one woman and two men. I stood entranced watching the colored stripes stretch and bend around their curves as they danced and rubbed their bodies together, much like the three men were doing in the men-only cube. But this time, the woman was sandwiched between the men as they bucked their hips against her from opposite sides.

I had to look closely to see their erections under the bands of light, but they were quite noticeable—and *large*. The man facing the woman's front side has his cock pressed up against her belly, while she stroked it sensuously with one of her hands. The man behind her had his tool between her legs and every time he swung his hips forward, I could see its head poke in and out under her mound. With her other hand, she caressed the underside of his cock and pressed it toward her opening. She turned her head and kissed the man behind her as the three engaged in an erotic tribal dance.

Not wanting to interrupt their concentration, my own hand fell to my crotch, and I began massaging my clit while I cupped and squeezed my breasts with my other hand. My mind raced ahead, thinking about all the different positions and permutations I could engage in with these three partners.

After a few minutes of erotic play, the man on the woman's backside angled his hips upward and the woman tilted her ass back to receive him. Their mouths opened in a silent moan as he slid his cock inside her. The man in front continued to hump the woman's belly, but now the woman had two hands free to clasp his cock and give him proper attention. As she and the man behind her rocked their hips together, the rainbow stripes slid over the other man's erection, making it look like a writhing anaconda.

*How I wanted that cock inside me!*

The movement of the man and the woman who were joined began to speed up and as I drooled from my soaking pussy, he slammed his hips against her ass, forcing her hands to move up and down on the other man's cock. She didn't need to do anything now, other than hold her hands tightly around his throbbing manhood. I was surprised how much of his organ I could see thrusting into the light, even with her grasping it hand-over-hand. It had to be at least nine inches long. As I inserted my fingers into my slit and began humping myself, I imagined directing it into my own quivering tunnel.

The three figures were now moving as one and their pace was accelerating toward an obvious climax. With one final thrust of his hips, the man in the rear slammed his cock deep inside the woman and pulled her hips toward his groin as he came inside her. I moaned out loud as my own climax rolled over me, our bodies heaving from the contractions consuming both of us. The man pulled his throbbing cock out of the woman's pussy and I could see it bobbing in the rainbow light as his seed coursed through his shaft. He leaned over and whispered something in the woman's ear, then left the room.

*Now's as good a time as ever to make my entrance,* I thought.

I figured I'd better get in there before the remaining couple got too hot and heavy. I wasn't sure if the man in front had come yet, but I sensed he wouldn't be disappointed to have *two* women in the enclosure giving him attention. I opened the door and stepped inside, and they turned toward me. The woman was still holding the man's dick in her hands, stroking it softly up and down. And he was still hard as a rock, in obvious need of satisfaction.

I walked up to the couple and without saying a word, I wrapped my hands around the woman's, feeling the heat emanating from the man's member. She released her hands to permit me freer access and I squeezed his pole tightly. It had to be at least six inches in circumference and even longer than I thought. I could feel him pulsating in my hands, and I leaned in to kiss him. He moaned softly as I flicked my thumb over his slick head, feeling his pre-cum leak onto my hand. The woman leaned forward and joined us in a three-way kiss while her hand cupped the man's balls.

I could feel his passion rising as the two of us gave him a glorious two-way handjob, but I wanted to save him for something else. There was no way I was going to let this beautiful cock go to waste by letting him cum in my hands. I began lowering myself, kissing his sculpted chest and washboard abs. His bush was neatly trimmed with just a bit of stubble on his pubis, and his balls were smooth as a baby's bottom. I really appreciated a man who shaved down there, especially one with such an impressive package.

When my head reached below his navel, I gobbled up the head of his tool like it was my last meal. I could only get about four inches of him inside my mouth, but I savored every bit of it with my swirling tongue. I hadn't sucked that many dicks in my life, but I knew a keeper when I saw one, and this was one spectacular johnson. While I sucked his manhood, the other woman moved behind him, squeezing his balls. Although maybe she was doing something *else* to

him back there, because suddenly his hip movements escalated in urgency.

I didn't mind the idea of him cumming in my mouth, but
I didn't want to siphon any of his virility before clamping
another part of my body around his impressive python. I
pulled my mouth off his cock and lifted myself up, licking his
sweating torso with my open tongue. When I reached his
face, I plunged my tongue into his mouth. The thrusting and
swirling action left little doubt that I wanted to be properly
fucked by him.

*Screw the other girl,* I thought. *She'd already gotten her piece
of the action—now it was my turn.*

I turned around and began rubbing my slick ass against
his dripping pole. Then I slipped his erection between my
cheeks and shifted slowly up and down, giving it a tanta-
lizing massage. He pulled back a little and grabbed his cock,
trying to steer it into my anus, but I wasn't having any of that.
Maybe later, if I was still in the mood, but right now I needed
that throbbing monster inside my pussy. I wanted to feel him
fucking me the old-fashioned way, filling me with his
manhood, stimulating my G-spot, stretching me to the limit.

I reached between my legs and grabbed the sticky head
of his prick and directed it toward my wet opening. He was
only too happy to oblige, and after I poked it inside the front
door, he slowly pushed it in all the way. I gasped at the thick-
ness and depth of his intrusion as I clamped down on his
throbbing meat like a bear trap. There was no way I was
letting him escape until I was fully satisfied. He reached
around and grabbed my tits with both hands, squeezing
them gently while he thrust his shaft in and out of my love

canal. I could feel my clitoral hood sliding back and forth over my nub as he pulled and stretched my labia with every thrust of his giant cock.

I could have easily come from this movement without any further stimulation, but as if reading my thoughts, the woman circled around and began rubbing her breasts against mine, heightening my ecstasy. As she kissed me passionately, I began moaning and grunting from the pleasure consuming me. My hands wrapped around her waist as I grasped her buttocks in each hand and pulled her toward me with each thrust of the man behind. We both panted in delight as we ground our pussies together.

Never had I felt such intense pleasure from so many different sensations at the same time. This was my first threesome, and it had already far exceeded my expectations. I would have been happy to come this way, sandwiched between two lovers, but perhaps sensing the newness of the experience for me, the woman pulled out of our lip lock and began to move her head down my body.

She cupped and played with my breasts, sucking and flicking my tender nipples with her soft, slippery tongue. I moaned, listening to the popping sound my erect nipples made when they slid in and out of her suckling mouth. I pulled her face into my chest, begging her to continue. But after a few minutes, she pulled away and moved lower. Slowly— tantalizingly—she kissed and nibbled her way down my body until she got to my soaking snatch. She paused and kissed it gently, then nibbled her way down the edges of my labia as the man slammed his cock in and out of me.

"Oh God!" I panted, practically fainting from the intensity of the pleasure building up inside me. The idea of being serviced on both ends by two different partners was driving me insane. I pushed my mound toward the woman's face and tilted my hips so my clit was level with her lips. When her tongue found my button and her lips surrounded me, I grabbed the back of her head with both hands and pulled her tightly toward me.

"Fuck, yes," I panted. "Fuck me," I shouted to no one in particular. I wanted to be fucked from both sides. *Fill me with your cock and flick me with your tongue,* I thought. *I want to soak you with my juices and feel you throbbing deep inside me.*

I slammed my mound into the woman's face and face-fucked her with all my energy as she sucked my clit into her mouth and rolled her tongue over its head. I was seconds away from having the strongest orgasm of my life.

"Yes—*yes!*" I screamed, as I bucked and whimpered from the intense pleasure racking my body. The man sensed I was about to come and I could feel his thrusting beginning to increase in intensity. I felt his hot breath on my back as he panted in unison with me. I looked down at the rainbow stripes washing over our thrashing bodies and closed my eyes, tilting my head back. This was as close to heaven as I could imagine.

When I was finally ready to come, I didn't hold anything back. I screamed like a wild animal, fucking the woman's face while the man slammed his python up inside me in a series of final rhythmic thrusts, spewing his honey inside me. I temporarily lost strength in my legs, but it didn't matter. The man's hard pole had me impaled like a cross, holding me suspended in the air as I gushed all over the woman's face.

When I finally stopped shaking and began to catch my breath, they both pulled away and turned to face me. We pressed together in a sublime three-way kiss, tasting each other's cum in our mouths. I opened my eyes and as I watched the spectrum of colors wash over our faces, and I couldn't help but smile.

I'd finally found my pot of gold at the end of the rainbow.

---

R eady for more erotic chills and thrills? Enjoy the next volume in Jade's Erotic Adventures:

*Hot yoga was never this steamy...*

**Sneak peek:**

*My eyes widened as Kayla grabbed her toes and began to lift them off the yoga mat until they were raised up in the air at the same height as her head. She'd opened herself up completely to the me, exposing her bare pussy and breasts in the most vulnerable way, daring me to ravish her magnificent body with my eyes...*

## READ MORE..

# VOLUME FOUR

---

## THE COSTUME PARTY

**1**

———

I woke up to the sound of my best friend Hannah calling me from the other end of my house. She'd let herself in early on a Saturday morning and for some reason was yelling at me as she ran up the stairs.

"Jade!" she hollered. "Where are you? I've got some exciting news!"

I rolled over and squinted at my clock on the nightstand. It was a little past eight. Saturdays were the only day of the week I allowed myself to sleep in, and I was more than a little ticked at her rude intrusion.

"Aren't you up yet?" she called. "Get up—you're not going to believe what I just heard."

I rolled over and wrapped my pillow around my ears as she dashed into my bedroom. She paused for a minute smiling at my feeble attempt to block her out of my morning daze, then she pounced on the bed below my curled-up knees.

"Wake up, sleepyhead!" she squealed, pushing my shoulders to rouse me from my slumber.

"This better be good," I said, raising my pillow a few inches and peering at her through thin eyes. "You know how much I worship my weekend sleep-ins."

"You'll be glad I woke you when you hear what I have to tell you," she said. "Besides, you're gonna want to get up and begin planning your day right away. We're going to need a few extra hours to go shopping."

I pulled my duvet cover over my shoulders and huffed.

"What could possibly be so important to drag me out of my soft and cozy bed this early in the morning?"

I peered outside, looking at the gray clouds hanging low in the late October skies. I was in no hurry to venture out into the chilly autumn air.

"Only the biggest private shindig of the year. Steve Bannon is hosting his annual Halloween party at his mansion on the lake, and we're invited!"

"Isn't that the party with all the A-list celebrities? How did you score an invitation?"

Hannah peered at me with a wicked look in her eyes.

"Let's just say I know somebody who knows somebody. Someone with whom I may have pulled a few strings to earn some special favors."

"I bet that's not the *only* thing you were pulling to earn those favors," I said, raising an eyebrow.

"Possibly," she smirked. "But I apparently impressed him enough with my naked gymnastics to land an invitation to this special event. Except this year, it's got an extra twist. This time it's going to be a *nude* costume party."

I lifted my head and propped the side of my face on a crooked elbow, suddenly intrigued.

"Isn't that an oxymoron? How can you be in costume and naked at the same time?"

Hannah smiled and handed me a gold-embossed card inscribed with fancy calligraphy writing. I felt the raised surface of the script on the tips of fingers, rubbing it gently trying to divine its meaning through my still bleary eyes. Somebody had gone to a great deal of effort to create an invitation card on par with the most extravagant wedding.

I pulled myself up and leaned against my headboard, slowly reading the message.

*You are cordially invited to attend my annual Halloween costume ball at my estate overlooking Lake Michigan.*

*This year I've added a special twist to make it even more interesting. You're encouraged to wear as little or as much trappings as you feel comfortable—including nothing at all beyond a simple mask. With everyone baring a little more than usual, who knows what kind of shenanigans might break out, and we're always mindful of protecting the anonymity of our special guests.*

*Of course, I encourage everyone to be playful and creative with their choice of costumes, as this is always the highlight of the event. As in previous years, there will be a special prize for the best costume of the evening and we hope you'll be suitably daring and inventive.*

*Feel free to bring a partner and let down your britches! As always, what happens at the Bannon residence stays at the*

*Bannon residence. I look forward to seeing you this Saturday, starting at midnight. We'll all have a ghoulish good time!*

I peered up at Hannah and grinned.

"No RSVP?"

"There's no need with a Steve Bannon invitation," she said. Everyone who's invited always goes. It's the go-to event of the year in the Chicago area. Models, actresses, rock stars, billionaires—everybody who's anybody in this town will be there. There's even a rumor that the Governor and his wife will attend this year's event."

I looked down at the card, rubbing my fingers over the embossed script.

"The invitation says you're allowed to bring a partner. Was that a condition of your little tryst with your friend—that you accompany him as his plus-one?"

Hannah peered at me devilishly as a tiny curl formed on the sides of her mouth.

"When I told him I had a friend who was even prettier than me and had a body to die for, he didn't hesitate to hand me an extra invitation. *You're* my plus-one, girl." She pulled another card out of her purse and handed it to me. "You know I'd never pass up an opportunity like this without bringing my bestie along to share in the fun."

I looked at Hannah with a quizzical look and shook my head in confusion.

"How are we ever going to find a decent Halloween costume on the Saturday before the end of the month? All the costume stores will be sold out of the best stuff."

Hannah kicked off her shoes and lifted the covers, then scooched in excitedly next to me against the headboard.

"I've been searching online for some ideas. We don't have to wear anything too elaborate, and there's no reason why we have to stick to a Halloween theme. Remember, this is a *nude* costume party. We already look pretty hot for a couple of girls nearing middle age. The less we wear, the better. Let's flaunt it while we've still got it!"

She pulled an iPad out of her purse and tapped the screen. A website opened showing a collection of sexy models wearing risqué costumes. She scrolled through the images, commenting on the various themes.

"Just look at some of these possibilities. We can play any role we like, wearing as much or as little as we please. Most of these costumes can be put together with a simple trip to Walmart and maybe a bit of needle and thread. Plus, we can easily remove one of two pieces from each outfit to reveal a bit more skin. The most important element is the headpiece. We just need something to conceal our identity and high-light our girly figures with a bit of flair."

Hannah paused at a picture of a sexy blonde wearing a Playboy bunny costume. She wore a tight corset and a rubber mask that covered the top half of her face with tall ears pointing up in the air.

"What about this one? You have to admit, it's pretty hot. You'd could even dispense with the bodice altogether and just keep the bunny tail on your naked ass. Imagine the looks you'd get prancing around his mansion in that costume!"

The images of sexy half-nude models wearing unusual masks reminded me of my encounter at the Fantasy Feast naked dinner party. Suddenly, I became mindful of the wetness that had begun building between my legs.

"Not bad," I said, shifting my weight uncomfortably off the wet spot on my sheets. "Show me some more."

Hannah flipped through a few more images and stopped at a picture of a sexy maid wearing a lacy dress, holding a feather duster in her hand. Her firm tits pressed against the flimsy fabric, creating an irresistible focal point from the sensuous shadows on her bosom.

"How about this?" she said. "You'd look stunning in this outfit. You'd be covering up just enough to drive every man and woman at that party absolutely crazy. And imagine all the fun you could have teasing the naked guests with your little duster!"

"*Intriguing...*" I said as I squeezed my thighs together, trying to quiet my burning clit.

The more images Hannah showed me, the more turned on I got. Whether it was from me imagining myself in the costumes or imagining myself playing with the guests dressed up in the provocative outfits, was unclear. Either way, the more my mind began to ponder the possibilities, the more excited I became about going to this event.

"The only problem is, it will be difficult to cover my face without looking unnatural in that outfit," I frowned. "Show me more costumes with masks."

Hannah refined her search by typing in the words *sexy mask costumes* and the screen refreshed showing a new set of models in racy outfits. Many of the themes revolved around superheroes, with the male models sporting Batman and

Superman motifs and the female models wearing Wonder Woman and Batgirl-type costumes.

"Not very original," I frowned. "I bet there'll be a ton of superhero costumes among all those egotistical celebrities. I'm looking for something a little different."

Hannah paused for a moment, then tapped on her photo library pulling up an image of me wearing a business suit painted on my naked body.

"Remember that time you went to the nude bodypainting workshop? You're a graphic artist. You can be virtually anything you want and show off all you wish with a little bit of well-disguised paint. Whether it's Catwoman, Black Widow, or Wonder Woman–all these characters wear is a mask and tight outfits to show off their beautiful physiques. You could even dress up like Mystique in the X-Men movie and wear absolutely nothing other than a full coat of body paint."

"Been there, done that," I said. "If I'm going to really enjoy myself, I want to wear something I've never worn before that will absolutely blow everyone away."

"You sure are a tough customer," Hannah said, shaking her head. "Let's try something a little different..."

She reopened her browser and typed in the words *naked masquerade costumes*. A gallery of Google images popped up with a collection of half-naked men and women.

"*Now* we're talking," I said, squirming on the bed as I scanned the toned bodies of the sexy models.

"Look at that one," Hannah said, pointing at the screen. "It's a picture of Rihanna at last year's Met Gala dressed as Nefertiti. With her sheer lace dress and silver headdress, it doesn't leave much to the imagination. A bit more makeup around the eyes, and you'd be able to mask your identity quite easily."

"That's pretty hot," I said, beginning to feel the sheets getting wetter and wetter between my legs. "She definitely looks fuckable. But it's been done before. I don't want to wear something half of these people will have already seen."

"Damn, girl, you're *impossible!* Remember, less is more. The idea is to show as much of our bodies as possible to attract the attention of all these beautiful people. You could get away with a simple mask, a painted emblem on your chest, and a shiny belt. Who really cares what you're wearing as long as you get the attention of the guests?"

"Humor me for a little longer," I said, squeezing Hannah's leg. "I'm starting to get a few ideas. I just need a bit more inspiration."

Hannah began flipping through the images more quickly until one picture suddenly caught my attention.

"Wait!" I said. "Go back a few frames. I saw something interesting..."

She scrolled back until an image of six men dressed in contrasting costumes popped up.

"That's the one," I said, scanning the image slowly.

"*The Village People*?" Hannah said. "That might be okay for a gay guy, but how could you possibly look sexy wearing any one of those cheesy costumes?"

My eyes darted back and forth between the sexy cowboy wearing chaps and the indian warrior wearing a feathered headdress and a skimpy loincloth. Suddenly I nodded as a mischievous smile formed on my face.

"What?" Hannah said. "What could you possibly be thinking?"

She glanced down at my breasts peeking above the covers, noticing my hardening nipples.

"Because I know gay dudes—even ones with hard bodies like these guys—don't do it for you. Where is your mind going with this idea?"

"I've decided what I'm going to wear," I said, crossing my arms over my chest. "But I'm going to keep it a secret until we get to the party. It'll be all the more fun and surprising if I reveal it at the last second. But I promise you, it'll be one-of-a-kind and extremely provocative."

Hannah's eyes darted across my face, trying to imagine what I had in mind.

"Now you've got *me* all excited thinking what you're going to do. Judging by your obvious state of arousal, your head is already at the party. Can I crawl under the covers with you and have some fun fantasizing which one of those costumes you're going to wear?"

"By all means," I said, disappearing under the covers with her. "Just imagine me as one of those hot dudes with his clothes off."

"Mmm," Hannah purred, slithering between my slippery thighs. "I'd rather imagine you as a hot *chick* with her clothes off."

"In a couple of days," I said, spreading my legs further apart and pulling her face into my steaming crotch. "You might be able to have it both ways."

**2**

---

Just after midnight on the day of the party, I pulled my car up beside a call box in front of a large wrought-iron gate protecting the entrance to Steve Bannon's estate. After providing our names and the identification numbers on the front of our invitation cards, the gates opened and we followed the curved driveway up to the front of a giant French-styled chateau. As a parking attendant approached our car, I turned to Hannah seated next to me and smiled.

"It's show time," I said.

"Not a moment too soon," she huffed. "I've been dying to see what you're wearing under that coat ever since you picked me up."

I'd intentionally worn a long western duster to cover my body all the way from my shoulders to my ankles. Part of it was meant to surprise Hannah when I finally reached the event, but it had much more to do with my desire to shock everyone else once I got in the front door. I reached behind my seat and pulled a thin black mask out of a bag on the floor and wrapped it around the top of my face.

Hannah's forehead wrinkled as she looked at me, still confused.

"Let me guess: Kato, Zorro, Nightshade?"

"You're moving in the right direction with the first two," I smiled, reaching back into the bag and pulling out a pair of western boots.

"Cowboy boots?" Hannah squinted. "I don't know my cowboy characters quite as well—"

"Maybe this will help," I said, donning a white Stetson.

Hannah looked at me blankly for a moment, then her eyes lit up, recognizing the familiar image of the famous cowboy with the white hat and black mask.

"The Lone Ranger?"

"Yes, but with a little twist. You'll have to wait for the full reveal until we get inside."

"You're such a tease," she said as I handed the attendant my keys and we stepped out of the car.

We paused for a moment, taking in the full scale of the Bannon estate close-up. The four-story mansion extended almost a hundred feet in either direction, with tall arched windows and ornate brickwork. The bright spotlights illuminating the front of the house lit up the entire courtyard, reflecting off Hannah's shiny Batgirl outfit.

"Holy shit!" she exclaimed. "This place is gigantic. We're going to have to drop *breadcrumbs* to not get lost in there."

"More like *caviar* or *foie gras*," I chuckled. "Something tells me everything about this affair is going to be top shelf."

"What are we waiting for?" Hannah giggled, rushing ahead of me toward the front door.

My gaze drifted down while I soaked up her tight ass in her black latex outfit. She had a beautiful hourglass figure, and the tight Batgirl costume highlighted every curve of her sexy body. I smiled as I imagined the two of us mingling among the high rollers. But I had a feeling they'd be focused on someone *else's* ass tonight.

With the large double entrance doors pulled back, we peered into the bright marble-floored foyer as we approached the front steps. A large crowd of costumed guests had already begun to gather in the main ballroom, and we could hear soft jazz music wafting out into the courtyard.

"Good evening ladies," a man wearing a crisply tailored tailcoat and black tie said as we stepped into the entrance hall.

He looked at my long shawl and smiled.

"May I check your coat, Madam?"

"Yes, thank you," I said, turning my back to assist him in its removal.

When he pulled the cape off my back and viewed my naked backside, I heard him gasp. To complement my Lone Ranger disguise, I'd chosen to wear a tight-fitting black leather vest and long black chaps with nothing underneath. My tight ass poked out the back of the open leggings, and I could feel him running his eyes up and down my body as he hesitated hanging my coat in the closet.

But when I turned around, both Hannah and the doorman took a step back in shock. On the front of my open pants, I wore a large dildo fashioned in the shape of a man's cock and balls, framed by two silver pistols on either side of my hips. The long phallus slapped against the sides of my naked thighs as it swung from side to side.

"Holy *fuck*, Jade!" Hannah squealed. "That's *outrageous*! Where did you ever come up with that idea?"

"Remember the Village People picture you showed me a few days ago? I decided to borrow elements of both the cowboy and the indian characters to create my own design." I shook my hips to juggle my equipment and smiled. "I thought it would be kind of fun playing *both* sides of coin, so to speak."

"Uh—*yeah*," she said, flicking her eyes between my tight bosom spilling over the top of my vest and my faux genitals. "I'd have to say you pulled it off. With that getup, I expect you'll be the center of attention all night long."

"Um," the doorman said, shyly interrupting. "May I have your tickets, please?"

"Of course," I said, rustling my rubber balls as I fished in the pocket of my chaps for my ticket. When the butler turned to collect Hannah's ticket, I could see the front of his pants tenting in obvious arousal.

"Enjoy your evening," he said, motioning for us to enter the ballroom.

"Oh, I have a feeling we will," Hannah winked, as she nodded toward the lengthening pole pushing down his pant leg.

A waiter approached us with tall glasses of champagne on a silver tray and did a double-take when he noticed the swinging package between my legs.

"Whoa boy," Hannah said to the server, taking two glasses off his unsteady tray. "We wouldn't want you to spill your load before we've sampled the goods."

As we moved into the main entrance hall, the patrons milling in small groups began to turn around to view the newly arriving guests. Suddenly, the gentle buzz of group conversation receded until the only sound we could hear was the hum of the background music. Everyone was so stunned taking in my outfit, they were literally dumbstruck with their mouths agape.

Many of the guests had chosen to wear predictable Halloween costumes with little bits of flesh showing here and there, but nobody was letting it all hang out quite as brazenly as I had. Amid the predictable sprinkling of ghosts and goblins, there was a profusion of superhero figures and Disney characters bedecked in various stages of undress. I shook my head at the lack of imagination of the high-powered group and began to wonder if the event was going to live up to Hannah's hyperbole.

"Damn, girl," she said. "It looks like you're going to be this evening's scene-stealer. You've already stopped the show. I don't know what everybody's thinking right now, but that thing looks so realistic, they must be wondering if you're a legit tranny wearing that impressive package."

I smiled a crooked grin, suddenly feeling self-conscious with all of the eyes in the room surveying my exposed body. Fortunately, a handsome couple dressed as Anthony and Cleopatra began to approach us, providing some distraction.

"Welcome to our little costume party," the man said, extending his hand to Hannah and me. "I'm Steve Bannon and this is my wife Genevieve. You'll have to excuse me, but I don't recognize either of you under your—*interesting* disguises."

I was taken aback by how handsome the eccentric billionaire looked close up. With his square jaw, dimpled cheeks and thick head of salt-and-pepper hair swept back in a dense poof, he looked like a slightly older version of the famous actor Patrick Dempsey. He wore a loose toga draped over his well-muscled chest, and I could see his pecs flexing as he shook my hand.

But I found his wife even more beguiling. Wearing a tight-fitting gold-lamé dress slitted at one side of her hips and a pretty beaded headdress, she looked like a dead-ringer for a young Elizabeth Taylor. As I ran my eyes shamelessly over her luscious figure, I felt a sudden dampness building under the weight of my latex balls pressing against my flaring clit.

"Jade," I introduced myself, not yet wanting to reveal my full identity.

"Hannah," my partner responded, politely shaking their hands.

"It appears that you two have already captured the attention of my guests," Bannon said, turning to appraise the congregation still gazing awkwardly in our direction. He extended his arm in the direction of the main hall and nodded. "Please, come in and mingle. There are so many fascinating people to meet. I'm sure we'll catch up with the two of you a little later this evening."

"I'll look forward to that," I said, smiling at Genevieve, lingering for a moment longer at her dazzling figure. She returned the gesture, widening her eyes as my member twitched while I held my palm over the handle of one of my six-shooters.

"Holy shit," Hannah said, as Bannon and his wife melted back into the crowd. "Did you see the way he was looking at you? He was practically *raping* you with his eyes. Something tells me this is going to be a very interesting night. It seems the men are even more enamored with your disguise than the women. Either there's a lot of bi-curious guys in here, or they're attracted to that whole futa thing."

"I dunno," I said. "I'm showing off a lot of *girl* parts too. Who's to say what they're more attracted to? But did you notice his wife? I'd far rather get into *her* pants."

"It's too bad that thing isn't animated," Hannah chuckled, glancing at my pendulous dick. "If you could actually get it up, you could probably have your way with just about everybody in this place."

"Who knows?" I said, winking at Hannah. "In my current state of arousal, I wouldn't be surprised if this thing had a life of its own."

Little did she know how much truth in this statement I was about to reveal before the evening was over.

**3**

———

After Bannon and his wife resumed mingling with the rest of the crowd, Hannah and I wandered into the main ballroom. At first, most of the assembled groups gave us a wide berth, unsure what to make of the two girls dressed in such revealing costumes. Hannah's latex Batgirl outfit clung to her naked body like a second skin, the shiny fabric accentuating every crease and curve like it was painted on her. And the cutouts on both sides of my leather chaps left little to the imagination, even with the modicum of cover provided by my fake genitals covering my bare mound.

I was glad to have the freedom to mill about the room for a while, surveying the faces and costumes of the high-powered gathering. I recognized a fair number of public figures from the senior ranks of the local political, business, and media fields. The mayor was there with his wife, dressed as Little Red Riding Hood and the Big Bad Wolf, which seemed fitting given the ongoing level of corruption at City

Hall. Bannon's business partner and fellow billionaire Kent Schiffer circled the room with a familiar supermodel, outfitted in matching red tights as Mr. Incredible and Elasta-girl. And our local news anchorman was paired with his pretty sidekick, dressed as Woody and Bo Peep from the movie Toy Story.

Many of the guests were dressed as famous characters from superhero movies or nursery rhyme stories, with most of the men playing the more dominant role. *Typical display of macho-entitled privilege*, I thought. *Why does it seem every man who achieves a certain degree of power have to lord it over everyone else, thinking they're better than the rest of us?* My cheeky cowboy costume seemed a perfect counterpoint to the heavy dose of testosterone permeating the room, mocking their oversize male egos as I swung my big dick around like I owned it.

As Hannah and I began mingling with the small cliques scattered around the room, I found it amusing that while most of the women praised my cocky outfit, their male partners seemed threatened by it, silently stealing glances at my huge dong while their wives and girlfriends chatted with me comfortably. I wasn't sure if it was because they felt intimidated by my outsize genitals, or because they were secretly fantasizing about fucking me.

As more and more people began gravitating toward us, intrigued by my outrageous costume, Hannah slowly drifted off to the other side of the room. I couldn't blame her, with everyone asking me silly questions like what it felt like to be a woman carrying a man's dick. For a while I amused them, swinging my hips from side to side and playfully grabbing my balls, flaunting my male persona.

But I soon tired of the incessant stares and never-ending quips about my tranny disguise, and began looking for an excuse to break away. Just as I was about to excuse myself to go to the ladies' room, the governor and his wife approached our group and introduced themselves. They were dressed in matching his and hers chef outfits, the only difference being that his wife wore a less poofy hat and a backless apron that showed off her sexy ass and legs.

"That's quite a provocative costume," the governor said, extending his hand to me. "I'm Jack Scanlon and this is my wife, Alicia."

"Pleased to meet you, Mr. Governor," I said, quickly seeing through his thin disguise. "But no less daring than your wife's, which I dare say is even *more* revealing."

"In some respects, possibly," he said. "Except you're revealing both sides of the coin."

"Heads *and* tails, you mean?" I smiled.

"In a manner of speaking," he said, temporarily at a loss for words by my sassy attitude. "Are you here alone tonight?"

I scanned the room and noticed Hannah chatting it up with a hunky guest dressed in a Tarzan outfit.

"It seems my partner is out looking for greener pastures. I guess she felt this one had been fully tilled."

"Oh?" the governor said, glancing at my pendulous prick. "Who's been doing most of the figurative plowing—you, or all these other farm animals?"

"At this point, I'd say everybody's just getting the lay of

the land," I said, dragging out the metaphor. "Surveying the landscape, deciding the best place to position their hoes."

"I see what you mean," the governor said, his eyes widening from my double entendre. "You seem to be particularly–*ambidextrous* in that respect."

"I'm just having fun pretending what it might be like to cultivate both sides of the field," I said, running my eyes up and down his wife's sexy body before locking eyes with her. "You never know when a particularly fertile plot might need tending."

"Well put, my lady."

"Please—call me Jade," I said, turning my attention to his wife, who'd been staring at my outfit the entire time. "What about you, Alicia? Have you been enjoying the evening so far?"

"Yes," she said, happy to deflect attention away from her overbearing husband for a moment. "So many interesting people and costumes."

"I find yours very alluring also," I said, staring at her plump breasts pressing against the front of her skimpy apron. "But it seems that all your fun parts are hidden from view, at least while we're talking face-to-face. It's only when you turn around that you reveal your adventurous side."

"I guess you'll just have to catch me when my back is turned then," she said, winking at me sexily.

"I'll definitely be keeping a lookout. Hopefully we can catch up later."

As much as I wanted to continue our playful flirtation, I knew I'd never have a chance for some alone time with her as long as I continued to engage them as a couple. Besides, I was getting tired of her husband's thinly veiled sexist comments.

"Will you excuse me for a moment while I use the restroom?"

"Of course," she said. "But be careful in there. It's not as simple for us ladies to pee standing up as it is for the men."

"Not to worry," I smiled. "Fortunately, this thing is easily removed. Though it might be kind of fun to try it just once."

"Will you be using the men's or the ladies' room?" the governor smirked.

"I'm pretty sure the toilets are unisex in this place," I said, gently admonishing him for another chauvinist remark. "Which will be a refreshing change from the usually cramped ladies' rooms we have to endure in other public places. Enjoy your evening. Perhaps we'll see each other a little later."

"We'll look forward to that," the governor smiled.

As I pulled away from the crowd, I shook my head at the impudent tone of the governor, ignoring his beautiful wife while he shamelessly flirted with me. Little did he know that I was far more impressed with Alicia than by the trappings of his high political office. I felt like I needed to wash myself off after dealing with his sexist attitude and while looking for a place to freshen up, I recognized the familiar red and white uniform of the mayor's wife as she waited outside the closed door of an adjacent anteroom. As I approached her from the side, I admired her shapely legs and full bosom pressing against her tight bodice. Her Little Red Riding Hood costume seemed the perfect outfit to highlight her youthful face and figure.

"You'd think we wouldn't have to wait to use a toilet in this place," I said, sauntering up next to her. "There must be at least twenty washrooms in this mansion."

"No doubt," she laughed. "But even in a place like this, with this many guests, unfortunately we ladies still have to wait to use the lavatory." She glanced down at my faux genitalia and smiled. "It's too bad they don't have his and hers toilets like in most public settings. With that getup, you'd probably get away with slipping into the men's room."

"Maybe," I said. "But I'd still have to pee sitting down. I'm just looking to freshen up anyway. I was hoping for a respite from all the overcharged testosterone out there."

"Tell me about it," she nodded. "I've been dealing with city politics from the other side for almost twenty years now. It's still very much an old-boys network in this business. Women are just treated as chattel, to be trotted out as eye candy whenever there's a public relations opportunity like this."

"That's partly why I wore this outfit," I admitted. "I thought it would be kind of fun to swing my own dick around all these heavy hitters at this posh event."

The washroom door suddenly swung open and a woman wearing a Victorian costume brushed past us, sneering at our haughty outfits.

"Judging by the heft of that thing," she said, "I'd say yours is the biggest one here by a large margin. Do you want to join me while I freshen up inside? It looks like the last thing you need right now is to stand outside alone while everybody wags their tongues at you."

"Thanks," I said. scurrying in behind her as we locked the

door, giggling like two schoolgirls. "I'm Jade, by the way," I said stretching out my hand.

"Haley," she said, grasping my hand firmly as she smiled into my eyes.

As we leaned in to the doublewide mirror over the marble vanity to check our lipstick and mascara, I noticed Haley's gaze drifting lower to check out my package.

"You know, if it weren't for the straps holding that apparatus onto your hips, I'd swear that thing was real," she said. "It's so life-like. Even your *testicles* look authentic."

"The whole thing is made out of a special latex engineered to mimic real skin. With all the advances in artificial dolls these days, it's amazing what they can do with sex toys."

"Do you mind if I—*touch* it?" she asked.

"I thought you'd never ask."

As I stepped back from the vanity, Haley turned to face me, reaching her hand down to touch my artificial cock.

"My God," she said, squeezing it firmly. "It even *feels* like a real dick. If only it could get hard, I shudder to think how big it would be angry."

As she reached further down to cup my balls, her face came closer to mine, and we kissed. I pressed my tongue into her mouth and she reached lower still, running her fingers over my moist labia. I purred in pleasure, pressing my crotch harder into her hips. She hiked up her skirt, and I was pleasantly surprised to see that she was completely naked underneath. Recognizing my opportunity to have a little fun, I positioned my hand over my right pistol, gently pumping the trigger. Slowly, my synthetic cock began to fill with air and inflate between her legs.

"What the—" Haley gasped, pulling back to see what was happening. "You've got to be kidding me. You can *animate* that thing?"

"In a manner of speaking," I said. "You want to give it a try?"

"*Hell* yes!" she said. "I'm so horny right now, I could fuck just about anything. But first, let me take a closer look at what I'm working with."

As I smiled at her wickedly, I pumped my trigger harder until my organ rose to a full ten inches of erect flesh. Haley couldn't help herself as she fell to the floor and took my member into her mouth while she proceeded to give me a pretend blowjob. As I watched her stretch her lips around my thick pole, I placed my hands behind her head and imagined fucking her face like a man. Although I was being far gentler than most, it was fun fantasizing being in the man's role for a change, having my way with my muse.

"That's it," I purred. "Suck my big cock, baby. Squeeze my balls while I fuck your pretty face."

Without hesitating, Haley reached underneath me and began rubbing my balls against my raging clit. The sensation was not unlike what I imagined a real man would be feeling as she stimulated my sex organ.

"Fuck, yes," I panted. "That feels good, Haley. I want to fuck you so bad."

Suddenly, she stood up and smiled at me.

"That makes *two* of us. I'm so turned-on, I could pop off any second."

She reached behind her, placing her hands on top of the vanity and lifted herself up onto the counter, hiking her skirt all the way up. I took one look at her glistening pussy and leaned in to kiss her passionately. She reached down and pointed my hard pecker toward her opening and when I pressed it into her, she gasped.

"Oh God, Jade," she groaned. "Your cock feels so good. Fill me up with your big dick. I want to feel your balls slapping against my pussy."

Her dirty talk got me even more worked up, and as I pressed my hips forward, she moaned loudly. As we began to grind our hips together, our tongues danced in each other's mouths. Haley flapped her thighs against me as I plowed in and out of her, grinding my clit against the underside of my rubbery balls. While we grunted and moaned with abandon, anybody who might have been waiting to use the restroom must have surely known what was going on inside. But neither one of us cared, lost in the moment by the rising feeling of ecstasy engulfing our joined bodies.

Suddenly, Haley wrapped her legs around my ass and pulled me even deeper inside her pussy.

"*Damn*, girl," she panted. "You're going to make me come with that big thumper of yours. Fill me up while I come all over your pretty pussy."

"Yes," I groaned. "I'm close too. I'm going to cum with you. God damn, I like fucking you."

"Here it comes," Haley moaned. "Take me over the edge."

I grabbed Haley's hips by both sides and pulled her strongly toward me, grinding my cock and balls as hard as I could against her while ramming my cock in and out of her sloshing pussy. Suddenly, a wave of passion rolled over me as my clit began pulsating against the underside of my faux balls.

"Oh God, Haley," I groaned. "Cum with me baby. Come all over my big dick."

"Yes!" Haley howled. "I can feel you pounding my G-spot. It feels soooo good!"

Suddenly, I felt Haley spraying all over my balls and mound as her pussy clenched down over my phallus while we ground our hips against one another. We moaned inside each other's mouths as we locked lips in a tight and passionate kiss. After what seemed like a full minute of shaking and convulsing in each other's arms, our breathing finally returned to normal, while we kissed with me still inside her.

"*Ahem*," a woman's voice called impatiently from outside the door, from someone waiting to use the facilities.

"I guess we'll have to vacate the premises," Haley smiled. "Though I could make love to you all night long."

"Same here," I said. "Let's clean up and get out of here. Maybe we can find a more private place to continue our fun."

While Haley pulled down her skirt and reapplied her smudged lipstick, I unfastened my appendage and washed it under the tap before reattaching it to my mound. When we finally got ourselves put back together, we opened the door and walked past a long line of stunned onlookers as their eyes widened in shock ogling my still-dripping, semi-hard cock.

**4**

———

It didn't take long after Haley and I returned to the main ballroom for her husband to spot us. While we giggled amongst ourselves about the pretentious costumes of all the men in the room masking their tiny peckers, the mayor approached us with an angry scowl on his face.

"Where've you been?" he barked at Haley, his ruddy, pockmarked face making his wolf costume look all the more ridiculous. "I've been looking all over for you. There are a lot of prominent people I wanted to introduce you to."

"Jade and I were just freshening up. No need to get your knickers in a twist, dear."

"*Freshening up*?" he said, darting his eyes back and forth between Haley's face and my tumescent cock. "How long does that take? You must have been gone for at least a half hour!"

"Well, you know how we women are when we hang out in

the ladies' room," she replied with a straight face. "There's no telling how long it might take to get ourselves put together in front of the mirror. You *do* want me to look pretty and proper for all your important friends, don't you?"

"I—suppose so," he stammered, distracted by my glistening joystick. He grabbed Haley's hand, trying to drag her away from me. "Come, I want you to meet one of my biggest fundraisers, Kent Schiffer."

As he steered Haley toward a gathering in the center of the room, she looked back at me with an apologetic expression, mouthing the words *later*. Soon after, Hannah came up behind me and cupped one of my bare cheeks with her hand.

"What was *that* all about?" she said. "It looked like the Big Bad Wolf was about to bite off his wife's head."

"He might as well have," I huffed. "The way he was acting as if he owned her. All these upper-class snobs seem interested in is congratulating themselves around their buddies while showing off their arm candy."

"He did seem a little distracted by you," Hannah said, noticing Haley peering in my direction with a flushed face. "And he wasn't the *only* one. What kind of trouble did you get into with his wife? You've got a strange glow about you."

"Nothing much," I lied. "We were just freshening up in the ladies' room, looking for an escape from all the overbearing egos in this place."

Hannah looked at me suspiciously, pinching her eyebrows as she peered at my puffy appendage.

"Well, judging by the flush on your chest and the sweat dripping down your ass, I'd say you were up to a little more than just fixing your makeup. If I didn't know better, I'd swear even your *dick* looks more excited than usual."

"We may have been touching up a bit more than just our *faces*," I admitted. "We started admiring each other's costumes and one thing led to another..."

Hannah reached down and squeezed my tumescent dildo, then her eyes widened as her lips curled up into a knowing smile.

"Is it just my imagination, or does it seem a little *bigger* than when we first came in? You better be careful—you could poke somebody's eye out with that thing."

"That's not the only thing it's good for poking," I grinned.

"No way!" she said, stepping back in mock indignation. "You were *fucking* the mayor's wife in the washroom? Did he have any inkling?"

"I don't think so. But judging by how much noise we were making in there, I imagine it won't take long for word to spread around the room."

"Not to worry–just stick with me, girl," Hannah said, moving closer to protect me from everyone's disapproving glares. "If any of these jokers cause you any trouble, I'll give them a batkick to the groin."

"I doubt that'll be necessary," I sighed, catching Hannah's Tarzan friend stealing glances at me from the open bar on the other side of the room. "Most of the men in here seem reluctant to engage me in any kind of conversation, let alone actually approach me in this getup. I don't know if they're more threatened by my provocative outfit or they're just afraid to admit they're attracted to a pretty girl with a big cock."

I noticed Tarzan moving to the other side of the bar to get a clearer look at me. I found it strange that he seemed so focused on me after Hannah had spent so much time with him earlier. Unlike me, I knew she had a preference for men, and I suspected she was hoping to land a wealthy boyfriend at this event.

"What about you?" I said, shifting my position to deflect Tarzan's gaze. "What kind of trouble have you been getting up to around all these society types?"

"Not as much as I'd like," Hannah frowned. "I've found a few interesting candidates, but so far everybody's been politely keeping their dicks in their pants."

"Well, you know how it is. With all their extra ornamentation, it might be kind of hard to just whip it out. Most of these guys seem to have gone to great lengths to gussy themselves up with all this embellishment."

"I know what you mean," Hannah said, pulling her tight latex skin down uncomfortably under her crotch. "I guess I didn't give this costume as much forethought as I should have. I'm sweating like a pig under here. I have to dismantle the whole thing just to go pee."

"Not exactly conducive to pulling off a quickie in this place," I chuckled.

"Not as easily as you," she grumbled. "You don't have to remove a single stitch of clothing to get your freak on. All you have to do is find a willing accomplice and insert your magic wand."

With Hannah's back turned away from the bar, I saw Tarzan adjusting his equipment under the counter. His loincloth had begun pouching in front of his penis, and he seemed to be getting more and more aroused watching me.

"What about that hunky Tarzan character I saw you flirting with earlier?" I said, hoping to redirect his attention. "He seems worthy of a little deconstruction."

"It crossed my mind, believe me," Hannah said. "But he seemed more interested in talking about everyone else in the room. Either he's just here for the people watching, or he's gay. I mean, I'm still a *catch*, right? Who can resist a sexy chick in this tight outfit? I was practically throwing myself at him."

Tarzan turned away from me holding his hands in front of his crotch, trying to keep his rising member from making too obvious an appearance. Then he suddenly stood up and exited through a door next to the bar.

"He's probably just trying to keep up appearances," I said. "It's a pretty snooty affair, you have to admit. People would likely get their nose out of joint if they caught a couple getting too carried away in public."

"That's what *powder rooms* are for, right?" Hannah grinned.

"Speaking of, I gotta go pee for real this time. Catch up with you in a bit?"

"Sure," Hannah said. "Just try not to dip your dick anywhere it doesn't belong this time. There's no telling what kind of hullabaloo it might generate if one of these heavy hitters caught you getting it on again with another one of their wives."

"Don't worry," I smiled. "I'll be staying far away from the ladies this time."

As soon as I left Hannah, a flock of men suddenly converged on her, no longer threatened by the presence of her sexy androgynous partner. But I was happy for the distraction, because there was something about this Tarzan hunk I needed to check out. He was the first man I'd met at the ball who'd demonstrated any genuine interest in me, and I wanted to see which persona he was more attracted to.

I meandered through the crowd making small talk with some of the guests then I ordered a cocktail at the bar and slipped quietly out the same door I'd seen Tarzan use. It led to a large wine cellar, darkened and chilled to a frigid fifty degrees. I looked around the room, catching sight of Tarzan huddled between two kegs with his hand moving suspiciously between his legs.

I strolled over in his direction and smiled when I noticed his predicament. His cock was at full mast, flapping up over his flimsy loincloth, high up against his belly. I nodded when I saw how well hung he was, his organ standing a good eight inches in length and at least two inches thick.

"Aren't you a bit underdressed for this place?" I asked.

"I suppose so," he said in a shaky voice. "But I didn't know where else to go." He looked down at his crotch with a sheepish expression, vainly trying to cover up his erection. "It seems I'm having a bit of a wardrobe malfunction."

"Is *that* what you call it?" I said. "Can I offer some help? Provide a little body heat at least? You're shivering in that skimpy outfit."

"Maybe," he hesitated, peering down at my even bigger cock hanging down over my naked belly. "At least you can provide some cover if anyone else comes in here."

As if on cue, the door on the other side of the wine cellar opened, and a uniformed waiter entered the room, walking in our direction. He appeared to be looking for a particular bottle, but when he caught sight of the two of us, he stopped and did a double-take. Without pausing, I stepped closer to Tarzan and flung my arms around him, pretending to make out. It was just the cover he needed, and this was the perfect excuse to get a little closer. The waiter smiled as he nodded toward us, then collected his items and exited the room.

"Thanks," Tarzan said, pulling away awkwardly. "This is beyond embarrassing. I can't seem to make this thing go down and I have nothing to cover up with."

"I can't imagine why you'd *want* to," I said, running my fingers over his hard chest muscles. "With a body like this, you should be showing off as much of it as you can."

He glanced down at my full breasts pressing up against him in my tight leather vest.

"I hadn't counted on getting quite so—*aroused* at this event," he stuttered. "I thought I'd be able to keep it together around all these stiff necks. This has never happened to me before in a public place..."

"Not to worry," I said. "This little accident will stay between us. But if you don't mind my asking, may I ask what's gotten you so worked up? I saw you looking in my direction, and all of a sudden you wanted to hide."

"I'm sorry," he said, his face flushing like a teenager. "I just couldn't help staring at you. I find you incredibly sexy, and with so much of you hanging out for everyone to see, I guess I just had a visceral reaction."

"I understand," I said, darting my eyes over his handsome

face, finding myself getting surprisingly turned by his shy demeanor. "But which *part* of me were you most attracted to? I'm hanging out on both sides."

"Both," he said, without hesitation. "You have a sexy body and you're absolutely stunning. But there's something especially alluring about a woman flaunting a man's genitals overtop their naked body. It's very—*ballsy* of you."

"You like *cocky* women, do you?" I said, leaning in towards him as I brushed my thick cock against his tight balls.

"In a manner of speaking," he huffed.

"Did you want to play with it?"

"May I?" he said. "I've never really touched another penis before..."

"You mean besides your *own*?" I kidded. "Is that what you were doing in here? Stroking it trying to make it go down before you went back into the ballroom?"

"I was so turned on, I didn't think there was any other way to get myself back together."

"Maybe I can help you with that," I smiled, reaching down and grasping his throbbing cock with my left hand. "Is this warming you up a little bit?"

"Yes," he panted, clutching my ass while he rocked his hips toward me, trying to create some much-needed friction against his throbbing hard-on. "But you've got goosebumps too. How can I help warm you up?"

I wasn't sure what he had in mind, but I wasn't interested in him fucking me in the usual manner. I'd long been fascinated seeing gay men play with themselves. I found one of the most erotic things was when they rubbed their erect cocks together. Something about the playful jousting of their erogenous parts always got me turned on.

"Well, we're both equipped with similar equipment," I said, raising an eyebrow. "I've always wondered what it would feel like to rub two cocks together..."

"Oh my God," Tarzan said. "I've fantasized about that too. But you're not exactly *functional* in the way most men are—"

"You might be surprised what this ladyboy is capable of," I grinned. "This little package comes equipped with a few extra features."

As I began stroking his hard-on, I squeezed the trigger of the pistol on my right hip, slowly inflating my rising pecker. Tarzan looked down and widened his eyes, seeing my love muscle inflating to its full ten inches. When it reached its maximum length, I placed it against the underside of his prick and began rocking my hips in tandem with his. Even though he was better endowed than most men, my giant phallus looked like an anaconda slithering up next to his garden snake. As the rubbery veins of my dildo rolled over the sensitive flesh on the tip of his rod, he shuddered and emitted a drop of dew out of his hole.

"Uhnnn," he groaned. "This is incredibly hot. I've always wondered what this would feel like, but to do it with such a sexy woman is a dream come true."

"You've always wanted to get it on with a *tranny*?" I smirked. "Well now you've got your wish."

I reached down and cupped my hands around both of our cocks and began humping him more vigorously. Tarzan groaned as he placed his hands against my chest, squeezing my breasts over my cowboy vest.

"Open it up," I nodded. "See what it's like to fuck a real ladyboy. I want to feel your hard pecs rubbing against my tits."

He didn't need any more encouragement as he fumbled with my buttons until he freed my boobs from their tight enclosure. When he saw my firm breasts bouncing on my chest, he circled them with his hands and pinched my nipples gently while I continued frotting our cocks together in my hands.

"Fucking hell," he said. "You are so hot. You are truly the woman of my dreams."

"And *man* also?" I smiled.

"Yes," he admitted. "I've long fantasized what it would be like to hold another man's penis in my hands."

"Why don't you take the driver's seat then?" I said, acknowledging his bisexual nature. "Let me admire the scenery for a while."

When I removed my hands, he placed his palms around our joined cocks and squeezed them together firmly. More precum oozed out of the head of his pole, and he moaned as he began to pick up the pace of his rocking motion. Neither one of us seemed interested in kissing, fixated on the appearance of our two big cocks frotting in and out of his hands. As he began to moan more loudly, I slapped my sweaty breasts against his hard chest. I could tell he was getting close to the point of no return, and I was eager to watch him cum with our cocks joined together.

"Yes, baby," I purred. "Let it come. Cum all over my big tits. Let me hear Tarzan's call of the wild."

Suddenly, he arched his back and thrust his dick as hard

as he could against my organ, pressing his balls tightly against mine. My clit throbbed as he shot one giant geyser after another between my boobs, cumming all over the underside of his chin and face.

"Fuckkkk!" he growled with each spurt. "I'm cumming all over your cock. *Uhn, uhn, uhn!*"

With each throb and spasm, he grunted like a wild animal until he was fully spent. When he finally recovered his strength, he looked up at me with gratitude.

"Thank you," he said. "I needed that. You were even more magnificent than I imagined."

"Glad I could be of service," I said. "Now you should get yourself back in there. Somewhere out there is your *real* Jane, waiting for you to scoop her up and take her away to your jungle."

"What about you?" he said, looking at me confused.

"I'm still looking for my Jane, too," I smiled.

The whole time neither one of us had so much as touched lips. All either one of us wanted was a quickie in the wine cellar, where we could live out one of our mutual boy-on-boy fantasies. As Tarzan tucked his pecker back under his loincloth and staggered out of the cellar, I smiled.

*That's one way to get it on with a man*, I thought. I wondered what other fantasies awaited me before the night would be over.

**5**

---

After Tarzan left the wine cellar, I found a sink nearby and cleaned myself up, removing all the cum that he'd splattered over my dildo and chest. Feeling flushed and sweaty, I decided to catch some fresh air before going back into the main room. A side door from the cellar led onto an expansive terrace overlooking the lake. Standing alone in a corner of the balcony stood the governor's wife Alicia with her back toward me. Her arms rested on the stone railing as she puffed a cigarette, leaning over with her naked ass jutting out behind her backless apron. My pussy fluttered as I admired her shapely figure, feeling the moisture accumulating on my lips tingling in the cool autumn air.

Alicia had one of the most magnificent backsides I'd ever beheld. Her long, slender legs were taut and shapely like a professional dancer's and her ass was as tight and firm as a teenager. The rising moonlight reflecting off Lake Michigan shimmered between the space in her thighs, illuminating the dark pit under her mound. It was almost as if she were daring me to approach her and fuck her from behind.

I surveyed the rest of balcony and seeing that we were alone, I began tiptoeing toward her. It was a calm and cloudless night and the light of the full moon shone brightly over the Bannon estate, revealing the splendor of its manicured gardens. Amidst autumn-speckled trees and perfectly manicured flower beds, lay a geometric hedge maze accented with stone sculptures and a flowing water fountain.

I paused for a moment to breathe in the floral scent of the breeze wafting in from the shore. I couldn't imagine a more romantic setting for a private encounter with my pretty temptress. As I edged closer toward her, I stepped on a small pebble and it went skittering over the stone tiles in Alicia's direction. She cocked her head and turned slightly in my direction, then bent lower on the handrail, taking another puff of her cigarette. Whoever she imagined approaching her from behind only increased the boldness of her seductive pose.

Maybe being the wife of the most powerful figure in the state gave her the confidence to blow off any would-be interlopers. Or maybe she was just bored and looking for an anonymous fling to mix up her dull political life. Whatever the reason, her self-assured nature turned me on even more and as the glistening slit of her pussy came into focus, I felt the wetness from my own sex beginning to run down the insides of my thighs. When I came within a few feet of her, she stood up with her arms extended on the balustrade and blew a stream of smoke high in the air.

"Beautiful night, isn't it?" she said to no one in particular.

"Spectacular," I said. "The view is truly magnificent in this light."

"Mmm," she replied, oblivious to the identity of her midnight paramour. "Were you admiring the landscaping?"

"Among other things," I said, staring at her bald snatch. "Everything is so perfectly balanced and neatly trimmed. It really makes you want to pause and appreciate Mother Nature."

Alicia took a step back with one of her legs, arching her ass higher.

"It would be a shame just to *look* at it," she said, "Nature is meant to be immersed in, don't you think?"

"Absolutely," I said, taking a step closer, brushing my bare breasts against her chilly back. "You never know what you might find until you make contact."

"Like the way a woman's nipples pucker when it's cold?"

"Or when they brush against a soft surface," I replied.

"Or her lover's skin," she said

She pressed her ass further toward me and touched my protruding organ, then gasped and turned her head in my direction, checking it before we made eye contact.

"And sometimes—" she mused, recognizing the familiar shape of my leather chaps. "Nature has a way of *surprising* us with her wonderful diversity."

"Do like surprises?" I teased.

"In the right circumstances."

I reached under the front of her apron and squeezed her breasts, pressing my cock harder between her legs. She reached underneath and began stroking my dildo against her wet cleft.

"I particularly like the way nature has a way of adapting to its surroundings—" I said, beginning to inflate my rubber penis with my pistol trigger. "Like the way it expands and contracts to fill the void in any particular situation."

"Yes," Alicia panted, running her hand up and down my giant shaft. "I'd like you to fill *my* void."

By now, my inflatable penis had reached its maximum length and Alicia was busy rubbing the bulbous head against her inflamed clit.

"Fuck me, Jade," she said, dispensing with any further pretense. "I've been fantasizing about you banging me with your beautiful dick all night long."

"As have I," I panted, angling the tip into her dripping opening. I've dreamt of pounding your beautiful ass from the moment we met."

"*Fuck* yes," she grunted, as I pressed myself inside her. "Pound me with your big cowboy dick. Let me feel your balls slapping up against me while you ride me."

As I began to hump her, I marveled at how enthralled all the guests seemed to be with my transgender persona—both male and female. Everyone seemed to want a piece of my girl-cock, no matter how they could get it. While I watched my drumstick pounding in and out of her hole, I had to admit it was kind of fun assuming the male role for a change. There was something strangely empowering about being connected to a man's cock, watching all these strangers bow to my made-up masculinity. As I grasped the sides of her hips and pulled her toward me, she moaned and gyrated her hips, holding on to the rail for support.

"God damn, girl," she hissed. "You feel so good inside me. I've never had a man fill me up quite this way before. I only wish you could cum inside me. I want to hear you get off with me."

There was something about the sight of my big phallus plowing into her tight little ass that was getting me especially worked up. Even though she wasn't providing direct stimulation to my lady parts, I could have come just watching the incredibly sexy scene that was unfolding before my eyes. But I'd been saving up one more special secret. I pressed a button on the inside of my handle and suddenly my balls began vibrating from a battery-operated motor embedded inside. As I pressed my scrotum against her underside, I was instantly taken to a whole new level of excitement.

"Holy shit!" she squealed. "That's *definitely* something no man has ever done to me. Grind your nuts against me, Jade. Trib me with your big fat balls."

"Fuck, yes," I growled, feeling the rising tide of ecstasy building within me.

I couldn't help smiling, acknowledging the multipurpose capability of my male equipment. Not too long ago I was frotting a man with my big firehose, and now I was tribbing a sexy woman with my vibrating balls. For a brief moment, I felt envious of a man's equipment, but as my pussy began throbbing and dripping over my strap-on apparatus, I became acutely aware of my true gender. I leaned forward and rubbed my tits against Alicia's back, pinching and rolling her nipples between my fingers.

"Can you feel my wetness, Alicia?" I panted. "Can you feel how much you're turning me on?"

She reached under my vibrating balls and inserted two fingers inside me, stroking the front of my G-spot.

"Yes," she grunted. "You feel exquisite. You're going to make me come soon. I want to feel you come with me."

"With every part of my body actively engaged in fucking her, I didn't need any further encouragement. Within seconds, a surge of energy coursed through me, as my pussy began clamping down over Alicia's fingers. At the same time, she hunched over and began shaking wildly as she gripped the railing with all her strength.

"Fuck, Jade!" she hissed. "I'm cumming! Pound my ass with your big dick. God, I'm cumming so hard!"

As the two of us grunted and shook in simultaneous orgasm with my buttocks clenching as I pressed my cock deep into her, I suddenly became conscious of the extra light that was being cast onto the terrace from the open windows of the ballroom. When we finally came down from our powerful climax, she turned around and gently kissed me.

"It seems we have an audience," she smiled, directing her eyes toward the adjacent wall.

I peered in the direction of the ballroom and noticed a giant crowd of onlookers staring out the windows with their eyes and mouths agape.

"Good," I said. "It's about time some of these snobs got a taste of the real world outside their sheltered cocoons.

"Maybe this will open their minds about the natural order of things."

With that, I lifted Alicia up onto the stone abutment and spread her legs far apart, pressing my still buzzing cock back inside her.

"If they want a show, let's really give them a show."

# 6

After Alicia and I came a second time in full view of the crowd, we took a moment to compose ourselves then walked back into the main ball-room as if nothing had happened. Neither one of us seemed to care that virtually everyone was staring at us as they continued gossiping in their little cliques. I didn't even bother to refasten my leather vest or deflate my dildo as my breasts bounced freely on my bare chest in tandem with my turgid hard-on.

The two of us approached the bar and ordered matching margaritas then giggled amongst ourselves about the way everyone was trying not to stare as they talked amongst themselves. In spite of the fact that they pretended to carry on normal conversations, it was obvious that they were still highly aroused by our little tête-a-tête.

"I think Mr. Incredible is regretting his wardrobe choice

right about now," Alicia chuckled, motioning toward the billionaire and his supermodel girlfriend.

I stole a glance in their direction and noticed Schiffer had a pronounced erection tenting the front of his tights.

"He's looking more like *Mr. Fantastic* with that cucumber wedged between his legs," I joked.

"And check out our favorite newscaster," she said. "It looks like Woody's popping a little Pinocchio of his own."

I peered at the anchorman and noticed him rearranging the front of his denims as a prominent bulge ran down one side of his pant legs.

"Ha," I chuckled. "I bet he's wishing he wore chaps like me."

I had to admit that I was enjoying the attention of all the powerful people in the room, particularly amongst the men who seemed especially attracted by my naked ladyboy costume.

"I don't know about *Jack* though," she said, furrowing her brow as her husband marched toward us with an angry expression on his face. "I have a feeling that his little willie will be even more shriveled than usual after watching you pound me with your big tool."

The governor stormed up to the bar and grabbed Alicia's hand, trying to ignore the pink pole jutting up from my lap.

"What is it, dear?" Alicia said, feigning surprise at her husband's indignation. "I was just enjoying a quiet drink with my new friend."

"That was hardly *quiet!*" he huffed, dragging her off her barstool. "Come on, it's time for us to go."

"But the party was just getting started," Alicia protested. "I was just starting to get warmed up."

The governor glanced down at my flaring joystick then glared at me.

"It looks like the two of you were getting more than just *warmed up.*"

"Oh, come on, Jack," Alicia said, trying to resist his advance. "We were just having a little fun. You said that you wanted me to get more comfortable around your political friends."

"Not *that* way!" he fumed. "You've made a fool out of me and embarrassed me in front of all my colleagues!"

Alicia tried to protest, but the governor pulled her away from the bar and stormed toward the entrance. After collecting their coats from the butler, they soon disappeared out the front door. Alarmed by the commotion, Hannah joined me at the bar and sat on Alicia's stool, taking a sip of her cocktail.

"Jesus, Jade," she said, slapping my dripping dildo. "You sure know how to rock the boat in these genteel affairs."

"That's not the *only* boat I was rocking around here," I said. "Were you watching the show like everybody else?"

"How could I miss it?" Hannah chuckled. "It only took one person to catch you fucking the governor's wife before the entire room joined in the spectacle. Not like they could have *ignored* it, with all the grunting and groaning the two of you were doing."

"I wasn't paying much attention. I was kind of lost in the moment."

"You sure looked like it," Hannah said. "I have to say, It

was an incredible turn-on watching you fuck her from behind. I could actually see your buttocks shaking when you came." She glanced down at my swollen cock and shook her head. "How does that work, exactly? I thought you were kind of detached from that thing."

"Not as much as you might imagine," I smiled. "Touch my balls to see for yourself."

Hannah placed her hand over my rubber scrotum and I switched on the vibrator, then her eyes suddenly flung open.

"Holy shit!" she said. "That thing really *is* fully animated. What else can it do? Spurt out fake cum?"

"As much as I wish it could, no. But these two extra tricks seem to be providing all the entertainment I need."

"I'd say so, judging by how loud the two of you were howling out there on the balcony. I fact, I've got a little girly hard-on of my own thinking what that would feel like inside me. I don't suppose we could find our own private alcove for a little fun, could we? I'm so horny right now, this costume is practically glued onto my body."

I glanced around the room and noticed that everybody was staring at us with disapproving expressions.

"Why not?" I said. "After that last escapade, it looks like all bets are off. There's not much to hide any more at this point."

I took Hannah's hand and began heading in the direction of the wine cellar, but Steve Bannon and his wife stepped in front of us, smiling like Cheshire Cats.

"It appears you've been enjoying my party even more than I could have imagined," he smirked, peering at my dripping dildo. "You seem to have gotten a rise out of more than a few of our guests this evening. I'd have to say you win the prize for the most inventive costume."

"I have to admit, it's been far less of a stuffy affair than I imagined." I glanced at Genevieve, noticing the slit in the side of her dress looking even more pronounced than before, revealing her hip bone above her barely concealed pussy. "I've found the conversation very stimulating."

"So it would seem," he said, staring at my tumescent totem. "Would you like to join my wife and me for a little nightcap in our private lounge? We've been admiring you all night long and would love to continue the conversation."

"Hmm," I said, raising an eyebrow toward Hannah. "Do you mind if I bring my friend along? We were just about to explore some private time of our own."

Bannon leered at Hannah's costume then smiled at her.

"I don't see why not," he said. "What do you think dear? Would you like to bring another partner into our little meeting?"

"The more the merrier," she smiled, jumping at the chance to have some more alone time with me. "Besides, now it'll be more evenly balanced. I'm not sure I could manage the two of you all by myself."

"Come then," Bannon said, leading us to a private elevator at the base of his stairs.

As we crossed the ballroom floor, the entire room followed our movement while my protruding penis waggled playfully between my legs. When we got in the elevator and the doors closed behind us, Bannon pressed button number four and smiled at Hannah and me.

"You've already explored many of the rooms in my

house," he said. "But I think you'll find the view particularly appealing from the top floor."

I glanced toward Hannah and saw that her pupils were already dilated in excitement. I didn't know if she was more impressed by the fact that Bannon's mansion had four floors and a personal elevator or that she was about to participate in a private orgy with the richest man in the Midwest.

When the lift stopped and the doors opened, we both gasped at the view. The elevator opened to an enormous bedroom with floor-to-ceiling windows providing a panoramic view of Lake Michigan. As impressed as I'd been with the view from his main floor balcony, from this elevation the lake seemed to stretch out in every direction forever. But the view on the *inside* was even more spectacular. Bannon's bedroom was almost as large as most people's houses, with giant expressionist paintings hanging on the walls, a huge wood-burning fireplace next to the bed, and a separate bar beside the sliding glass windows.

"Would you like something to drink?" he said, lifting a crystal decanter off the table. "Perhaps a glass of brandy? I've got a thirty-year-old bottle of Hennessey that I've been meaning to open for a special event."

As much as I admired his impressive collection of personal effects, I was far more attracted to the elaborate trimmings of his beautiful wife.

"That would be lovely," I said, smiling at Genevieve.

Bannon handed each of us a large goblet filled with cognac, then he pressed a remote control device and the large window panes began to separate, bringing in a gust of cool air.

"Would you like to move to the balcony? The view is even more magical at this time of the night."

"Sure," I said, checking with Hannah to make sure she was still feeling comfortable. She simply peered back at me with wide eyes and nodded silently. We stepped out onto the deck and Bannon motioned to a wicker settee encircling a bubbling Jacuzzi.

"It might be a bit warmer next to the hot tub," he said, extending his hand toward the tub. "Please—make yourselves comfortable."

Hannan and I took a spot next to one another, while Bannon and his wife sat kitty-corner to us, a few feet to our left. The view of the lake was magnificent with the light of the full moon reflecting off the ripples like an evening sunset on a secluded beach. A cool breeze wafted in from the shore, and I pulled my vest over my exposed abdomen.

"Feel free to dip your toes in the water," he said. "Or climb right in if you prefer. It's chillier outside than usual tonight."

"I wouldn't mind getting out of these boots," I said, kicking off my footwear and placing my feet in the churning water.

Then I turned to Hannah and smiled.

"This feels heavenly, Han. Why don't you join me?"

She motioned to her all-in-one ensemble and frowned.

"It's not quite as simple for me as it is for you."

"Don't be concerned about *us*," Bannon grinned. "We're all adults here. Besides, I think we've seen just about everything already tonight. No one's watching this time besides Genevieve and me."

Hannah peered at me for a moment and I nodded. I'd

never known her to be shy in these kinds of circumstances and it didn't take long for her to shed her clothes and slide under the bubbling water.

"Mmm," she purred, glancing up at me. "It's lovely. You should come in. These jets are good for massaging more than just your feet."

I looked toward Bannon and his wife and they smiled with a knowing grin.

"You said you wanted to find a private spot to continue your engagement," he said. "Don't let us stop you. We'll just finish our brandies while you two make yourselves comfortable."

He glanced down at my bobbing tool then peered back up at me.

"Is your equipment waterproof?"

"It should be," I said, winking toward Hannah. "Would you like me to keep it on?"

"I think we would," Bannon grinned. "I'd love to see how you use that thing close-up. How about you, dear? Are you interested in watching Jade play with her magic wand again?"

"Absolutely," Genevieve said, staring me directly in the eye. "I'd love to see her make another pretty girl come with her big man-cock."

I pulled off my chaps and vest and squeezed the trigger on my pistol to re-inflate my shaft to its full length then pressed the button on the handle to turn on the vibrator. Bannon and Genevieve squinted at the humming device, and I smiled at them as I slipped under the surface next to Hannah.

She scooted up next to me and lowered her hand under

the water, stroking my phallus as she caressed the inside of my thighs. I turned toward her and we embraced in a passionate kiss. I could feel the jets of the Jacuzzi shooting between our breasts as we rubbed our tits together while she lifted her leg, straddling my hips. Within seconds, she lowered herself onto my pole and wrapped her arms around my back. As she began to rock her hips together with mine, I glanced up and made eye contact with Bannon and his wife. I noticed the front of his toga was tenting between his legs and Genevieve's hand was moving up and down as he smiled lasciviously toward us.

"Damn, Jade," Hannah groaned as I embedded my rod deep inside her. "That thing feels amazing. Fuck me with your big cock. Rub your balls on my cunt. I can feel it vibrating."

"Mmm," I sighed, as her tits mashed up against mine in the swirling water. "Squeeze my dick, Hannah. Let's put on a nice show for our hosts."

By now, Bannon had dispensed with any form of modesty, flinging his toga to the side where I could see his throbbing erection standing up between his spread legs. Judging by the size of his wife's hand, he appeared to have a decent-sized hard-on, but nowhere near as large as my own. Genevieve had apparently gotten just worked up watching Hannah and me fucking under the swirling water, and before long she kicked off her heels and hiked up her dress, sitting down over her husband's cock while she faced us. As I darted my eyes between her husband's prick thrusting in and out of her pussy and her dark eyes, our mouths began to open in mutual pleasure.

It was an incredible turn-on watching Genevieve's sexy body squirming over her husband's cock as she watched the two of us writhing in the churning water. Whether she was more excited getting fucked by her husband while two pretty girls watched them get it on or by the sight of Hannan and me enjoying ourselves underneath the surface, it didn't matter. Before long, all four of us were moaning loudly as we watched each other fuck our partners with abandon.

Hannah was the first to go off, as she started shaking wildly on my hips.

"Oh God, Jade," she groaned. "I'm cumming! Ram it inside me. Let me feel your balls slap up against me. Uhnnnnnn!"

Seeing Hannah having a powerful orgasm on top of me soon put Bannon over the edge as he grunted with his shaft pulsing inside his wife's pussy. Although he was staring at me, I was more interested in watching the expression on Genevieve's face as she returned my gaze with glassy eyes. I could tell that she was close, but needed a little extra stimulation to reach her goal.

As she locked eyes on me, she placed her hand over the front of her mound and began jerking her protruding nub. As her eyes opened progressively wider, I leaned forward and lifted my ass over one of the jets behind me. While the water gushed against my quivering opening, the vibrating balls pressed against my clit, and I felt a surge of pleasure engulfing my body.

"I'm close," I panted, locking eyes with Bannon's wife. "Come for me, Genevieve. Let me watch you come all over my big dick."

Even though she was planted on her husband's cock, we

were both thinking the same thing. In that moment of mutual ecstasy, we were both imagining that it was *my* cock embedded in her pussy instead of her husband's.

"Yes, Jade!" she howled. "I'm cumming! I feel you inside me. I want you so bad. Oh *Gawd*..."

While the four of us panted and groaned in simultaneous climax, I glanced at Bannon, noticing him watching me with a wild look in his eye. Locked on me with laser focus, he had a strange, almost animalistic expression. I wasn't sure what he was channeling at that moment, but I could tell it wasn't his wife he was thinking about.

After we all settled down, Genevieve lifted herself off her husband's cock and slid in the water next to Hannah and me. She cuddled up beside me and her hand disappeared under the water, and soon after I felt her caressing my vibrating dildo. As Hannah leaned over to kiss her, Bannon stood up with his penis dripping a string of cum, motioning with his head inside his bed chamber.

"Why don't we all go back inside?" he said. "There'll be more room for us to play and we can watch each other better on the bed. Something tells me there's still a lot of pent-up energy between you girls."

Genevieve stepped up out of the tub first and led me by the hand into the bedroom as Hannah scampered in behind us, shivering. Bannon returned from his washroom and threw each of us a towel. Then he walked over to the bed and sat on the edge, beckoning for the rest of us to join him.

"Come," he said. "Let's share the wealth. There's plenty to go around."

"What did you have in mind?" I said, raising my eyebrows.

After the Tarzan episode, I wasn't sure what part of me he was more interested in.

"There's enough parts between us for us to create an interesting *foursome*, don't you think?" he smirked.

As we all lay down on the bed and began exploring each other's bodies, Bannon seemed immediately drawn to my cock. As he sucked on my nipples, he reached down and began stroking my phallus while he masturbated himself with his other hand. While Hannah and Jenny intertwined their legs and began rubbing their pussies together, Bannon lowered himself down my abdomen until his face was directly in front of my giant pole. Suddenly, he stretched his lips around the head and began sucking it while he jerked his hand over his own dripping dick. Within seconds, he began moaning loudly, as he jetted squirts of cum all over his stomach.

Seeing her husband getting off so quickly again, Genevieve sat up and peered at the two of us with a sly smile.

"You seem quite enamored with Jade's cock, dear. I have an idea, if you're game for a little four-way fun. How would you like a *real* cock inside you this time, Hannah?"

Hannah looked at Genevieve then back at her husband, and smiled. There was little doubt that she'd fantasized about being fucked by the hot billionaire for a long time.

"*Definitely*," she said.

"Lie down face up on the bed," Genevieve instructed. "That way we can *both* have access to you. And *Jade*," she purred, with a gleam in her eye. "Why don't you choose whatever outlet looks most enticing to you among the three of us?"

As Genevieve spread her thighs over Hannah's face and lowered her pussy onto her lips, Bannon pulled Hannah's legs apart and straddled her opening with his dripping dick. As I watched them begin to fuck my best friend like she was a piece of meat, something inside me snapped. There was something about the way Bannon thought he could use her any way he wanted that pissed me off.

*Just another self-righteous rich asshole*, I thought. *This guy needs to be put in his place.*

As I kneeled behind him watching the two of them grinding their bodies against Hannah, Genevieve looked up at me and smiled. She glanced down toward her husband's ass and nodded. It was almost like she was *begging* me to fuck him from behind.

As the sides of my lips slowly curled up in acknowledgement, I brushed my erect dildo over Bannon's cheeks. Instead of flinching, he leaned further forward until I could see his balls waggling above Hannah's pussy. His asshole puckered as he thrust in and out of her, and for the first time in my life, I sensed the attraction of anal sex. There was something incredibly sexy and empowering about fucking a man up the ass. Now I knew why gay men separated into tops and bottoms. Just as with lesbian couples, one had to be the dominant one and one was meant to be the submissive one.

And *this* time, it was *my* turn to be the dominant one. Only in a way I'd never envisioned.

I lifted the tip of my pole, still glistening with Hannah's juices, and pointed it toward Bannon's opening. As I pressed it against his pucker, he grunted and pushed back gently.

*So he likes being fucked by a woman?* I thought. *It's time to show him who's really in charge here.*

I grabbed the sides of his hips and slowly pressed my cock deeper inside him. It felt strange and titillating at the same time to be fucking a man with my faux hard-on. As my balls pressed back against my clit, I imagined what it would feel like for a man to fuck another man this way. Suddenly, all the times I'd felt used by men who fucked from behind came flooding back. I thrust my dick as far into Bannon's ass as I could and began pounding my hips against his butt cheeks.

As his hole stretched as far as it could go by my coke-can-width hard-on, I found myself enjoying the feeling of thrusting in and out of him. Strangely, Genevieve seemed to be enjoying the show almost as much as me, as she writhed and moaned on Hannah's face while watching the two of us.

"Yes, Jade," she grunted. "Fuck Jack's ass. Make him your bitch. I want to watch him get off while you have your way with him."

Whether it was the sight of her pretty body twisting over Hannah's face or the sense of power I felt fucking her husband, I soon felt the familiar wall of pleasure beginning to overtake me. As I pressed my balls tight against his ass, creating more friction against my clit, I began to moan approaching my peak.

"Damn this is hot," I grunted. "I'm going to come soon. Watch me cum inside your husband's ass, Genevieve."

"Yes," she groaned, suddenly shifting her gaze to her husband's eyes.

I wasn't sure if she was communing with him at that

moment or she just enjoyed seeing him at his most vulnerable moment. Either way, the sight of her convulsing over Hannah's mouth as she reached her own orgasm soon opened my floodgates. I pulled Bannon's ass hard toward me as I thrust my cock one last time deep into him, squirting all over my vibrating balls and Hannah's pussy. Within seconds, all four of us were howling in mutual ecstasy as we pounded and quivered atop one another in a mass of sweaty flesh. When we finally collapsed onto the bed in exhaustion, Genevieve leaned over and kissed me, whispering in my ear.

"Thanks for putting my husband in his rightful place," she mewed. "You have no idea how much both of us needed that."

---

R*eady for more erotic chills and thrills? Enjoy the next volume in Jade's Erotic Adventures:*

*Getting wet in the steam room was never this much fun...*

### *Sneak peek:*

*I didn't need any more encouragement as I began to feel the pleasurable sensations spreading throughout my body. The rising steam from the coal stove had increased the room temperature to well over one hundred degrees and I didn't need any more excuses to fully disrobe. I took my gown off my shoulders and threw it on the bench beside me and spread my legs wide apart to let the girls see my glistening vulva...*

## READ MORE..

# VOLUME FIVE

## NUDE CRUISE

## EXOTIC VOYAGE

My exhilarating encounters at the dinner party, the dark room, and naked yoga had whet my appetite for new adventures. But each of these experiences, as stimulating and fulfilling as they were in their own right, were one-time affairs. In each case, it hadn't taken long for me to yearn for something new, something more. I wanted an *all-in-one* adventure, where I could move from one new experience to another without having to search for the next one. I wanted my own erotic *Disneyland*.

I knew if I could find such diverse activities online, there must be a whole underworld of swingers looking for something similar. Surely some enterprising operator would see the potential in putting together some kind of package deal. I sat down in front of my computer, opened up my browser, and typed in the words 'all-inclusive erotic adventure.'

A surprising number of 'clothing-optional' resort listings came up. I clicked on the first one, but it just showed the usual pictures of pretty pools, beaches, and guests suites, with a vague description of an 'upscale retreat for an adventurous lifestyle experience'. A little further down the page, I saw a blog article titled *Inside a nudist sex resort*. The article described an adventure traveler's experience at a resort where couples romped on nude beaches, swam in nude pools, and 'hooked up' in private cabins.

*Definitely a little too tame-sounding for me.*

I clicked on the next page of search results, where I saw a link titled *Nude Cruise — Explore Your Erotic Fantasies*.

*This looks interesting.*

I clicked on the link and a webpage opened showing pictures of naked people climbing walls, dancing in water fountains, and wrestling in a muddy pit.

*That looks a little different,* I thought.

At the top of the webpage, there was a tab titled *Fantasy Menu*. I clicked on the link, and a list of sexy-sounding shipboard activities appeared:

Peak Sensation
House of Holes
Fantasy Fountain
Sensuous Steam Room
Masquerade Ball
Sexy Games Room
Get Down Disco
Cybersex Rules
Private View Rooms
Intimate Massage
FourPlay

I clicked on the first one and a photo appeared showing naked men and women scaling a climbing wall with unusual foot and hand holds. Instead of the usual jug and pocket holds, the 'grips' were in the shape of dildos and artificial vaginas, where climbers could pause to 'rest' and 'recharge their batteries' as they scaled the wall. A description under the photo read:

*Challenge yourself to a climbing wall like no other. The higher you go, the more stimulating the experience becomes. Reward yourself at each new level, where you'll find a new wall feature to stimulate and excite every part of your body, as you seek the peak experience at the top of the mountain. All while safely strapped into a comfortable harness that permits a maximum range of movement and accessibility.*

*That sounds like an incredible turn on,* I thought.

The idea of fucking a dildo strapped to a wall while people watched me from below sounded insanely sexy. My pussy began to twitch as I imagined the idea.

What's this next one—*House of Holes*?

I clicked on the next listed activity, and a picture appeared showing various nude men and women pressing their hips and buttocks against a wall with scattered holes. The look of ecstasy on their faces left little doubt as to what was happening on the other side. The description read:

*Hook up with a stranger on the other side of a wall through your own personal intimate portal. You can choose to 'give', 'receive', or 'merge' with a partner of either sex in an erotic and completely anonymous connection. Or you can choose to simply watch, as other couples get their groove on in this sensuous and erotic House of Holes.*

*Damn, that sounds dirty. And fun.*

I'd heard of glory holes before, but I'd always thought of them as skanky places where gay men went to get an anonymous blow job. The idea of engaging in heterosexual sex or touching pussies with another woman through my own private portal was different. And highly stimulating. My left hand dropped down between my legs and I began to rub my clit as I continued exploring the website.

*What happens in the Sexy Games Room?*

I clicked on the next activity, which displayed a photo of naked men and women in contorted positions atop a polka-dot-covered mat. Their hips and asses were pressed together while they stretched their arms and legs around each other. The caption read:

*Play interactive nude games with your fellow guests where the rules and rewards are wide open. With Naked Twister, stretch into increasingly difficult and erotic positions as you try to reach around, over, and under your naked partners. Or try Naked Poker where the 'loser' must engage in increasingly erotic situations in full view of their playing partners. Or jump into the Naked Mud Wrestling pit and try to wrestle your partner into submission, all while surrounded in sensuous mud.*

*Fuck, yes!* I thought. *These guys know how to organize an erotic party.*

I didn't need to click any more of the fantasy activities to know this was the sort of erotic travel destination that I had in mind. It promised to be an immersive, stimulating experience with multiple partners and exciting activities. As always though, I needed to be sure it would be clean and safe. I searched the page and found a tab marked *Conditions*, which read:

*Every Nude Cruise guest must provide a certified report from a verified medical testing lab, indicating negative for sexually communicated diseases. The report must be dated within one week of your ship's departure date. Clothing is optional for all activities. Security staff are available at all venues to ensure the safety of guests and to ensure that all interaction occurs only with express consent.*

*Fair enough,* I thought. *The medical test requirement shows this is a class act. You can't be too careful about these things.*

I clicked the Booking tab and viewed the calendar for available dates. The next cruise departed from Miami in two weeks' time. I'd have to move a few things around and schedule a two-hour flight, but one of the joys of my job as a freelance graphic designer meant I could choose my own vacation days. I booked a private cabin with a Queen-size bed, then I tore my panties off and plunged my fingers into my pussy as I fantasized about all the shipboard activities I'd soon be participating in.

2
___

## SETTING SAIL

On the scheduled day of my departure, my whole body was buzzing with excitement. This was my first cruise, and I didn't know what to expect. Besides my fear of seasickness, I was a little nervous about the idea of parading around nude in public. I'd picked up some anti-nausea pills at the pharmacy, but I had butterflies in my stomach for an entirely different reason.

So far, my excursions into the realm of public sex and nudity had been fairly anonymous. At the dinner party, I could hide behind my masquerade mask. In the dark room, the special light effects concealed my identity. Even at my naked yoga class, everybody was so busy concentrating on their poses that it was really only my partner who had a close-up view of me.

But on this 'clothing-optional' cruise, I'd be going about my everyday routines in plain view of hundreds of strangers. Granted, some of the activities sounded highly erotic and fun. But the idea of sitting down for dinner or even just sunbathing in the nude gave me the willies. I'd packed some skimpy bikinis in case I got cold feet, but I didn't want to be the only one wearing clothes if everyone else was naked.

When I arrived at the cruise terminal, it was a hive of activity. There were hundreds of people waiting to go through security, and the building was buzzing with chatter and public announcements. I pulled out my boarding pass and looked for the sign directing me to my designated gate. Just like at airport security, there were multiple lines of people placing their bags on conveyor belts going through an X-ray machine. When it was my turn, I took off my shoes and opened my roller-bag to remove my liquids.

"That won't be necessary, ma'am," a handsome security attendant said.

"Oh?" I murmured, confused.

"No need to remove your shoes or any items from your bag," he said. "Security procedures for cruise ships aren't as stringent as they are for air travel."

I smiled and nodded sheepishly as I pulled my sandals back on.

"Unless you're carrying something metal, of course. That'll set our machine off."

"No, of course not," I said, blushing from all the attention I was getting holding up the line. But now I was worried about the vibrator I'd packed in my luggage.

*Who needs to bring a vibrator on a naked sex cruise, anyway?* I chided myself.

"I'll just need to see your boarding pass," the security agent said.

I showed him my pass, and he directed me to stand in line behind the pass-through body scanner. As I waited for my turn, I looked around at my fellow boarding passengers. Most of them were fairly young, in their 20s and 30s, but there were also some older couples who were apparently looking for a little adventure to spice up their marriages. I noticed a few people checking each other out. Most of them didn't make eye contact for very long, but I wasn't the only one undressing some of the hot passengers with my eyes.

I caught a tanned gentleman in the adjacent line running his eyes up and down my body. I'd intentionally worn skinny jeans and a tight blouse for the first day to show off my best assets. I stood up tall and lifted my chest to display my cleavage. He had a nice ass, strong arms, and beautiful skin. When our eyes met, he smiled at me, and I could feel the blood rushing to my face again.

*Come on, Jade,* I admonished myself. *Get a hold of yourself. If you're going to be this self-conscious fully clothed, how are you ever going to be comfortable walking around in the nude?*

I returned my attention to the X-ray machine as my bag disappeared under the cover. I watched the face of the security agent as he scanned the monitor for any suspicious contents, then breathed a sigh of relief when I saw my bag pop out the other end.

"Ma'am?" the agent at the opposite side of the body scanner said, motioning for me to step through.

I'd been so worried my vibrator would set off the X-ray machine, that I hadn't realized I was holding up the line again. I nodded self-consciously, then walked through the pass-through stand, making eye contact with the security agent to ensure I wouldn't set off any other alarms. After he nodded that I was clear, I picked my bag off the X-ray belt and looked for the sign to the check-in area. By now, I was sure that half the passengers in the security area were cursing in bewilderment at my awkward travel etiquette, and I was glad to find a respite at the end of a new line.

"That's a pretty big bag for a short cruise," a woman's voice said, as I heard someone step up behind me.

I turned around and looked into the eyes of a stunning brunette about my same height.

"Um, well, you know," I stammered. "It's mostly makeup and toiletries and that sort of thing. We women can't be shorthanded about these things."

I could feel the flush in my cheeks again, caught off guard by her disarming beauty.

"No, I suppose not," she said, smiling at my innocence. "Although something tells me *makeup* will be the least of our concerns on this trip."

Her confidence and bold manner was rapidly sending blood flowing to another part of my body.

"Is this your first time with this cruise operator?" I asked, not wanting to state the obvious.

"This is my third Fantasy Cruise. Once you dip your toes in, it's kind of addicting." Her eyes darted across my face, appraising my demeanor. "How about you?"

"It's my first time. I'm a bit nervous, to be honest. You know, about all the..."

"Yeah, there's a lot of that," she said. "But there's nothing to worry about. We're all in the same boat, so to speak. You get used to it pretty fast. It's actually quite liberating. Not having to dress up and put on airs. Nudity is a great equalizer."

I took a quick glance at her tight and tanned body. She was wearing loose fitting linen shorts and a tight T-shirt displaying a cruise ship sailing into the sunset. Her legs were long and shapely, and her firm breasts sat up high on her chest.

"Some of us are a little more equal than others, I'm afraid."

She scanned my figure and smiled.

"I don't think you have anything to worry about. You're gorgeous. As long as you don't mind being the center of attention with a body like that."

I puffed out my cheeks and exhaled heavily.

"That's exactly what I'm worried about. I'm not used to being the center of attention. At least not in a public setting with all my clothes off."

"What deck is your cabin on?" she asked.

I fumbled for my travel papers and pulled out my boarding pass.

"E deck," I said. "They told me that if I chose a cabin nearer the water line, I have a better chance of avoiding seasickness."

"That's my deck too. Stick with me girl, and I'll show you around. There are plenty of ways to take your mind off the motion of the boat. The key is to not stay in one place too long. With so many interesting shipboard activities, your stomach will be the *last* thing you'll be thinking about."

She held out her hand and smiled at me.

"My name's Heather."

"Jade," I said, shaking her hand softly. "Thanks, Heather. I could use a wing woman, or shipmate, or whatever you're supposed to call your cruise partner these days."

"It's a deal," Heather said, winking at me. "We'll be *partners in crime.*"

I reached the front of the line and saw one of the check-in agents motioning for me to come to her station.

"I'll wait for you past check-in," I said, suddenly mindful of the increasing dampness building between my legs.

3

---

# RECEPTION

After clearing through Check-in, Heather guided me through the final boarding process then we walked together toward our rooms on E deck. We agreed to meet thirty minutes later when we'd go to the guest reception in the main lounge on the top deck. Our rooms were in the same hall, so after saying temporary goodbyes, I continued down the hall toward my stateroom.

When I opened my door, I was surprised by how small my room was. The Queen-size bed seemed to take up almost all of the space, with a tiny adjoining closet and small desk beside the wall-mounted TV. I went into the bathroom and was disappointed to see a stand-up shower with no tub. I knew that space aboard a cruise ship was at a premium, but I wasn't expecting it to feel so claustrophobic.

I unpacked my toiletries and placed them on the tiny sink, then carried my small carry-on case and placed it on the bed. There was a small sliding window beside my bed, and I immediately walked over and slid it open to breathe in some fresh air. I could see a flotilla of small boats moving about the bay opposite our ship, and I immediately regretted not upgrading to a larger room with balcony.

*I bet Heather has a bigger room,* I thought. *I'm such a light-weight at this cruise thing.*

I was looking forward to picking her brain for other tips about optimizing my shipboard experience. Not to mention picking over the *rest* of her body. I couldn't wait to see her naked and run my hands over her tight ass and breasts.

The porter had taken my larger roller case, and I didn't have much of a change of clothes in my carry-on bag. Heather had said not to worry too much about what to wear for the reception since most first-time guests chose not to go fully nude at the first activity. Nevertheless, I wanted to get with the program and ease myself into the idea of being naked on board, so I removed my bra and unbuttoned my silk blouse three buttons to reveal my cleavage.

I went into the washroom and looked at myself in the small mirror. The soft silk rubbing against my nipples had already stimulated them to an aroused state, and they protruded against the thin fabric, creating two conspicuous nodes. I smiled at how full and firm my breasts looked in my revealing blouse and hoped they'd attract Heather's attention too. I put on a new coat of light red lipstick and touched up my mascara, then grabbed my purse and headed down the hall toward Heather's room.

When she opened her door and I saw what she was wearing, it took my breath away. She wore a see-through gauzy top that barely concealed her large breasts through the sheer material. I stared shamelessly at her figure, wanting to flip her loose top up over her waist and devour her firm, round tits. To top it off, she'd let her long brown hair down and it shone with iridescent hues of amber and gold. She looked absolutely ravishing, and I was already regretting my wardrobe choice.

"Damn, girl," I said. "You're a feast for sore eyes. Who needs hors d'oeuvres when the main course is standing right here in front of me."

"That can be arranged," she said. "Come on in. Let's freshen up before heading over to the reception."

Heather motioned me into her room and I stepped inside. As I suspected, her room was larger than mine, with a small sitting room next to her bed and French doors leading out to a balcony.

"I knew I should have upgraded to a suite," I frowned. "I'm already beginning to feel claustrophobic in my tiny little cabin."

I looked out her French doors toward the open bay.

"Do you mind if I check out your view?"

"Of course. Make yourself comfortable. You're welcome to hang at my place anytime you're feeling closed in. I'll just be a couple more minutes."

Heather disappeared into the washroom, and I slid the side doors open and stepped out onto her balcony. I could smell the fresh salty air from the sea and I closed my eyes as I breathed it in.

*This is definitely the way to travel*, I thought. *Next time*, I reminded myself, *remember to get a full-size suite with balcony.*

After a few minutes, Heather emerged from the washroom looking even more beautiful than before, and I couldn't help shaking my head.

"I'm feeling terribly overdressed. You look like you're getting in the swing of this nude cruise thing already. Should I find something skimpier to wear?"

"Nonsense," Heather said. "You look perfect." Her eyes traced a line down to my aroused nipples protruding against my blouse. "You're revealing just the right amount for the meet and greet. I guarantee you'll be getting a lot of attention in that tight outfit."

I glanced down at her tanned legs and sandals.

"But you're showing a lot more...skin. Am I going to be the only one covering up my whole body?"

"Not at all. Most first-timers come to the initial reception dressed pretty conservative. It takes a couple of days for people to get comfortable being in the buff around their fellow passengers. By the second or third day, everybody will be strolling around buck naked. After the reception there's a dance, where the lights get turned down. You'll have plenty of opportunity to shed some of your clothes then."

As Heather walked toward me, I watched her breasts jiggle under her sheer blouse. When she stood in front of me, I stared at her tits and soft brown nipples. I couldn't stop myself.

"May I?" I said, looking gently into her eyes.

"I thought you'd never ask," she smiled.

I lifted her top and cupped her breasts in my hands and squeezed them softly. They were full and firm, and perfectly shaped, straight out of a centerfold. I noticed her areolas contract and her nipples begin to extend. I rolled them gently between my thumbs and forefingers, and she leaned in to kiss me. When our lips met, I pushed my body toward hers and pressed my hips against hers. She grabbed the back of my head and pulled me closer as our tongues danced around each other's mouths. I could have fucked her right then and there, but after a long lingering kiss, she pulled away.

"There'll be plenty of time for this later," she said. "Let's go meet some new people at the reception. This is a *nude cruise*, remember? We don't want to be holed up in our cabin the whole time, do we?"

"I suppose not," I said, slightly disappointed. My head knew she was right, but the ache in my pussy disagreed. I wanted her right now, and I didn't feel like sharing her with anybody else.

"Come on," she said, grabbing my hand, pulling me toward the door. "Let's go trip the night fantastic."

---

When we got to the top deck, Heather led me to a large open lounge with floor-to-ceiling windows offering a commanding view of the bay. I hadn't realized the ship had already left the pier, and I saw that we were steaming past South Pointe Park toward the open sea.

There were hundreds of people milling around the room, and Heather clasped my hand as she led me toward the bar. I was glad almost everybody was fully clothed, ranging from shorts and T-shirts to camisoles and bikini bottoms. A few veteran Fantasy Cruise travelers had been bold enough to go topless, but for the most part, it was a fairly low-key affair.

"What'll you have, ladies?" a handsome bartender wearing a white dress shirt and bowtie asked.

"I'll have a watermelon vodka," I said.

"I'd like some sex on the beach please," Heather said.

"Coming right up," the bartender smiled.

"You're so naughty," I teased Heather.

"Hey, when in Rome..." she said.

I turned and looked around the room. Heather had given me good advice about what to wear, and I began to feel more relaxed.

"You were right about the dress code tonight," I said. "Though the bartender seems a little formal. Are the staff always dressed so prim and proper?"

"They're always *dressed*, if that's what you mean. It's company policy that staff always must wear clothes, even on a nude cruise. Something about maintaining their professionalism, I suppose. It kind of helps to separate the staff from the guests, especially when you need something. The officers dress in navy whites, and the servers typically wear black pants, vests, and bow ties."

I watched the bartender approach us as he returned from the other end of the bar.

"Are they allowed to...you know...*hook up* with guests?" I asked.

"Officially it's a no-no, but whatever enterprising staff chooses to do when they're off duty, is nobody's business. If they get caught cavorting with passengers they can technically be fired, but it's pretty hard not to dip your toe in the water every now and then with so many flirty naked passengers floating around."

"I see your point," I said, as a pretty topless girl walked past us.

"Here you go, ladies," the bartender said, placing our drinks in front of us.

"Come on," Heather said, picking up her glass. "Let's go mingle."

For the next hour or so, Heather and I stuck together as we wandered from one cluster of passengers to another, making small talk. Nobody seemed to want to address the elephant in the room, mostly sticking with safe subjects like where we were from, what we did for a living, and if we'd been on a Fantasy Cruise before.

But everybody was definitely checking each other out. Although most of us were technically fully 'dressed', there was plenty enough skin showing to get a good idea of what we'd look like naked. Most of the men wore tight T-shirts or open shirts, revealing plenty of chiseled pecs and abs. The women wore skimpy bikinis, or flimsy camisoles and miniskirts. It was a feast for the eyes, and I soaked it all in. After a little while, I spotted the tall gentleman who I'd made eye contact with in the security line, and I gently steered Heather in his direction.

"I see you managed to survive the security gauntlet," he said to me, as I shimmied up next to him.

"Barely," I laughed. "I wasn't sure who was going to arrest me first—the security guards for my smuggled contraband or the passengers who were steaming about me holding up the line."

"It wasn't so bad," he smiled. "Traveling on a ship is easier than a plane. Is this your first time?"

"Yes," I said. "How about you?"

"This is my second trip. I guess I had some unfinished business from my first time around. There's so much to do on this big ship—one week hardly seems to be enough time to take it all in."

I paused for a moment as I appraised his body. He was wearing creme-colored linen pants and sandals, with a loose-fitting short-sleeved Bermuda shirt. But it was unbuttoned enough to show the cleft rippling between his chiseled pecs as he motioned with his powerful arms. His dark eyes beckoned to me, as I began to fantasize about falling into his arms.

"I'm Marc," he said, extending his hand.

"Jade," I said, feeling his large fingers envelop me. I turned toward Heather. "And this is my partner in crime, Heather."

Marc smiled as he looked at Heather, trying to keep his gaze concentrated above her barely concealed breasts.

"Are you two sisters?" he said. "Because I have seen such a lovely pair since Giselle and Patricia Bundchen."

"If you're talking about Jade and me," Heather teased, "no." Then she grabbed her breasts and shook them provocatively. "But if you're talking about my girls here, I'll take that as a compliment."

"Either way," Marc said, "I mean it as a compliment."

A woman's voice suddenly came over the room's public address system to break the sexual tension. The three of us turned toward the stage, where a woman wearing white shorts and a pressed shirt was standing holding a mic.

"Good evening, Fantasy Cruise travelers!" she said, raising her voice in welcome.

A loud cheer filled the room from the attending guests.

"My name's Ashley, and I'll be your cruise director. For those of you who are traveling on your maiden voyage with Fantasy Cruise, welcome. And for those of you returning for more fun and games, I promise you won't be disappointed. We've added even more fantasy activities to uplift and stimulate you.

"All of you should have found the brochure with our full Fantasy Menu on your nightstand when you checked into your staterooms, but we have lots more here on the desk beside the stage. Whenever you have any questions, just come see me any time. I'll be here the rest of the evening, and you can find my office mid-ship next to the Poseidon Restaurant on Deck B. Or just ring me at triple-two on your in-room phone.

"But now, let's get this party started with our first Fantasy Dance!" she hollered.

The suddenly lights dimmed and flashing lights began circulating the room. The sound of Marvin Gaye's *Let's Get it On* began booming over the speakers, and Heather, Marc and I began swaying our hips together in unison. Heather turned toward me and began shaking her ass suggestively in Marc's direction.

*He's dreamy!* she mouthed to me.

*Damn straight*, I returned, widening my eyes in agreement.

Marc simply smiled at me as he pretended to grind his hips against Heather's ass.

*My first fantasy cruise was off to a promising start.*

4

———

# GETTING DOWN

**F**or the next hour or so, Heather, Marc and I got our groove on as the swirling lights from the disco ball flashed over the writhing crowd. With the sun beginning to set over the horizon, the room became increasingly dark, and some brave passengers began shedding their clothes. Heather was the first to take off her skimpy top, and after another ten minutes of bumping and grinding with her and Marc, I soon followed suit. Not long after, Marc ripped off his shirt and threw it on a growing pile beside the stage.

It felt fabulous to be semi-nude, and we shamelessly rubbed our bodies together as the sexy music played in the background. It didn't take long for us to remove our clothes completely as we got more and more worked up by the suggestive lyrics. When Donna Summer's *Love to Love You Baby* came over the speakers, we moved in close and rolled our hips and chests together, our passion rising in tandem with the singer's orgiastic moans. I could feel Marc's cock hardening against our bodies as my wetness commingled with Heather's on our skin. As usual, Heather made the first move.

"Let's get out of here," she panted in our ears, and we didn't even bother to pick up our clothes as the three of us pranced out of the lounge. Bypassing the elevator, Heather led the way down the closest stairwell while we raced down the three flights to E deck. We giggled our way down the hall past a few other half-dressed passengers as we headed toward Heather's room. When we got to her door, I looked at her blankly, wondering how we were going to get in. We were all stark naked, and none of us were carrying a room key.

"Shit!" I said to Heather. "What now? Maybe we can find a secluded spot on the deck—"

"Not to worry," she said. "I've been in this predicament before, and I've taken precautions."

She kneeled down on the floor and peered through the small crack under the base of her door. Then she reached into the space with her fingers and pulled a credit-card-sized room key out across the carpet.

"Shazam!" she said, standing up and displaying her room key triumphantly. "A lady is prepared for every contingency."

She fumbled with the key in the lock then pushed open the door, and the three of us scrambled into her room. As soon as the door closed, Heather jumped up onto Marc and threw her legs around his hips. He turned and pinned her against the door, and they started kissing passionately. I rubbed my breasts against his sweaty back and moved my hand between his legs. I could feel his hard cock pointing down between Heather's legs, and I rubbed it against her soaking pussy. It didn't take long for the three of us to be coated in her slippery juices.

I squeezed Marc's balls gently as he contracted his glutes and pressed harder against Heather. All three of us were panting, wanting a piece of his meat. Suddenly, he swung around and carried Heather toward the bed with her still clinging to his hips. He placed one knee on the bed and lowered her onto its surface, then pressed his body against hers. Not wanting to interrupt their rhythm, I stood and watched as my sticky hand moved between my legs.

At this point, I was so turned on I could have come just watching Heather and Marc make love. But Heather had other plans, and she twisted her body and flipped Marc over, straddling his hips. She motioned for me to join them on the bed and I kneeled down beside her and kissed her on her lips. I could feel her body writhing over Marc's midsection, and I ran my hands down her stomach to feel their connection. Marc's hard cock was flat against his stomach as Heather rolled back and forth over it with her wet pussy. I played with her clit and she began to moan in my mouth.

Then she began lowering herself until our mouths were inches away from Marc's throbbing phallus. She swung her leg over to Marc's opposite side and his penis popped up into an acute sixty-degree angle, pointing toward his head. In the soft moonlight streaming through Heather's balcony doors, I could see that it was large, straight, and magnificent. The head glistened with a mixture of pre-cum and Heather's juices, and we both wrapped our fingers around it.

While we gave him a slow, two-handed massage, Marc sighed and thrust his manhood into our pliant hands. After a couple of minutes, Heather lowered her head and took him into her mouth, as I cupped his balls and played with the space between his testicles and anus. Marc moaned and began to roll his hips more aggressively, obviously enjoying Heather's attention on his cock. I could hear his passion rising and I began to feel his balls tighten and rise up. I knew it wouldn't take long for him to come with the combined effect of two beautiful women attending to his erogenous area.

Heather must have sensed it too because she lifted her head off his dick and leaned over and kissed me. Marc began to raise himself up wanting to get in on the action, but Heather extended her right hand and pushed him back onto the bed. He quickly got the message and watched the two of us while we explored each other's bodies. I cupped Heather's tits again and rolled her nipples between my fingers, then we pressed our chests together and tribbed our nipples while we fucked each other's mouths with our tongues.

By this time, all three of us were ready for some direct stimulation, and I hesitated, unsure where to go next. It was my first time in a threesome—at least one where I had this degree of control—and I didn't want to leave anyone hanging. Heather suddenly lifted her right leg and swung it over Marc's stomach, then did the same with her other leg until she was straddling his hips from the side. She motioned for me to do the same, then we pulled each other forward until our vulvas touched Marc's throbbing member on opposite sides. It was an incredible sensation feeling the heat of his hard cock sandwiched between our two pussies. Heather and

I wasted no time moving our hips up and down, giving Marc an entirely new type of erotic massage.

The three of us were now getting direct stimulation, and Heather and I moaned in each other's mouths as we rubbed our soaking pussies together against Marc's pointed cock. I could feel our combined wetness running between my legs, as I pushed harder against Marc's warm and wonderful joystick. I wrapped my arms around Heather's waist and pulled her closer toward me. By now, we were all moaning in abandon and nearing the tipping point. I tilted my hips downward a bit and pressed my clit against the side of Marc's cock. Heather and I were humping him hard now, and our tits rubbed together as sweat streamed down our stomachs. This was an entirely new kind of tribbing that I'd never experienced before, and the image of the three of us joined together soon put me over the edge.

I threw my head back and let out a primal scream as Heather and I thrashed our hips together and gushed all over Marc's throbbing hard-on. We kissed for another minute as we came down from our high, then we separated and peered at Marc. He had a silly smile on his face, but his cock was still pointing up, bobbing gently over his stomach from the pulse flowing through its veins. I ran my hand over my stomach to see if I could detect any sign of semen on me, then I looked at Heather and shook my head to signal that he hadn't come yet.

"Good boy," she said, leaning over to give him a long, lingering kiss.

Then she shifted her body until her hips were behind his head, and she looked at me, silently nodding. I knew her intent immediately, and I swung my legs over Marc's midsection, straddling his hips in her direction. She lifted herself up, placing her pussy over his face, then lowered herself onto his eager mouth. I could see her eyes roll back in her head as he took her swollen clit between his lips and began to suck her, and she began to grind her hips into his face.

I didn't need any more encouragement. I grabbed Marc's thick schlong and directed the tip toward my quivering opening. I teased him for just a second, rubbing his sticky head against my clit and vulva, then I lowered myself onto him until his mound pressed firmly against my clit. As Heather and I locked eyes, I convulsed in a mini-orgasm.

It was an unbelievably hot sight watching each other fuck this adonis from opposite ends as we watched our passion rising. I began to rock my hips in unison with Heather, and I could feel Marc's hips answering the call. I loved the feeling of his big cock filling me up, and he knew how to move his hips to give my clit direct stimulation. The combined feeling of my clit grinding into his mound and the head of his cock rubbing against my G-spot was driving me crazy. I began moaning more loudly as I stepped up the pace of my humping action, while Heather and I clasped hands.

I wanted to make this last as long as I could, but the sights and sounds of three beautiful people joining together in an erotic union was too much. I could feel my orgasm welling deep inside me and I made one final push down hard onto Marc's cock as I squeezed Heather's hands like a vice. When I finally came, I grunted like a wild animal as my body spasmed over Marc's hips while I looked Heather straight in her eyes.

I guess that was too much for Marc too, because he grabbed my hips with two hands and thrust his hips into the air, lifting me off the mattress as I felt his cock throbbing in rhythmic contractions inside my pussy. With him moaning into her pussy and her seeing me have a powerful orgasm, it soon put Heather over the edge. Just as I was beginning to feel the last of my contractions subside, her hands squeezed mine hard and her eyelids narrowed as she clamped her thighs around Marc's head. She growled like a dog in heat as I watched the pleasure roll over her pretty face. The whole time we never took our eyes off one another.

When she finally collected her breath and came down from her orgasm, she smiled at me. We were both thinking the same thing. My new partner in crime and I had found our first accomplice.

Later that evening, Marc returned to his room and Heather and I continued to make love into the wee hours. By 3:00 a.m., we were both spent, and we fell asleep sprawled naked atop the bed sheets, as a cool breeze from the ocean wafted over our sweaty bodies. When the morning sun streamed through her balcony door, Heather rolled over and caressed my breast.

"Morning, Sunshine," she said, as my eyes slowly flitted open.

"Morning, Beautiful," I said, moving in closer to give her a kiss.

"That was quite a first night we had together."

"Mmmm, yes," I said, tasting her sweet tongue in my mouth. "Hopefully the first of many."

"I hope so too. But I don't want to steal all your time and attention on this cruise. The main idea is to mix it up and take advantage of as many activities as you can in the limited time you have available."

"Can't we do that together?" I asked.

"Some of them, for sure. But I think some of the other activities you might enjoy more on your own."

"What about our new friend Marc?"

"I'm pretty sure he'll want to get out there on his own and sow some more of his oats. But he left his room number on my nightstand, so we might have a chance to hook up with him again before the cruise is over."

I looked out the open balcony doors at the sun shimmering over the open sea.

"You've done this before. What activity do you recommend we try next?"

"Most people like to ease into this whole nudity thing. Let's head up to the pool and do some people watching while we work on our tans. There's also a cool fountain on the top deck that's quite fun and refreshing. But first, I think we should get something to eat. I don't know about you, but I'm famished!"

"Me too. I think we burned enough calories last night for *three* meals. But first I'd like to return to my cabin to freshen up. What do you recommend I wear to breakfast?"

"It'll be pretty hot up top. A bikini and sandals should be enough. You'll just be taking it all off pretty soon anyway. You don't want to have to carry a bunch of clothes around with you."

"That reminds me," I suddenly remembered. "I've still got to retrieve my stuff from last night in the lounge."

"Something tells me you're not going to need jeans and a

blouse for a while. We can pick that up on our return to our cabins later in the day. Did you want to borrow my shawl to get back to your room?"

I smiled at Heather's thoughtfulness.

"I'm just a few doors down. Judging by last night, half the people on the ship are already nude, so a little more streaking down the hall shouldn't hurt me."

"You're going to need a key to get in though. I'm guessing you didn't think of my trick."

Heather leaned over and picked up her room phone then tapped some numbers on the dial.

"Yes," she spoke into the phone, "my friend's lost her key for room E48. Can you send someone down with a replacement? She's in my room, E32. Thank you."

Ten minutes later, there was a soft tap on Heather's door.

"Maybe I'll take you up on that shawl offer after all," I said.

Heather smiled and went to her closet and held the garment open for me as I slid my arms into it.

"Meet you in the Poseidon Restaurant in an hour?" she said.

"Deal," I said, giving her a quick kiss.

I opened the door, gave Heather a playful shake of my ass, then followed the porter back to my room.

---

After breakfast, Heather led me to the main pool on the top deck, where scores of people were lounging naked on deck chairs and playing in the water. A series of interconnected pools simulated the look of a tropical lagoon, complete with life-size palm trees and small cabanas. We found a couple of open lounge chairs not far from the bar, and Heather asked me to mind them for us while she went to get a couple of drinks.

While she was gone, I made a quick scan of the scene. Virtually everybody was already naked, and it was a busy hive of activity. On one end of the lagoon, a large waterslide deposited screaming guests into the splashing water. In an adjacent basin, a small group of people were playing water polo. On the other side of the patio, a few passengers were skipping through a water fountain like a bunch of playful toddlers. It was all pretty surreal, and I paused to take it all in.

"Checking out all the action?" Heather said, returning from the bar and handing me a drink.

"Mmm, yes," I said, taking a sip of my pina colada. "There's certainly a lot of...*diversions*."

"Are you referring to all the naked people or the activities?"

"Both," I said, scanning the bodies of some of the men walking around the pool. "It's strange, though. Everybody seems so...*asexual*. I would have thought more people would be, you know, *aroused*, seeing each other naked."

"That's the thing about us all being in the same boat, so to speak. Like I said earlier, nudity is the great equalizer. Everybody gets used to it pretty quickly, and before you know it they're walking around like it's a normal walk in the park." Heather paused as she appraised my demeanor. "Are you disappointed?"

"Not really. I just expected the men in particular would be showing more sign of, you know, *interest*. The cruise operator billed this as more of a sex cruise than a nude cruise."

Heather smiled, as she lay back on her lounge chair.

"Believe me, there'll be plenty of opportunity for you to get down and dirty on this cruise. There's more going on than might first appear. For instance, take a look at that woman standing in the fountain on the other side of the patio."

I peered across the pool and saw a naked woman in her twenties standing over some jets of water spraying up from the surface. She had a strange look on her face as she spread her legs and squatted over the stream.

"It looks like she's having an enema," I laughed.

"I think she's directing the spray to a *different* part of her body," Heather said.

The look on the woman's face changed to one of pleasure as she began to shimmy her hips over the water stream. Suddenly the spray started pulsing like a shower head, and she let out a low moan.

I crossed my legs, beginning to feel a tingle in my pussy.

"I see what you mean," I said. "Now I see why they call it the Fantasy Fountain."

Heather noticed me squirming on my chair.

"Do you feel like giving it a try?"

"In a sec. Let me enjoy her experience first."

The woman suddenly grabbed her tits with her hands and pushed them up, as the spray from the patio surface gushed up over her abdomen and washed over her face. She was grunting and groaning now and moving her hips more rhythmically over the jet.

"Fuck, that's hot," I said.

"Kind of a nice way to cool off on a hot day like this."

"It looks like it might take the edge off in more ways than one."

Suddenly, the woman began screaming, as her body convulsed and her hips shook in rhythmic spasms. There was no doubt to us or any of the many other spectators that she had just enjoyed a powerful orgasm. When she staggered out of the fountain back toward her lounge chair, a small round of applause rose from around the pool.

"What do you think?" Heather said. "Are you up for it?"

"Now that I know I'm going to have an audience, I wouldn't mind some company. Will you come with me?"

"I think I will," Heather said, winking at me. "Let's toss these bikinis first. We don't want anything getting in the way of all the fun."

Heather nonchalantly unclasped her bikini top behind her back then stepped out of her bottoms. I'd almost forgotten how beautiful she was, and her tanned body looked magnificent in the bright sunshine. Her shaved pussy left nothing to the imagination, and I could see her nub poking out of her labia at the top of her pussy.

"Damn girl," I said, opening my eyes wide. "You're never afraid to let it all hang out."

"It's called a *fantasy cruise*, right? Let's live out our fantasies. Get those clothes off and let's go have some fun!"

I pulled off my top and bottom and threw them on my lounge chair, then Heather and I scampered around the pool past a throng of curious onlookers. When we got in the fountain, it was actually quite refreshing. The water was warm, but it felt cool against my hot skin in the blazing sun. The water jets were spread a few feet apart, facing different directions with alternating pulsing patterns. Some were a constant stream and some stopped and started periodically, while others pulsed at different speeds like an overhead shower faucet.

Heather and I stepped into the sprays and danced around for a minute, laughing and holding hands. Then we came together and kissed, rubbing our bodies together as the spray shot up between us, soaking our faces. Suddenly, I no longer cared about being naked in full view of the other pool guests. I was lost in the deluge of sensations I felt from the water jets spraying against my ass and Heather rubbing her body against mine.

We shifted position until we found a spot in the fountain where a steady stream directed toward our pussies. Then we pushed our mounds together so the stream sprayed directly against our touching clits. I opened my mouth and gasped as Heather smiled at me. This was a once-in-a-lifetime experience, and I wanted to enjoy every moment of it with her.

Suddenly, two more sprays began jetting at a forty-five-degree angle from behind each of us, and we bent our knees to give the spray direct access to our rosebuds.

"Oh my God!" I said to Heather, as my eyes flew open.

"Is this *arousing* enough for you?" she said, grinding her clit against mine.

"Fuck, yes!"

Just when I thought it couldn't get any more intense, the

steady spray directed toward our clits began pulsing in strong, flickering streams.

"Uhnn," I moaned, closing my eyes at the intense feeling of pleasure I was experiencing from every part of my body.

"Enjoy, Baby," Heather said, as she thrust her tongue into my mouth, swaying her hips in tandem with mine.

I could feel the passion rising quickly inside me, and there was no way I could hold it back any longer.

"Fuck, I'm coming!" I said, as my pussy clenched inside me and I became weak in the knees. "Ohh, Ohh, Ohh," I panted into Heather's mouth, feeling the waves roll over me. Heather grunted into my mouth and I felt her hips shudder against mine as she reached her own peak. We moaned out loud together as the warm water from the jets sprayed all over our ecstatic faces.

When we finally came down from our orgasms, we held each other over the gentle spray, leaning against one another in exhaustion. When we separated, a loud cheer rose from around the pool from the appreciative crowd.

*I guess this won't to be so hard getting used to after all,* I thought.

6

## PEAK SENSATIONS

Heather and I spent the rest of the day lounging around the pool, people watching. We made a few new friends and got some more cabin numbers, but mostly we just wanted to relax and scope out our next move. Heather said if we didn't pace ourselves, we'd either be too sore or exhausted to partake in some of the more adventurous shipboard activities. After perusing the ship's Fantasy Menu, we both agreed our next rendezvous would be at the climbing wall.

I went back to my cabin alone that night planning to get a good night's sleep, with visions of naked climbers exposing themselves as they scaled the cliff. I woke up refreshed the next morning, eager to try out the next erotic challenge. When I met Heather at the breakfast buffet, the room was filled with naked passengers filling their plates with hardly a sideways glance. I guess she'd been right about everybody getting comfortable being in the nude by the third day.

As she explained to me what to expect at the climbing wall, my eyes widened in anticipation. It sounded terrifying and exciting at the same time.

"Do people ever *fall*?" I asked.

"Everyone's strapped into a harness and they have spotters to maintain tension on the rope holding you up, so even if you do slip, it's perfectly safe."

I frowned at the thought of other people watching my naked body from below.

"So I'll have some stranger watching my bare ass as I stretch my legs and move up the wall?"

"Yes, but that's part of the fun of it. Knowing other people are watching you as you get higher and higher is quite titillating, for both you and the observers. Plus, the staff doing the rope work are usually pretty buff, so it's kind of hot."

The idea of exposing my body while I stimulated myself on the wall reminded me of my Dinner Party experience. I squirmed in my seat reflecting back on the memory of Jasmine playing with me under the table while my fellow diners looked on.

"Tell me more about the unique 'features' on the wall."

"Besides the usual cup and lip-shaped ledges for gaining a comfortable hand and foot hold, there are other more *erotic* holds to clasp onto along the way."

"Such as?"

"For starters, some of the lips vibrate, so you can pause and get a little extra stimulation whenever you're feeling in the mood."

I pictured the idea of being in a harness clinging to a wall while sex toys stimulated my private parts.

"Now I see why they strap you in," I said. "I could barely maintain my balance on solid ground at the fountain yesterday, the more worked up I got. I can imagine how weak in the knees people might get, stimulated in a similar manner while climbing a challenging wall."

"Exactly," Heather said. "Especially the higher you go. The stimulation gets more and more intense the higher you climb."

"How so?"

"The features start out pretty tame at the bottom, just little nodules to rub against. But then they start vibrating, like little magic bullets. They get progressively larger and more animated the higher you go. If you make it all the way to the top, they've got some full-size dildos that twist and rotate to really give you a ride."

"Mmm," I said, feeling the moisture beginning to build inside my pussy. "Just like my favorite rabbit vibrator."

"Kind of like that. Except this time, you're suspended twenty-five feet off the ground in full view of your spotter and any other spectators while you get off."

Suddenly I had a burning need to have something inside me.

"That sounds pretty hot."

Heather raised her eyebrows and nodded.

"There's something about the whole idea that's very arousing. I think you'll find it's quite a different experience."

I wrinkled my forehead as I pondered the possibilities.

"What about the guys? Are there similar erotic features for *them* to enjoy on the wall?"

"Definitely. The wall holds alternate between 'innies' and

'outies', so everybody has a chance to enjoy. Many of them are fashioned in the form of flexible lips, pussies, and anuses, where men can insert their dongs along the way and get a similar thrill. Near the top, they become animated with internal vibrators, just like the bullets and dildos for the ladies. It's quite arousing to watch the men and women stop and fuck the life-like features along the way."

I shook my head and grimaced at a new thought.

"What about all the...*by-products* deposited along the way? It must get pretty slippery and gross before long. I wouldn't want to place my hands or my pussy anywhere near some dude's day-old cum."

Heather scrunched her nose and laughed.

"Not to worry. The ship operators have got it all figured out. After every new climber comes down from the wall, they cover the wall in a tarp and wash it down with high-powered steam water jets. They keep it all very antiseptic."

I clenched my legs together, trying to stimulate my burning clit. I couldn't wait to give it a try.

"What do you say?" Heather said. "Are you up for it?"

"Definitely. My pussy's ready to climb on just about anything right now!"

---

When we got to the wall, I was surprised by how tall it was. It towered at least thirty feet straight up, with foot and hand holds separated a few feet apart. It was odd but strangely arousing to see the artificial vulvas and dildos sticking out from its surface. Two naked people were already strapped into hip harnesses at the base of the wall, a man and a woman both appearing to be in their mid-20s.

They spoke with familiarity to one another, so I assumed they were a couple. What a thrill I thought it must be for the pair to experience this together. A small crowd of friends and onlookers were gathered a few feet further back from the wall, egging the couple on. As Heather had described, two buff staff members held thick ropes in their hands, which looped up over an extended wheel at the top of the structure. The other end dangled down the front of the facade and clasped securely to the front of their harnesses.

"Are you ready?" the man said, looking at his partner.

She nodded silently, then reached up for the first hand-hold and placed her foot onto a lip at the base of the wall. Heather looked at me and smiled. The idea of doing this in tandem appealed to me, and I hoped that the two of us would have our turn soon. It was strange watching the climbers spread their legs and bend their asses as they stretched to reach the next higher holds. I could see the man's balls hanging between his thighs and his penis wobbling back and forth as he swung from one placement to the other. They both seemed so focused on figuring out their path of ascent that they barely paused to rest.

But about half way up, the woman suddenly paused and pushed her hips against the wall. I could see a small ball-shaped object resting between her thighs, nestled against her vulva. A gentle vibrating noise emanated from the area. She looked over at her partner and smiled, encouraging him to find a similar place to rest. He glanced to his left and saw an orange ring protruding from the wall. He stepped up and over until his cock was level with the ring then he positioned his flaccid member inside the hole. Suddenly the ring started vibrating, and the man threw his head back. I could see his cock hardening and lengthening as he positioned the vibrating ring around the glans of his penis. He turned toward his partner and they giggled while they gently humped the wall together.

"Higher! Higher!" their friends urged them on from the bottom of the wall.

The two reluctantly disengaged from their fixed positions and resumed their climb up the wall. About five feet higher up, the woman came upon a curved rubber dildo protruding about three inches from the surface, and she paused over it then lowered her pussy until it disappeared inside her hole. She started humping the small dildo to cheers from the crowd. I was glad everybody's attention was focused on the wall, because my fingers had already begun circling my clit as I matched the woman's hip movements.

The man noticed a new feature on his side of the wall, this time mimicking the lips and tongue of a woman. He didn't hesitate to slip his now fully erect cock inside the orifice and begin to moan as he deep-throated his artificial lover. Both he and his partner began speeding up the movement of their hips and it looked like one or both of them might come soon. But the crowd at the base of the wall weren't quite ready.

"Get to the pussy and the dick at the top!" someone shouted. "You're almost there!"

The couple glanced at one another then looked down and shook their heads in mock frustration. Then they peered up the wall and resumed their climb. All the while, the two staff members holding the ropes held the lines taut while pretending to be uninterested in the actions of the climbers. But I noticed the telltale bulge in their pants that belied their disinterest. I looked over at Heather and saw that her hand had slipped between her legs too.

The couple picked up their climbing speed with new determination, and it didn't take long for them to near the top of the wall, where the woman was presented with a large purple dildo and the man with a gaping artificial pussy. The woman placed her lips around the dildo and pretended to give it blowjob while the man pushed his face into the artificial vulva and shook his head playfully. The crowd below erupted in a loud cheer.

"Fuck it! Fuck it! Fuck it!" they chanted in unison.

The woman climbed a few feet higher, then placed the big dildo inside her pussy, and relaxed her legs. The staff member holding her rope bent his knees, clasping the end of the rope tightly with two hands. He'd obviously been in this situation before, and he braced himself for the shifting load. Just a few feet away on the other side of the wall, the man positioned himself adjacent to the artificial vulva and inserted his dick into the hole.

"Whomp! Whomp! Whomp!" chanted their friends down below, in encouragement.

With everybody's attention focused on the wall, Heather suddenly moved behind me and squeezed my breast with one hand, while she slipped her fingers inside my cunny from behind. I could hear vibrating sounds emanating from the artificial pussy and dildo, and the man and the woman clenched their buttocks as they began to fuck their sex toys more vigorously. They peered over at one another and mouthed something, and I could hear their breathing escalating in urgency.

Heather began to speed up the pace of her ministrations, and I fucked her fingers as I pretended it was me on the wall. Within a minute or so, the couple's bodies began convulsing, and their arms and legs suddenly became rigid. Heather held me tightly while I clamped down hard on her hand as I came at the same time with the couple on the wall.

The handlers held the couple's lines firmly until they pushed away from the edifice and were gently lowered. When they got to the bottom and removed their harnesses, their friends surrounded them in a group hug, jumping up and down in celebration. The staff ordered everybody to step ten feet back from the wall, then a canvas tarp descended from the top and hot jets began cleaning the surface. I could feel the steam rising above the tarp as a rivulet of water began pooling at the base of the structure, draining into a grated hole beside the podium.

I turned around and looked at Heather. She raised her eyebrows to signal if I was game to try it next. I simply nodded my head and smiled. I could feel my own rivulet of warm liquid running down my legs.

## 7

## HOUSE OF HOLES

After they finished sanitizing the wall, Heather and I took our turn on it. Most of the spectators had moved on after the previous couple came down, but it was still unnerving being watched so closely by our rope handlers. As usual, Heather took the lead sitting over the erotic extrusions, and the look of delight on her face soon encouraged me to do the same. We came multiple times grinding our pussies into the various devices, culminating with two powerful orgasms on the large dildos at the top of the wall.

We spent a few more hours lounging around the pool, then Heather encouraged me to strike out on my own. I protested briefly, still not entirely comfortable with the idea of engaging in public sex by myself, but she suggested a few venues that might provide an opportunity for more privacy. After a quick lunch, I reluctantly began exploring the ship.

My first stop was the Sexy Games Room. It was filled with

various contraptions, where solo men and women were getting fucked by automated machines. At one station, a woman bent over on all fours, while a large plastic dildo pounded in and out of her pussy. At another one, a man sat on a chair humping a life-like silicone doll, while he squeezed her fake tits and thrust his tongue into her fellatio-shaped mouth. In the corner of the room, a pretty co-ed straddled a device that looked like a pommel horse, as she bucked and writhed atop its vibrating saddle.

It all seemed so surreal and impersonal for me. I wanted a *human* connection, like the one Heather and I shared at the fantasy fountain. I scanned the activity menu and considered going for an Intimate Massage, thinking at least this way I'd have some human touch, and then I remembered one of Heather's recommendations. The description for the House of Holes sounded intriguing:

*Hook up with a stranger on the other side of a wall through your own personal intimate portal. You can choose to 'give', 'receive', or 'merge' with a partner of either sex in an erotic and completely anonymous connection. Or you can choose to simply watch, as other couples get their groove on in this sensuous and erotic 'House of Holes'.*

*Yes,* I thought, *'merging' with a partner is exactly what I need.* The notion of engaging with someone through my own personal 'glory hole', reminded me of the fun I'd had playing with hidden strangers in the Dark Room.

When I got to the venue and opened the door, the first thing I noticed was the sound. A cacophony of moans and grunts greeted me, as a variety of naked men and women shimmied their hips, asses, and mouths against the vinyl-coated walls. The lights were dimmed, but I could see the unmistakable shape of erect penises and vulvas poking through various small holes scattered around the room.

People on the other side were shaking their hips trying to get the attention of someone from inside the room, but everybody was already engaged in some form of coupling. One man was humping the wall, being serviced by someone from the other side. Another one kneeled on the floor giving head to a well-endowed fellow who thrust his cock vigorously into his consort's eager mouth. Not far away, a woman bent over rubbing her ass against the wall, where another man plunged his cock through the hole into her pussy.

But the whole scene somehow left me cold. It struck me as cheap and dirty. Medical clearance or not, I couldn't get on board with the idea of connecting with some other stranger's private parts in such an impersonal way. Just as I was about to leave the room, I noticed a neon sign in the corner reading 'Private View Rooms'.

*Private* definitely sounded more appealing. And being able to *see* my partner was more along my lines.

I opened the door and entered a dimmed hall with closed doors lining both sides. Most of them were locked with a sign reading 'Occupied', but a little further down the hall I found one marked 'Vacant'. I turned the handle and stepped into a small room. It had a single vinyl chair facing a floor-to-ceiling glass wall with a one-foot diameter hole cut in the middle. On the other side of the glass was a similar room with an empty chair.

I turned and locked my door, then checked the chair to see if it was clean. There were no visible marks or residue, but I ran my hand over its smooth surface just to be sure. Even the vinyl floor looked like it had just been cleaned, reflecting the light from the single overhead incandescent lamp.

*At least they clean up after themselves pretty well*, I nodded, as I sat down on the chair and waited for someone to enter the adjacent room.

I expected a man looking for a simulated adult video store glory hole experience, but I was pleasantly surprised when a slim young Asian girl opened the door. She paused for a moment and appraised me seated in my chair with my legs slightly ajar, then she turned around and locked her door from the inside. She was carrying something but she kept it hidden from my view as she turned around.

We could have easily talked if we'd wanted to, with a large enough hole in the glass to carry on a private conversation. But we both seemed to want to just *look* for the time being. She sat down on her chair and placed the hidden object behind her, then spread her legs apart. She had a petite figure with firm B-cup breasts and a small V-shaped patch of pubic hair on her mound that pointed toward a protruding nub at the top of her labia. She had large eyes with long lashes, and she smiled at me as she began to run her hands over her body.

I watched her for a moment, as I felt the juices from my pussy puddle on the chair in front of me. She placed her hands on the inside of her thighs and pulled them slowly toward her apex, then continued moving them up toward her chest. She squeezed her tits then pushed them up and tilted her head down, sucking each of her nipples.

I wanted a piece of her so badly, but I was enjoying her little striptease. I cupped my left breast with one hand and I began to play with my clit with my other, spreading my legs further apart. She did the same and pointed her toes, as she opened her mouth, signaling her pleasure. I could hear a soft moan emanating through the hole in the glass as she flitted her eyes and began to rock her hips on her chair.

By now I was thoroughly soaked, feeling the intensity rising in my loins. I slipped the fingers from my other hand into my pussy as I rubbed my clit more forcefully. The Asian girl suddenly thrust both of her hands into her love box and began fucking herself with a two-handed motion, rocking her chest in tandem with her hips. The sound of her juices sloshing around as she finger-fucked herself with both hands ratcheted my excitement up another level.

I could feel my orgasm beginning to build as I let out a low moan. The girl spread her legs wider until they were virtually straight out to her sides. I marveled at her flexibility, reminding me of my naked yoga experience with Kayla and Neve. We were groaning in tandem as we each fucked our own pussies, alternating our line of sight between our sopping pussies and our glazed-over eyes. Suddenly the girl's chest began to heave, and she grunted a staccato burst of moans as she hunched over in orgasmic spasms. That was enough to put me over the edge, and I growled like a wild animal as I gushed all over the chair in front of me. It was incredibly erotic watching each other come with only a few feet separating us between the clear pane of glass.

But now I was ready for a more personal connection. After I came down from my high, I stood up and walked toward the glass and motioned for her to do the same. She walked slowly toward the hole in the partition, then placed her palms flat against the glass at shoulder height. She was even prettier up close, with big brown eyes, high cheekbones, and full pouty lips. I placed my hands over hers and we moved our faces toward the glass until our lips touched on the cool surface. There was something about being this close to another naked woman and not being able to touch her that I found highly arousing.

Our opposite hands traced a path down the side of the glass and we reached through the hole to touch each other's pussies. I groaned when I felt the heat of her box and her fingers touching my clit. We lowered our bodies a few more inches to gain better access to our midsections while still peering into one another's eyes. I stuck out my tongue and began to lick the glass, showing that I was ready for a more personal touch.

I bent my knees a little further and her fingers slipped out of me as I squatted down over the hole in front of her pussy. She pushed her hips into the glass to try to give me better access, but it felt awkward tilting my head through the hole trying to get to her clit with my tongue. Sensing my frustration, she suddenly stepped back from the glass then lifted her right leg straight up and placed her heel against the glass beside her shoulder. Then she pushed her body forward until her legs were pressed flat against the glass in a perfect split.

Her open vulva was now pushing through the hole

directly toward my face. I didn't hesitate to take her little button into my mouth and roll it around my tongue like a peppermint candy. Her lubrication coated my face as she ground her pussy against my cheeks. I reached through the hole and wrapped my arm around her hips, pulling her harder toward me. She moaned softly and whimpered as she fucked my face. I inserted two fingers into her love canal as I sucked and flicked her little cocklet in my mouth. Then I curled my fingers in a come-hither motion against her G-spot and she bent her knees, pressing her pussy harder against my face and fingers. Her moans were growing in intensity and my heart raced at the idea of her coming on my face. I pushed my fingers deeper inside and circled her clit more quickly with my tongue. Suddenly, she howled as her pussy clamped over my fingers in a long series of hard contractions. I held my face still while she gushed all over me.

If I could have squeezed my whole body through the narrow opening in the glass, I would have pounced on her right then and there and tribbed her hard until we both came together. Instead, I slowly raised myself up until my face was at the same level as hers and kissed her gently against the glass. She smiled at me and blinked twice as if to say 'thank you'. Then she turned around and walked toward the chair and picked up the object which she'd gone to such pains to hide from me. She held it up in the dim light and smiled. It was a long two-sided flexible dildo, anatomically correct on both ends, shaped like a two-headed penis.

*Fuck, yes,* I thought. *That's what I'm talking about.*

I wanted to fuck this girl so badly, and the two-sided

dildo was just what the doctor ordered. She walked up to the glass and held it up in front of me, then licked it up and down the shaft. Then she placed one end in her mouth and simulated fellatio over the silicone glans.

*Please,* I mouthed through the glass. *I need it inside of me now.*

Demonstrating my urgency, I turned around and placed my ass against the open hole, then bent over to present my open pussy to her. She pushed the dildo through the hole and rubbed it back and forth across my vulva, and I shuddered in pleasure. I bucked my hips against the phallus and pressed my ass harder against the glass, signaling that I wanted her to place it inside me.

When she finally did, I almost fainted in pleasure. The feeling of the thick dildo pushing inside me from behind was exquisite. She pushed it as far as it would go, then I felt some slack on the device as she turned around and faced her ass toward me. I didn't need to look to know what she was doing, as I felt the pressure of the dildo when she pushed the other end inside her own pussy.

When our buttocks touched through the open glass, we groaned as we began to simultaneously fuck the giant phallus. I could feel her juices coating the dildo on the other end as our pussies sloshed and bucked against our imaginary partner. The girl began to whimper as we ground our asses together, trying to come over the thick joystick between our legs. It didn't take long for us to reach our peak as we screamed and shook in simultaneous orgasms on the writhing snake embedded inside us.

It took us over a minute before we were ready to disengage, when the girl finally separated herself from the two-headed dildo and pulled it out of my throbbing pussy. I turned around and placed my lips against the glass, and we kissed one last time before she silently picked up the dildo and exited the room. No words had been necessary the entire time we shared our intimate connection.

Just as I was turning to leave, a buff young man entered the room the girl had just left. I took one look at his large swinging cock and shook my head.

*I wouldn't mind a taste of the real thing,* I thought.

8

———

## STRAIGHT FLUSH

After I had another go with my new partner in the private view room, I staggered back to my room, sore and exhausted. I slept like a log that night, dreaming of animated cocks and pussies attached to life-like trees, as I walked through a magical forest. When I woke up in the morning, I lay in a giant wet spot atop my leaking cunny and rubbed another one out before showering and heading upstairs to meet Heather for breakfast.

She laughed when I told her about my strange dream, and we entertained each other over lox and pineapple with stories of our experiences from the previous day. She seemed interested in my private view room encounter, but when I told her about my disappointment with the games room, her ears perked up.

"You didn't explore the *other* games rooms?" she said.

"What other games rooms? I only found the one with the holes in the wall."

"There are lots of others that you might find interesting. One of my favorites is the Card Lounge."

"What happens there?"

"It's where groups of people meet to play card games."

"That doesn't sound very interesting."

"It *is* when everybody's naked and they play by different rules."

Heather noticed Marc heading back from the buffet and motioned for him to join them. Virtually everybody was now walking around the ship completely naked, paying little mind to the jiggling breasts and penises as people went about their daily routines.

"Good morning, ladies," Marc said, as he approached our table. "How have you found your shipboard experience so far?"

I took a good long look at Marc's body before he sat down, refreshing my memory from our first night together. Standing well over six feet tall, his well-muscled torso and arms rippled in the bright light streaming through the windows on the top deck. His penis was flaccid, but still hanging a healthy five to six inches as it swung gently above his nicely shaved balls. I picked a thick piece of pineapple from my plate, remembering what his dick felt like standing straight up.

"I think the word is...*eclectic*," I said, sucking the dripping fruit between my lips.

Marc sat down quickly on the other side of our booth to hide his growing erection and smiled.

"There's certainly no shortage of diversions," he said,

scooping a large forkful of scrambled eggs into his mouth. "Have you had a favorite experience?"

"You mean besides our little tryst with you?" Heather said, grabbing a sausage from his plate and biting it in half.

"Of course I knew that would be your highlight," Marc said, continued the tease. "I was referring to the venues."

"The climbing wall was fun," Heather said. "But I think Jade may have experienced a different kind of high in one of the private view rooms yesterday."

"Oh? You like those sexy holes, do you?"

"Some holes were a little sexier than others," I said.

"Jade found the rest of the games room a bit underwhelming. I was suggesting she try her hand at a little strip poker. Care to join us after breakfast?"

"Just the three of us?" Marc said.

"I think we need a plus-one to balance things out. Maybe we can persuade one of the guys from the House of Holes to take his dick out of the wall and find a more interesting use for it."

Marc stretched his lips and nodded.

"Game on," he said, finishing his sausage and eggs.

---

When we got to the card room, we saw an empty round glass table with a pack of playing cards and four trays of betting chips. Heather excused herself for a moment, then returned a few minutes later holding a college-age boy's hand. He looked a little perplexed as he stared at the three of us and the empty table.

"*Three's* a lot more fun than one, don't you think?" she said to the young man. "Plus, there's no barriers here to limit your engagement. Are you ready to play some sexy games?"

He paused for a moment, then stuck out his hand.

"I'm Liam," he said, signaling his assent.

After we all introduced ourselves, we took alternating seats at the table and Heather cracked open the pack of cards.

"What are we playing?" Liam enquired.

"Five card stud," Heather said, winking at me. "With two *real* studs. You *do* know how to play poker, Liam?"

"Yes, but what are the stakes? I didn't bring any money..."

"You're so cute," Heather said. "We're not playing for money. We're playing for *favors*. The rule is that whoever wins each hand, gets to command one or more of us to perform some kind of act. Whoever ends up with the most chips at the end of the hour gets to propose a special group activity. The only limitation is that no one is allowed to come until the very end."

"That makes it a little more interesting," Marc said.

"And challenging," Liam said, crossing his legs to hide his growing erection under the table.

"Right then," Heather said, pulling two red chips from her tray. "The ante is ten dinars."

"Dinars?" Liam said.

"It's just *play* money, remember? They gain *real* value a little later."

Heather dealt one card face down to each player then one more face up. We each looked at our hole cards and placed our bets. Liam placed the largest stake in the pile, then Heather dealt another set of cards face up. Liam showed two Kings and threw in one of his three black chips.

"Too steep for me," Marc huffed, pushing his cards into the waste pile.

Heather displayed two tens, and I had a Jack-high.

Heather matched Liam's bet, and I decided to fold. She dealt the fourth card to herself and Liam. Heather got a Queen, while Liam showed an Ace.

"Hooo!" Marc cheered, as he rubbed his hands together. "Now it's getting interesting. Think hard about what you want the ladies to do for you, Liam."

"I'm *already* hard," Liam said.

I looked through the table top between his legs and saw his good-sized cock pointing straight up on his belly.

Marc reached into his tray and tossed another black marker on the table. Heather paused trying to read his face, then she glanced beneath the table at his throbbing cock.

"I think he's bluffing," she said. "I'll match your bet and raise you one hundred." She threw down her last two black chips then dealt the last card face up. She got another ten and Liam got a six.

Liam didn't hesitate to throw his last black chip in the pot.

"I call," he said, then he turned over his hole card and revealed three Kings.

"Whoa," Heather said, opening her eyes wide in surprise. She turned over her card and revealed a two. Liam had won the hand.

"Well played, young man," Heather said. "Your wish is our command. What would you like us to do?"

Liam ran his eyes up and down Heather's figure and smiled.

"I want you to spread your legs and play with yourself."

Heather pushed her chair back from the table to give everyone a commanding view of her crotch, then she spread her legs apart. She began to circle her clit, while she stared Liam directly in the eyes. His breathing increased as his gaze wandered between her legs. She began to move her hips on the chair, and Liam's hand dropped down to his lap where he began rubbing his cock.

"Hey!" Heather admonished. "That's not allowed. You get to watch only."

"But you said as long as we don't cum—"

"There'll be plenty of time for that later. I want you boys to save those nice big hard-ons for the main event."

Heather sat back up and handed the remaining pack of cards to Liam.

"Your turn to deal," she said.

"That's it?" Liam said. "That was hardly worth three hundred dinars!"

Heather placed her moist fingers in her mouth and licked off her juices.

"You better play your hand wisely the rest of the way, then. Now you've got some extra cash to up the ante. We're just getting started."

Liam collected the pot from the middle of the table, then we all threw in two blue chips for the next round. Liam dealt the cards, and I won the next round with a full house.

I looked at Marc and Liam and licked my lips. I noticed that Liam's dick had lost some of its firmness, but Marc's was rapidly elongating under the table. I wondered how far he'd be willing to go with this game.

"I want Liam to suck Marc's cock," I said.

"What?" Liam said, his eyes flying open. "But I'm not...*gay*."

"It's just a game," Heather said. "No one's going to cum in your mouth, right Marc? At least not yet. Besides, how do you know if you don't like it until you try? Now get down there and suck that bratwurst."

Marc swung his chair out, and I noticed his cock was standing at full mast. Apparently at least *one* of the boys liked the idea of sucking another guy. Liam walked around the table and kneeled down in front of Marc. He stared at the tip of Marc's manhood, unsure what to do.

"Go on," Heather said. "It won't bite you. Just think of it as a popsicle. A very large warm popsicle."

Marc pulled his arms around behind his chair and clasped his hands together to give Liam freer access.

Liam opened his mouth and slowly lowered himself over the head of Marc's joystick. At first he just held it there, but after a few seconds he began to bob his head as Marc slowly swung his hips. They both seemed to be enjoying it, and I had to fight hard to keep my hands away from my steaming pussy. The sight of seeing two hetero men going at it was incredibly erotic. I wanted to see if I could push it a little further.

"Now play with his balls," I ordered.

Liam paused and peered up at me out of the corner of his

eyes, and I simply nodded. Marc pushed his hips toward the end of his seat until his tight balls poked over the edge. Liam reached up and cupped them then rolled them gently between his fingers. His own cock had resumed its full length and was bobbing against his flat stomach. It was obvious that he was getting turned on by the experience, and I saw his tongue begin to roll around in his mouth as he circled the head of Marc's cock. Marc let out a groan and lifted his hips higher. I would have happily forfeited the game at that moment to watch Marc cum in Liam's mouth, but Heather interjected to remind us of the rules.

"Okay, I think that's enough for this round," she said. "You boys seem to be having a little bit too much fun."

Liam sheepishly disengaged from Marc and returned to his seat at the other side of the table. We resumed the game, with each round ratcheted up the degree of engagement between the players. Marc won the next round and asked Heather to sit in my lap while we tribbed each other for a couple of minutes. Then Heather won the next round and asked the men to do the same as we watched them jack their two cocks together between their bellies. By the time our hour was up, all four of us were worked up enough to jump each other bones. When we counted our chips, Heather had eked out Liam for the largest residual.

"What now?" Liam said, his cock bobbing on his stomach, already leaking pre-cum.

"I ended up with the highest winnings," Heather said, "so I get to decide on the final group activity. And I think we should all come back to my cabin."

We didn't bother to clean up the table as we quickly

found the nearest exit. Unlike our first night together when we'd scurried down the stairs to her stateroom, this time we took the elevator down the three levels to her floor. But the tension in the lift was palpable as none of us said a word to one another, holding our collective breath in anticipation of what would come next.

## 9

## FOUR PLAY

When we got to Heather's room, nobody was sure who should make the first move. When it was just the three of us, Heather hadn't hesitated to jump the only man in the room, but this time we had to figure out what to do with Liam. The obvious thing would have been for us to pair up as two hetero couples, but Heather had seen enough in the games room to have other ideas.

"You boys lie down on the bed with your feet facing each other," she ordered.

Marc and Liam dutifully lay on the mattress as Heather instructed.

"Now bend your knees and move together until your cock and balls are touching one another."

I looked at Heather inquisitively, wondering what she had planned. We'd already seen the men frotting their cocks together in the games room, and I was eager for some of my own touching.

She glanced at Marc and Liam's glistening cocks throbbing against each other and smiled at me.

"Do you want to go first or me?"

I pinched my eyebrows for a second, then gasped when I understood her intention. The idea of having two cocks inside me was something I hadn't yet experienced. I moved toward the bed and kneeled on the mattress straddling the two men, facing Liam. I'd already watched Marc come inside me, this time I wanted to picture a younger man's reaction.

The men paused for a moment, unsure what I wanted. They were probably thinking of the classic DP maneuver, where one would fuck me in my pussy while the other fucked me up the ass. But I had a better idea. Ever since I saw them rubbing their cocks together in the game room, I'd fantasized about grasping them both inside my pussy. Both men were well hung, measuring together at least three times the girth of an average man's erect penis, but I figured if my anatomy could accommodate a baby's head during childbirth, surely it could take the equivalent of two good sized English cucumbers.

I reached around behind my ass and clasped their two penises together then slowly lowered my pussy until it touched the wet heads of their joined hard-ons. Marc's was a little bit longer, so it pushed its way through first, as I felt my lips widen to accommodate his large organ. Slowly sitting down another inch, I could feel Liam's cockhead pressing me apart still further, and I moaned as I felt my pussy stretch to take them both inside me. With both of them lying flat on their backs on the mattress, there was little they could do with the full weight of my body pressing down over their hips. I relished the feeling of control, watching Liam's face contorting in pleasure as my love tunnel squeezed over their joined cocks.

I slowly lowered myself until I felt my vulva resting on Liam's stubbly pubis. I was glad I'd placed Marc in the posterior position, where he had a little more room to sheath his larger cock. I began to use my thigh muscles to move up and down over their connected meat and reflected back on the Asian girl's two-headed cock from the view room the previous day. Two double pricks in as many days was a new milestone for me.

It seemed as if every nook and crevice of my pussy was filled up by the hot, throbbing manhood of these two virile men. I humped them faster, knowing it wouldn't to take long for all of us to come after the long buildup in the game room. Before long, Heather decided she wanted a piece of the action, and I could hear Marc's muffled moans behind me as she sat over his face. The look on Liam's face was priceless. I wasn't sure which he was enjoying more—the feeling of having his cock deeply embedded in my wet pussy, or the feeling of having Marc's throbbing member next to his.

His mouth was wide open as he moaned loudly in pleasure, and I knew he wouldn't be long to this world. I placed my hands over his tight pecs and squeezed the two-headed python inside me as I felt a powerful urge welling inside me. Heather suddenly reached around my back and squeezed my tits and we all howled in unison. When I came, I bucked wildly over the two men as I felt their cocks pulsing together, flooding me inside with their honey.

I sat there for a minute savoring the feeling of having two hard dicks inside me, as I peered out Heather's balcony window at the sun setting over the ocean. This cruise had been one hell of an adventure, and I didn't know if or when I'd have another chance like this again. I wanted to make it last as long as possible.

***

Ready for more erotic chills and thrills? Check out the entire collection of stories in *Jade's Erotic Adventures* in your favorite online store:

*Click to view your favourites...*